NASHVILLE NIGHTS 1

SARAH PIRTLE

Cover Design and Formatting by Kate | Kate Decided to Design

www.katedecidedtodesign.com

Edited by Erica Rogers | Logophile Editing Services

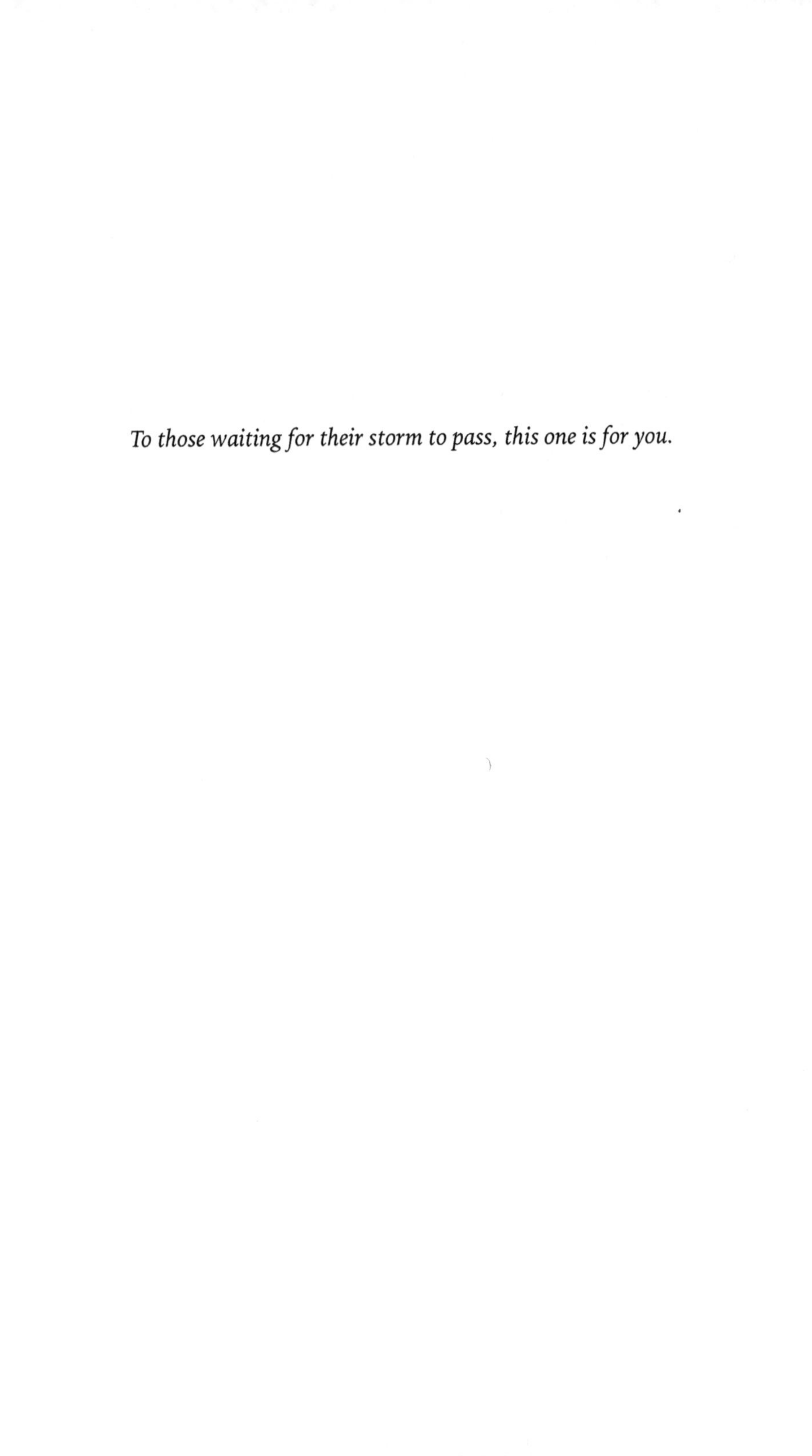

To those waiting for their storm to pass, this one is for you.

Playlist

listen on spotify

how do you sleep - sam smith
under your radar - miss fortune
golden hour - jvke
dirty thoughts - bonnie x clyde
bad habits - ed sheeran
potions - slander & said the sky
rescue me - thirty seconds to mars
it's you - ali gatie
lights down low - max
silence - marshmello (ft. khalid)
every time you leave - i prevail
smile - juice wrld & the weeknd
malibu nights - lany
just pretend - bad omens
please don't go - joel adams
you're not alone - the broken view
never stop (wedding version) - safetysuit

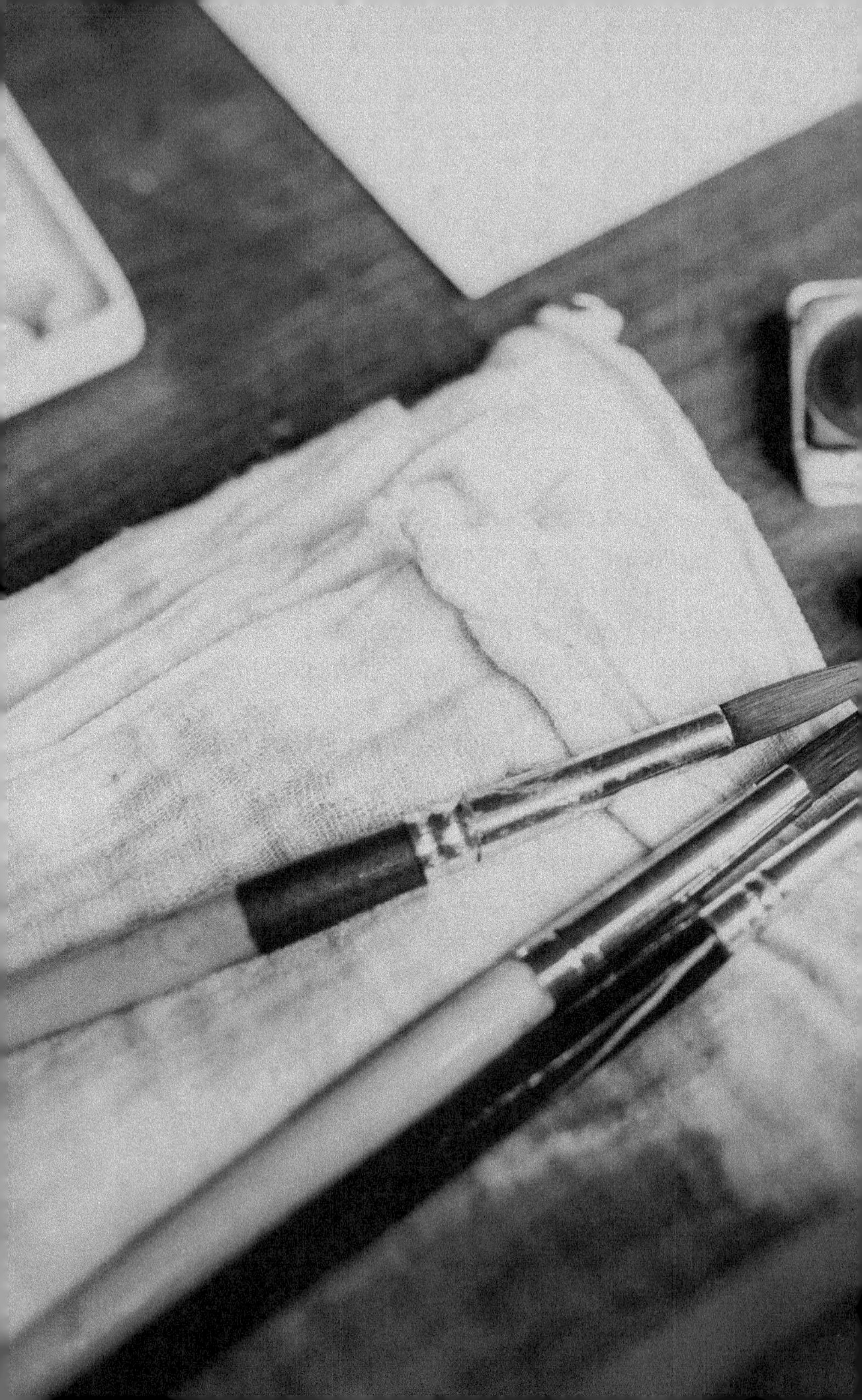

Chapter 1

Shane

As the heartache of moving away from California settles in, I am reminded of the day I moved out here six years ago to attend art school at California College of the Arts. I was more than ready to get out of my hometown, leaving all the tragedy and horrible memories behind. Instead of experiencing joy and excitement for my new adventure, I was drowning in my sudden grief and heartache. I struggled during my first year away; keeping in close contact with my three best friends back home and pouring myself into my art, helped a lot.

Life in San Francisco turned out to not be so bad. I met my boyfriend, Pete, during my senior year of college. I had been at the beach, painting the waves crashing up on shore and the beautiful sunset; taking in the calming scenery around me. I've had a deep connection with the ocean since moving here. The symbolism of the way the ocean waters can come and wipe the sand clean, giving it a fresh start resonates deeply with me. The waves acted as calming

music to my ears as I watched beachgoers surf, run, sunbathe, and –
stop directly in front of me.

There stood Pete, in a freaking sweater vest and khakis on the
beach, talking away on the phone, planted directly in front of where I
had my canvas set up. I couldn't see any of my previous inspiration,
and while I tried to be patient, thinking he was bound to move sometime, he did not. I finally piped up and let him know he was blocking
my view. I hadn't bothered hiding my look of annoyance when he
looked over at me with a smug look saying, *"Maybe I am the view."*

I giggled like a schoolgirl at the remark that I now find extremely
egotistical. We talked for a while before exchanging numbers, and the
rest is history. We were dating within a week, and I moved in with
him a couple of months later.

In the same year, right before graduating college, I also landed a
job working at an art gallery run by Hugh Burgess. I was lucky
enough to nail the interview and land the job as an assistant curator.
My dream has always been to have my own art hung in a studio someday, but this job was a great way to get my foot in the door. Every
artist knows making good, connecting relationships is just as important as the art itself. I have worked there for about two years now, the
same duration Pete and I have been dating.

Things have been a little different between us lately, though. He
has been working late nights at the accounting firm he works for, and I
spend any spare time I have painting in one of the "creative spaces" as
Hugh calls them, at *The Gallery*. Yes, the name of the art gallery I work
at is called *The Gallery*. Because in Hugh's mind, it's the only one.

I try to be intentional when Pete and I are both home, which is
rare. I am always asking him if he wants to go out to dinner, or even
take a night walk on the beach, but he always claims to be too tired
and goes straight to sleep. In a last-ditch effort to revive our relationship, I decided to surprise him at work today for our two year anniversary and take him lunch from his favorite sushi place.

Imagine how completely shocked I was when, instead, I caught
him in the act of cheating on me with his secretary, *Mandy*. I hadn't

seen her at her desk outside, so I just walked in. So confident, big grin on my face, hopeful I would be able to mend whatever part of our relationship was still hanging by a thread. Ugh, how humiliating. He wasn't just kind of cheating on me either, this was a full service, the door should have been locked, the relationship was over immediately, type of cheating.

I decided in the heat of the moment to throw the sushi right at him. It probably wasn't the most mature route, but I did feel a smidge better when a wasabi roll went rogue, slapping Mandy across the face. I let him know *very* clearly I would be gone when he got home, and to lose my number. In case the idiot wasn't smart enough to figure out for himself that I was done, with a capital DONE, with him.

I rushed out of the office, trying my best to catch my breath when I got to my Jeep. I have never been so hurt and embarrassed in my life. Not even when my parents started swing dancing at my sweet sixteen, and that felt mortifying at the time. I immediately put my car in drive and peeled out of the parking lot. I only got so far down the street before my vision was too blurry to drive. I decided to pull over and call Taylor.

Taylor Clark has been my best friend since birth, she is more like a sister to me, since I never had any of my own. Our mothers were best friends growing up, so it felt so natural for us to cling to each other and remain best friends as we got older. I'm glad things happened the way they did for us because I wouldn't have been able to pick a better best friend for myself if I tried. Amidst my breakdown, I just have to call her to tell her what happened and find out what the hell I was supposed to do now.

"Hello? Shane, is everything okay?" she asks, probably hearing my sobs as soon as she answered the phone.

"He cheated on me, Taylor." I manage to choke out between the tears.

"That bastard!" she yells. "How did you find out? Are you okay? Do I need to fly out and kick his scrawny ass?" she fires off the questions while rifling through something on the other end of the line. I wouldn't doubt if she was actually trying to pack a bag to fly out here and do just that.

Taylor has always been very protective and takes no bullshit from anyone. She would 100% come kick his ass if I said yes. I let out a laugh through my tears.

"I found out when I walked in to surprise him with lunch, but he was already having Mandy." She gasps. "I'm not really okay, I just found out the person I've loved for 2 years is banging someone else behind my back. But, no, don't fly out here. Just tell me what to do, Tay." I break into a sob again.

I hear her sigh. "Shaney, I am so sorry. He's trash for doing this to you, and I *will* kick his ass one day for this. What do you *want* to do?" her question has my mind swirling.

I run through different plans and ideas of how I could manage to live out here alone.

I lived on campus during college so I never had to find a place of my own or a roommate. Right after I graduated, I moved in with Pete and we split the rent. I have never lived on my own out here, and I know all too well that I won't be able to afford it with my current salary.

Finding someone off the internet to room with just sounds like a recipe for disaster, so I'm left with zero ideas at the end of my thought process.

"I don't know. I don't want to leave California, I love my job at *The Gallery* and working for Hugh. He's the best boss I could ever ask for, and he's taken me under his wing showing me the ropes of gallery work. But I just don't see how I could manage it. You know how I feel about living with strangers, but I can't afford to live alone. I have no idea what to do." I let out a shaky breath.

"Well, given everything you just said I know this may not be ideal. But, my guest room is available. If you want to come back home, it's yours." She offers.

Living with Taylor is the most appealing thought of the hour. She works as an ER nurse and her hours are crazy sometimes, but living with each other is something we've always talked about. We both hated that we weren't able to experience college life together, but I got a scholarship to one of the best art schools in California and I couldn't turn it down.

I'm not sure San Francisco ever truly felt like my home, I was here for the sole purpose of chasing my dreams, furthering my career and doing it on a scholarship. But nowhere has really felt like home since I left Nashville. Even when I moved in with Pete, everything was *his;* I felt more like a house guest than anything.

I hate the idea of leaving *The Gallery* so much, but maybe one day I'll make my way back out here to it. Maybe one day I'll call this place home. For now, it looks like my best and most attainable option is going back home to live with my best friend.

"Are you sure, Tay? What happened to your old roommate? Tana, right? I thought she like, just moved in." I ask, remembering our conversation about her new roommate Tana last month. "Ugh, she was so nasty, Shane. If she hadn't bailed on me, I was on the verge of kicking her out." The thought of Taylor ever kicking anyone out was wild to me, because even though she's feisty as hell, she's still kind and doesn't like to hurt other people's feelings.

"You were not," I argue back.

"She clipped her toenails in the kitchen Shane. In. The. Motherf-reaking. KITCHEN!" she yells back, making me hold my phone further from my ear. "She was disgusting and one very well-manicured foot out the door." She makes a gagging noise into the phone making me laugh.

"Well, I promise not to cut my toenails in the kitchen." I laugh.

"Does that mean you're coming home?" she sounds so excited.

"I'm coming home," I say softly, trying to reel in my emotions about leaving the city I've called home for the past six years. Taylor squeals on the other end of the line.

"I can't wait, Shaney!" I smile at the response. Knowing my best friend is so excited to have me stay with her makes the other hard decisions worth it.

"Me either. Now, I have to go pack my shit and quit my job." A job that I love and adore – a job that it's absolutely killing me to leave.

"You got this, boo. Text me later." I can hear the sympathy in her voice.

"Will do. Love you."

"Love you too!" We hang up the phone and I take one more deep, cleansing breath before heading to the home I have shared with Pete for two years, to get all of my belongings and cram them into my jeep. Seeing as how the apartment and all the furniture were Pete's, everything I have to pack should easily fit.

The Gallery is one of the most beautiful places I have ever seen, and I don't say that because I'm biased. The beauty of it makes it even harder to walk up to for what I know is the final time. The outside of the building is whitewashed brick with some of the natural brick still exposed. It has massive arched windows that let in the best natural light, and the glass doors push open into the foyer. There's a round desk that sits underneath a crystal chandelier where Sherry is always stationed to welcome guests and direct them when needed.

When I walk in, I smile at Sherry who is, no surprise, standing behind the counter.

"Hey Sherry, is Hugh in his office?" I ask.

"Yeah. He shouldn't be too busy, you could probably just go back and knock." She waves her hand toward his office, gesturing for me to walk on back.

"Okay, thanks." I try to hide the anxiousness in my voice, but I think it just makes me sound overly cheery. This is going to go swell. I get back to Hugh's office and take a shaky breath in before knocking.

"Come on in." Hugh's smooth swagger-like voice calls. I walk in and when he looks up at me, the biggest grin comes across his face. *Shit.*

"Shane, what a pleasant surprise. I thought you were off today."

His brows draw together as he reads my expression. "Everything alright?" he asks. I sigh and shake my head because I'm afraid if I speak right now, a stream of tears will follow.

"Have a seat." He motions for me to sit in one of the armchairs across from his desk. His office is as immaculately styled, as is he. Hugh is one of the most attractive and well-dressed 40-year-old men I've ever met. He salt and peppered early in life and completely owns the look. At six feet tall and perfectly toned, the man is a walking sculpture. He's always dressed in cropped dress slacks, a fitted button-down shirt, and loafers with a belt and watch to match.

His office is no different. Completely modern in style, and extremely neat. He has a glass desk with only a computer, notepad, and writing stationery on it. There are bookshelves lining the back wall, full of books, art awards, degrees, and funky art pieces – *of course*. There's a large table off to one side where artists can show him their work if they get so lucky. Two armchairs and a small table between them with a water pitcher and glasses sit across from him. Where I am currently planted, trying to choke down the lump in my throat to find words to say why I'm here.

"You don't look well, would you like a glass of water?" he offers.

"No, thank you." I clear my throat. Hugh sits back, crossing his hands behind his head.

"What can I do for you today?"

"Well, I actually came to tell you I might be quitting," I admit, looking down at my hands in my lap, unable to meet his gaze. "Effective – like, today." I finally look up and see the surprise on his face.

"Well, that definitely wasn't where I thought this was going. May I ask why?" he sits up, placing his forearms on his desk, staring more curiously at me now. I let out a long breath.

"You may, but the answer might be a little more drama than you bargained for," I warn.

"Go on," He quirks a brow.

"Well. I caught my boyfriend cheating on me today. It's our two-year anniversary. Seeing as I was living with him, I am currently homeless. I don't have any close friends out here that I could room with, and my salary won't be enough for me to support myself. Not that I don't appreciate what I do make in my position, I do, honestly. I will not be finding a roommate on the internet because I want to live to see next year. And I am basically out of options outside of moving back home." I get the words out as quickly as possible not wanting to bore Hugh with the mess that is me, Shane.

I'm sitting here, waiting for him to respond, to tell me to hop on the next train at the hot mess express and he'll see me never, when he shocks me instead.

"I am very sorry to hear about this horrible anniversary you're having. Sounds like you're better off without him." He raises his brows as if you say *And you better believe that.* "As far as your salary and living situation, I wish I could be of more help. Right now we wouldn't be able to offer you more pay for your position, and I could look into some of my rental properties and see if we could work out some sort of agreement, but that would take time, and it seems as though that is not something you have right now.

"I wish there was more I could do for you Shane, truly." He gives an apologetic look.

"Hugh, you have been the best mentor and boss ever since I started here 2 years ago, I couldn't possibly ask you for more than that. I will miss working here and under your expertise, immensely." He stands and rounds his desk, and I push to my feet as well. He offers his hand and I accept.

"If you ever make your way back to San Francisco, we would love to have you back as part of our team. I see potential in you, Shane. You're on your way to being something great." Tears begin to well in my eyes again and I nod.

"Thank you," I clear my throat, these stupid emotions need to leave me alone.

"Do you mind if I grab my things from the room I use to paint?" I ask.

"Of course not. Take your time." He smiles and walks me to the door. "Good luck, on your next adventure."

I collect my things from the creative space Hugh allowed me to use for the duration of my employment. I look around and am devastated when I can't find a certain piece I had painted. I looked the room over twice, but it was useless, it was empty and the painting wasn't there. I pack everything else in my Jeep, then head to Pete's to pack the rest of my belongings. Looks like I'm going home. I open my phone to the group text to let the rest of the girls know what's going on.

ME

Looks like Nashville just got a new resident. 👑

TAYLOR

New roomie, YAY!

LEAH

So, we missed something?

LAUREN

It appears so. 😬

ME

Girls' night as soon as I'm back and I'll explain everything.

TAYLOR

Check in often so we know you're not getting crazy murdered by truckers. 😏

ME

And on that note... I won't be sleeping until I'm back.

After packing the rest of my belongings from Pete's house, I head to grab a coffee, before I'm back on the road. This is going to be the longest trip of my life.

Chapter 2

Shane

I HAVE BEEN on the road for 30+ hours, sleeping in motel rooms that left something to be desired and eating nothing but fast food. I feel gross, to say the least, but I am finally nearing the end of this long ass trip back home. After listening to my travel playlist one too many times and not vibing at all with my latest audiobook narrator, I call Taylor over the Bluetooth in my Jeep to let her know my ETA.

I cannot wait for a shower and to sleep on a bed I am confident doesn't have a family of roaches living beneath it. I shudder at the thought as Taylor answers the phone.

"Shaney! Thank god, you're still alive!"

"Yes, yes. I am still alive. I smell like crusty motel and cheeseburgers, but I am alive." An enormous yawn takes over my body at that moment. I'm beyond ready to get out of this car.

"Okay. Ew. But that's okay girl. I have my guest room all made up for you. I figured you'd want to shower and get some sleep. However, I do have a little surprise for you when you get here." She says mischievously. I have a feeling I know what said surprise is, but I will play along for her sake.

"You're a lifesaver, and I can't wait. I love surprises." I wag my eyebrows before realizing she can't see my face. "Umm, Tay?" I question.

"Yeah?"

"You have disinfected the kitchen since Tana, right?" I ask cautiously.

"Ugh, YES! I considered burning the whole place down, but I settled on disinfectant by the gallon because I kind of like it here." She says playfully. I huff out a tired laugh as I see the mile marker to my exit.

"I should be there in about 20 minutes," I tell her, taking a sip from my latest coffee cup. Soon to join the other 5 on the passenger side floorboard.

"See you soon, *roomie*," Taylor says before hanging up the phone.

I look in my rear-view mirror to see my Jeep packed floor to ceiling with my bags and paintings. I still couldn't believe everything that transpired over the last couple of days, so many things changed so quickly. I am no longer in a long-term relationship or working for a gallery owner I love. Instead, I am single, road-tripping back home, alone, with everything I own crammed into my Jeep, and jobless.

Jobless.

I groan at the thought. I never would have imagined that I would spend 4 years attending art school, graduating at the top of my class, just to end up jobless so soon after graduating. I have absolutely no idea what's next for me. If I will find an art-related job or if I will settle on something that's good cash flow for now. If I will be living with Taylor for a while or if I'll be able to afford my own place eventually.

Maybe I'll end up working a job that pays well and be able to move back to San Francisco to work with Hugh again. Being the optimist that I am, I won't worry too much about it. I have some money in my savings to live off of for a little while. It will definitely stretch further in Nashville, living with Taylor, than if I were alone in SanFran.

I turn on my blinker and turn onto Taylor's street. Her neighborhood is seriously the cutest. Everyone's lawns are perfectly manicured and there are small trees with their supporting mechanisms still attached planted in most yards since they are all new builds. Even the flower beds with shrubs that are beginning to die, because it's the dead of winter, manage to look well kept. My suspicions about the surprise are confirmed when I see two cars parked outside, belonging to Leah and Lauren.

We met Leah Gates and Lauren Long in middle school when we all got put together for a group project. We spent the entire week taking turns working on it at each other's houses, and once we bonded over how hot we all thought our history teacher was, the rest was... well, history. After that, we did everything together, and the fact that we've stayed friends into our 20s is something very special to me. I would do anything for these girls– they've become my family.

I pull into the driveway where they left a spot open for me, quickly turn off the engine and hop out. Before I make it around the front of my car, my three best friends come barrelling out of Taylor's house running right towards me. In a matter of seconds, I am completely enveloped in their hugs.

God, I've missed them.

"I missed you guys so much!" I say, my face buried in a mess of red and brown hair. Taylor pulls back first, removing the red curls from the bunch that was threatening to suffocate me.

"We missed you too, bitch!" she shouts back, making all of us laugh.

"Oh my god, Taylor. Did you need to shout that so loud, the whole neighborhood probably heard you?" Leah laughs. Leah is the youngest of the group – I mean, we're all the same age, but her birthday is last so we always give her shit about it. However, she's the most level-headed out of the four of us. Always being the most reasonable when it comes to... well, everything.

"Of course she did, she wouldn't be Taylor if she didn't." Lauren chimes in, brushing a strand of Taylor's wild red hair out of her face.

"Plus it's true. We missed our bitch!" Lauren yells out even louder than Taylor had. Leah rolls her eyes, shaking her head in disapproval. Lauren, I'd say, is probably the second most feisty of the bunch. She and Taylor hold down the lets have a good time, fuck the world attitudes, and I'm settled somewhere between their wild sides and Leah's voice of reasoning. I've always been a more go-with-the-flow type, and it fits in our group dynamic perfectly.

"Okay okay, let's get all your shit in the house already." Taylor directs as she breaks up the group huddle. When we walk over to the Jeep, I pop the hatch open and we all stand there staring at it.

"Oh my god, Shane, did a grizzly bear pack your car?" Taylor asks. Her eyes wide as she looks at me. I shrug my shoulders and yank some canvases out to hand her.

"I was in a bit of a rush, Tay," I say and stick my tongue out at her. She playfully rolls her eyes and grabs the rest of my paint supplies.

After grabbing all of my stuff and shutting the trunk back, Taylor swings her arm over my shoulder and we walk inside, Lauren and Leah right on our heels holding duffle bags and boxes of shoes.

Taking an immediate left once inside the house, Taylor sets my canvases on top of the small kitchen table. At the same time Leah, Lauren, and I drop my bags and boxes of shoes on the floor beside it. I stand there taking in the sight of her cute little house, as she walks over to the small island and pours us each a glass of wine.

I have always loved Taylor's house because it is so freaking cozy. The outside is painted cornflower blue, with white trim and columns on the front porch. When you walk inside there are coat hooks on the wall to the right and an entrance to a small dining area to the left.

The dining area leads straight to the kitchen, which I am obsessed with. She has navy blue cabinets, white marble countertops, and stainless steel appliances. There's a small island in the kitchen that has the same color scheme of navy and marble, with just enough room for two barstools on one side.

There's a door to the left of the kitchen that leads to Taylor's master bedroom, then windows that look out to her little backyard. In the living room, there's a small gray sectional, covered in throw pillows and knit blankets.

Her fireplace is whitewashed and sits in the far left corner, right next to the tv stand – which I'm sure has all of our favorite movies inside. There's a small hallway off the living room that leads to the guest room and guest bath, which I will be calling home for the foreseeable future.

There are candles burning everywhere you look, which has the house constantly smelling like vanilla or baked goods. I want to curl up on the couch and take a nap every time I'm here.

"Okay!" Taylor announces, startling me from my thoughts. "I know you need a shower Shaney because you were not lying about smelling like a crusty cheeseburger." She scrunches her nose at me.

"I said crusty motel *and cheeseburgers*. Though I'm not sure that statement helps me." I laugh.

"Anyways," she continues, "you go take a shower, and we will order food. Then it's full-on girls' night." She raised her wine glass in the air, and the three of us followed suit, clinking our glasses together.

I grab my bags and haul them into what is now my bedroom. I find my way to the guest bathroom, which is conveniently right across from my room, and tie my long blonde hair into a bun on top of my head and wash my face. I walk over and turn the shower on and let the water run so hot it steams up the whole bathroom. After I drop my travel clothes into a pile on the floor and step in the shower, I am able to immediately feel all the muscles in my body relax. I take a deep breath and tears start falling down my face. Because this is the first moment I really let myself relax since I walked into Pete's office.

I don't even try to stop the tears. My whole life changed in two days' time. I have no idea what I am doing next. I just up and left the only life and job I've known since starting college and meeting Pete.

Traveling across the country to come back home. No job prospects, and no place of my own, and it scares the hell out of me.

I am so grateful for Taylor allowing me to call her guest room home for now. This is the second time in my life I've lost everything and moved away. Only this time I moved back to where it all fell apart the first time. I feel like there's something poetic about that, I just can't manage to see it right now.

Tomorrow I think I will go out and start looking for a job while Taylor is at work. I can't just sit around and do nothing. I *won't* just sit around and do nothing.

After taking an in-depth shower that made the water run cold, which was very much needed, I get out and dry my hair. I throw on my CCA sweatshirt and some joggers before joining the girls. As much as I want to just crawl into bed and sleep away the last few days, I am really excited to catch up with them.

When I walk into the living room, take-out containers from our favorite local Italian restaurant cover the entire coffee table. They're all sitting around talking and giggling.

"I'm *not* lying, I walk in there to give this man a blanket and he's just butt ass naked on the bed. Nobody even warned me!" Taylor dramatically waves her hands around.

"Umm. Do I even want to know?" I laugh, as I plop down on the couch next to her.

"No!" Leah and Lauren shout in unison.

"So the other night I'm at work and some old man came in from a car accident and someone told me he needed a warm blanket, so I'm sitting there thinking oh, this poor old man, I'll grab him a blanket, he's been through so much, right? HE WAS COMPLETELY NAKED! Because *no one told me* that car accident patients get stripped all the way down to check for injuries." Taylor yells. "I threw the blanket at him and ran out of the room."

"Taylor, you didn't." I gasp.

"Yes, the hell I did." She shrugs and tips her wine glass back until it's empty. I shake my head in disbelief, even though I fully believe it. Just another reminder as to why I stuck with art when Taylor tried to convince me to go into nursing with her.

"Okay, so let's get into it. What the hell happened with that rat bastard ex-boyfriend of yours?" Lauren says.

"Wow, okay. So we're just...doing this." I cough trying not to choke on the wine I just drank. They all settle into their places on the couch, holding their take-out containers and drinks. I take a deep breath in, "okay, where do you want me to start?" they all look at each other and then back to me.

"The beginning," they say.

So I do.

I tell them about how he had become much more distant lately. He would work late into the night several nights a week, and was always glued to his phone when we were together.

Because of that, I would spend more time at the art studio than at home because it just didn't feel right anymore. Then the big finale was when I made a surprise visit to his work for our anniversary and found him going down on Mandy right there on his desk. They all laughed hysterically when I told them a sushi roll slapped Mandy across the face.

"As it freaking should," Leah said, bobbing her head back and forth.

Then they all comforted me and reassured me when I questioned why I wasn't good enough for him. Questioning why he would cheat on me, and trying to pinpoint where exactly it all went wrong. Why he had chosen to cheat and humiliate me like that, instead of just ending things?

"What a fucking asshole. I really am gonna kick his ass next time I see him." Taylor said, slamming her take-out container on the coffee table.

"Well, hopefully, you won't see him ever again. I'm so done with men that it's ridiculous." I proclaim.

"Oh please, you are not. You just need a *good* man. One that's worthy of you and all the goodness you possess." Lauren says. Maybe she's right, but for now, the jury is out on every last one of them. I don't see myself trusting so easily after this whole debacle, so swearing off all men seems like my best bet.

"Okay, so if we are done with the info spill on Pete. Can we talk about anything else?" Taylor goes to open her mouth to speak but I interrupt, "anything besides naked old men in the ER," I say with a pointed stare in her direction. She sighs and rolls her eyes. "Leah, how are those little munchkins you teach every day?" I ask.

Leah had talked about being a teacher ever since we worked on that group project together in middle school. She said she wanted to teach Kindergarten because it was the cutest age, however from some of the stories I've heard I think it might also be the sassiest age. She went to UT to get her degree and is currently taking online classes to get her master's.

"They're as crazy as ever. One of them brought me a frog the other day after recess and I almost screamed. I had to very politely tell little Oscar that frogs needed to stay outside so they can find their way back home." Taylor makes gagging noises, bringing our attention to her.

"There's no way I wouldn't have thrown the whole kid back outside." She says waving her hand in front of her face. I shake my head as if to dismiss the comment then turn my attention to Lauren.

"What about you Lu, how's business been for the best realtor in Nashville?" Lauren is the most sought-after real estate agent in Nashville. I'm convinced the girl could sell a cardboard box to God himself if the pitch was right.

"It's been steady, I have been absolutely booked the last few months. I am hoping to get a bit of a break here soon though. People usually don't want to be moving during the holidays." She shrugs. With it being the beginning of December, Lauren usually hits the start of her slow season which lasts from now through the New Year. Then it's back to business booming.

Before I can respond and tell her I might be using her to find me a place, a yawn completely takes over my body.

"Okay, I think that's enough catching up for tonight. Let's let our poor girl sleep." Leah says, patting my head. "We will have plenty of time for girls' nights now that she's back." Everyone stands to clean the coffee table off, throwing away empty containers and taking wine glasses to the sink.

"Yeah, I guess I better hit the sheets. I have to start looking for a job tomorrow." I say optimistically. We all finish cleaning up the living room and hug Leah and Lauren goodbye. Before I make my way back to my room I run up to Taylor, throwing my arms around her neck. "Thank you, for being the best friend I could ever ask for. I don't know what I would have done without you." Her curly red hair tickles my face, but I don't move until she does. She takes a step back looking at me, her grayish-blue eyes, locking with my own.

"Sisters forever." She kisses my cheek and leans back again. I squeeze her arms, scrunching my nose to try and fight back tears.

"Sisters forever." I let her go and walk back to my room and strip my joggers off, leaving me in only my sweatshirt and underwear. I turn on the fan, plug up my phone, and crawl under the big down comforter. Burrowing into bed I can't help but think about how this was probably going to be the best sleep I've had in ages.

Chapter 3

CLOSING down the bar last night has me absolutely dragging this morning. When I opened Chattahoochies a couple of years ago, I didn't plan to just open it and hire a crew to run it. I wanted to be there, serving the locals who made this place what it was. A place of solitude for the misfits and outcasts in this crazy town, who others seemed to turn away or flat-out ignore.

I put my heart and soul into this place to make it different, and everyone knew it. When I got out of the Navy a few years back, I was in a pretty awful place. Serving for 12 years really leaves you with some scars, both mental and physical. I decided after a while that I needed something to keep me busy. Something to give me a purpose and get me up and out of the house every day. The bar has proven to do just that, as I spend most of my days and nights there.

I try to keep a healthy balance in my life outside of the bar. I will go to the shooting range or the gym with my best friend, Tucker, or get other shit done that needs doing. Sometimes I like to take Riley to our special place for a run, but besides that, I'm more of a home-body.

Being a bar owner myself I don't really have the desire to go out to someone else's bar when I'm off. So most of my downtime I spent at home with my girl Riley. Riley is a Belgian Malinois and was my service dog when I was a Navy SEAL, and she is the best one I could have asked for. She's been the only constant in my life through all the good shit and the worst shit. Well, except for Tucker, but I prefer Riley's company most days. Though I wouldn't tell him that.

Today, I decided to drag my ass out of bed and hit the gym with Tuck before going in to look over the books at the bar. The less exciting part of the job, but it still needs to be done. I make my way to Brüman's, the coffee shop that is just a few doors down from the gym, because there is no way I am getting through a workout without some caffeine. *I'm getting too old for this shit.*

After grabbing my coffee from Clara, the overzealous barista who is always much too chipper this early in the morning. I head out the door towards the gym.

I make my way down the sidewalk while trying to set my workout goal for the day on my smartwatch when suddenly my coffee is spilled all over me.

"Shit!" I mutter as the hot coffee pours over my arm and hand. I look up and notice I have run directly into a woman standing outside the empty building on the strip, not just any woman, but probably the most gorgeous woman I have ever seen.

"Oh my god, are you okay?" she asks, before looking down at her own shirt a few moments later. "Dammit," she whispers as she wipes the coffee off of her shirt.

"I am so sorry, I was just looking in the window and I didn't even see you coming," she says quickly before bending down to grab my empty cup. I shake the coffee off my hand and arm before grabbing the cup from her.

"Yeah, it's fine, don't worry about it." I grump and toss the cup in a nearby trash can.

She finishes dabbing the coffee spots from her sweatshirt and tosses her hair behind her. She has blonde hair that is set in loose waves, it falls down her back, stopping just at her waist. She's wearing a white sweatshirt *that is now stained thanks to me*, ripped blue jeans that hug her curves just right, and a pair of tan and white sneakers.

She looks up at me, as I stand over a head taller than her, and when I look down to meet her gaze, the first thing I notice is her eyes. The sun hits her insanely blue eyes just right and I am drawn to them immediately. They have a line of darker blue surrounding a much lighter, sky blue. Strokes of dark blue swirled in like lighting through the lighter blue parts, and dammit if I couldn't pull my attention away from them.

"You owe me a new sweatshirt." She raises a brow but her voice is all tease.

"Is that so?" I say as I clear my throat. Hoping the way I was just staring at her eyes wasn't completely obvious. She gives me a puzzled look.

"Umm, I'd say so." She waves her hands up and down her torso, pointing out the rather large coffee stain on her otherwise pristinely white sweatshirt.

"Well. It *was* an accident, so I'm not sure why I'm suddenly in charge of replacing your clothes." I argue back. "Maybe you shouldn't absentmindedly stand right in the middle of the sidewalk."

I'm not sure why I am arguing with this woman. Even I know that I sound like an asshole right now; I think I would stand here arguing with her all day if it meant I got to be around her a little longer, her presence is intoxicating. I wouldn't even mind replacing her freaking sweatshirt if I knew what the hell a CCA was. But here I am, arguing. She stands there staring at me, but her ocean eyes suddenly have a fire behind them.

"Are you seriously blaming *me* for not paying attention?" she lowers her sunglasses onto her face, clearly done with this conversation. Fine by me.

"Maybe *you* should take your head out of your ass and pay attention to where you're going." She walks past me and struts towards the coffee shop. I turn around to watch her go, the crease in her jeans from her perfectly round ass has my mind somewhere it should *not* be. When my eyes make their way back up to hers, I catch her looking back at me. I wink at her, making her narrow her gaze at me right before she walks through the door of the coffee shop. When I look down at my watch, I realize I am now late to meet Tucker at the gym.

"Bout time your ass showed up. Where have you been? You usually beat me here." Tucker hassles me as soon as I step in the door.

Tucker has been my best friend since middle school. I had been getting bullied every day by some of the older kids and one day Tucker saw it happening and stepped in. He was the only person that ever stood up for me. I guess his brotherly instinct kicked in for *me* that day.

He was very protective over his younger brother, Tank, so his instincts to stand up for others were strong. We've been friends ever since. When I told him I was going into the Navy, after spending two very unfulfilling years in college, he shocked the hell out of me and enlisted with me. We went through hell and back together, and he'd become more like a brother to me with each passing day.

Since we got out and have been back home he's been working on building his business as an architect. We try to go to the gym or the range together as often as we can and he even pitches in at the bar from time to time when we're slammed. He's always there when I need him, and I'm not sure I'd ever be able to repay him for everything he's done for me.

"Yeah, sorry. I ran into someone on the way over." I say as I make my way over to the weight bench.

"Oh yeah, anyone I know?" he inquires.

"No idea. I literally ran *into* her. Spilled my coffee all over the damn place, her included." I admit.

"And you *didn't* get her name?" Tucker asks in amusement.

"Nope, but she did tell me I owed her a new sweatshirt. Then told me I should take my head out of my ass and watch where I'm walking." I laugh and toss my stuff on the ground.

"Damn, I like this girl already." Tucker teases, swatting at me with his towel.

"We doing this or not?" I swat back at him.

"Ready when you are Prince Charming." He bows with his arms outstretched. *Asshole.*

After Tucker and I finished up at the gym, I went home to shower instead of using the showers there. I was picking up Riley before going to the bar anyways, so I figured I would enjoy my own shower today.

When we get to the bar, we walk in the back door. The staff that is already here getting ready to open for lunch, greet Riley and give her all the attention she adores so much. I take the moment to walk back to the office and she follows soon after, laying at my feet as she always does. I'm trying my best to stay focused on my work, but those damn ocean-blue eyes keep invading my thoughts. This shit is going to take longer than I thought.

Chapter 4

Shane

I STOPPED in front of an empty storefront on my way to get coffee, before running errands and job hunting. I stood there thinking about how it would make such a great art studio. I pictured the wooden chandeliers I would hang above the front windows and how I would display different pieces each week until they sold. I tried getting a better look inside to see what other potential it may have but I couldn't see much. As I was stepping back and taking one final look at the outside, I was hit by *The Hulk*, apparently, and was suddenly covered in coffee.

"Shit!" the deep voice muttered, startling me and drawing my attention to where the hot coffee had landed on his arm and hand.

The man is built like what I imagine a Viking god would be sculpted after. He has dark brown hair that is cut high and tight, but is much longer on the top, and dark brown facial hair that lines his perfectly chiseled jaw. He has a muscular chest, and arms that are covered in tattoos and strained against the sleeves of his NAVY t-shirt. The tattoos on his arms go all the way down his hands and to his knuckles, which I find insanely hot. He stands at least a head taller than me, if not more. I quickly realize the coffee he's shaking off his arm is on me too. I wipe at my sweatshirt, to no avail, and ask if he is okay. When I look up at him, I get a glimpse of his gorgeous eyes. They are a deep, swimmable blue color with a sort of sadness behind them.

When I jokingly told him he owed me a new sweatshirt he was less than pleasant about it. Telling me I shouldn't stand in the middle of the sidewalk. Like, who the hell says that to someone they just walked directly into because *they* weren't paying attention? Today was not the day, *Viking Hulk*.

"Maybe you should take your head out of your ass and pay attention to where *you're* going," I announce as I stomp off towards the coffee shop. Before opening the door I glance back at where he stands, and the man freaking winks at me.

The audacity.

Wait, am I blushing?

I walk into the coffee shop and march up to the counter. The barista looks me up and down, smiling. "Can I get you a scone with your coffee?" she laughs in amusement.

"What?" I furrow my brow, having no idea what she is talking about. She points down to my sweatshirt and I realize she's referring to the big coffee stain on it. This is my favorite white sweatshirt from college, and it is a total goner. I sigh and look back up at her, forcing a smile.

"I'll take an iced vanilla latte to go. Hold the scone." I smile, genuinely this time, able now to appreciate her wit from before. I grab some cash from my wallet to pay and drop a little in the tip jar. A few moments later she hands me my latte and I'm on my way.

Despite the run-in with the extremely hot, mildly rude coffee spiller, who ruined my favorite sweatshirt, I am optimistic about my day looking for a job.

With that optimism *and* the need for a new top, among some other items, I decide to do a little shopping before I go and put in applications at the places I have written down. I had been in such a hurry to pack and get the hell out of Pete's apartment that I left most of my skincare and shower items there. Thankfully my makeup bag was in my Jeep that day because I would not want to replace all the contents of that bag. I'm not sure I can even afford that right now.

While driving around town, sipping my iced latte, I run my Jeep through the car wash before heading to the store. Two days on the road doesn't exactly leave a car looking its best. Now that she's looking shiny and new, I pull into the store so I can grab all the essentials I am lacking. First thing I looked for is a top to change into, since I didn't want to be applying for jobs looking like a slob. I change in my car and look down at the time. It's just now 11 AM, so I figure I will make my way to the places I listed to apply at.

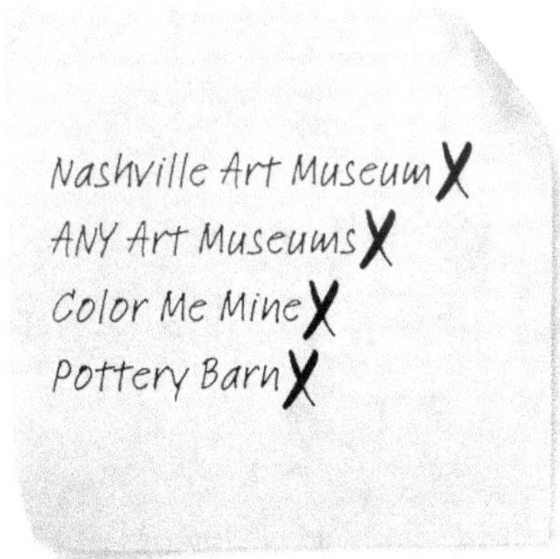

Well... this isn't going great.

ME

Can we please go out tonight? I need a mental break from applying - and getting turned down for jobs.

TAYLOR

I'm in. Where are we going?

LAUREN

Someone at work just told me about this cool bar. I'll get the address.

LEAH

It's Tuesday...

ME

TAYLOR

LAUREN

LEAH

OH MY GOD OKAY. What time?

ME

5 o'clock.

"Lauren, what the hell is this place?" Taylor whips her head around to face her as we stand on the sidewalk outside of the bar. The sign hanging above the door reads Chattahoochies.

"Luther said it's a really cool place. Come on, let's just go in." Lauren rolls her eyes at Taylor's dramatic questioning.

"What kind of name is Chattahoochies anyways?" Taylor huffs, folding her arms over her chest.

"Can we just go in and drink before I become a full-time chattahoochie?" I ask, being the first to walk towards the door. When we walk in, the inside matches the name. Unique as hell.

I look around taking in all the eclectic aspects of this place. It isn't a sports bar, or a bar and grill. It looks to be something of a biker-dive bar/pool hall hybrid. The actual bar is in the center of the back wall, with an oddly shaped, natural wood bar top and a bright neon sign with the bar name hanging above it. There is a hallway off to the left that leads to the restrooms, and pool tables are placed to the right of the bar, with a neon 8-ball sign on the wall.

Black and white photos of, what appeared to be, different biker gangs flood the walls around the pool tables. Between the bar and a random door in the corner, there's a jukebox that is playing Metallica. Pub tables fill the middle of the floor, while the wall to the left is lined with booths. One booth is reserved and has a single beer sitting on the table, with photos on the wall above of men in uniform and a plaque that reads *For our Fallen Soldiers - Until Valhalla*. The rest of the walls are covered in Viking-style weapons and shields. This is by far the coolest bar I have ever walked into.

"Let's just sit at the bar," I pull my attention from the reserved table and walk over to the bar.

Once we get seated, the woman behind the bar looks up at us, "What can I get you, ladies?" She's wearing a cut-up t-shirt with the bar name on it and loose-fitting torn-up jeans. Her makeup is fierce as hell with a thick winged liner and dark lipstick. She has her jet-black hair pulled up in a clip with a few loose pieces falling on the sides of her face. The name tag she has on the side of her shirt reads *Ruby*.

"Well, *Ruby*, what do you have that will wash away getting cheated on on your anniversary, quitting a job you love, moving 2,000 miles back home, and getting turned down for every *single* job you've applied for?" I ask, with a sarcastic smile. The sarcasm isn't towards her though, she seems perfectly pleasant – the sarcasm is directed toward my life.

"Tequila it is." She pours a shot and slides it over.

"Make it four," I say. She looks at me with wide eyes, and my friends follow suit.

"Oh my god, you guys, they're not all for me. 1,2,3,4." I count, pointing at each of us.

"Hell yeah, guess it's a shots night!" Taylor cheers.

"I'm off tomorrow, let's do it." Lauren drums her hands on the bar.

"Fuck it, those kids are watching a movie tomorrow," Leah says, surrendering her sober Tuesday night.

"And this is why you're my best friends," I hold my shot glass up.

"Cheers!" we all sing out in unison.

After tipping back our shots, and slamming the glasses back on the bar top, I look back at Ruby.

"This place is incredible. I have never seen someplace so, unique." I waved my hand around the bar. Her gaze follows my hand gestures and she smiles.

"Yeah, Max really poured himself into this place." She shakes her head.

"Max?" I repeated in question.

"Yeah, Max Mullins. He opened the bar a couple of years ago, after getting out of the Navy. He was a Navy SEAL, the dude is a total badass but he's too humble to flaunt it. He's also a great boss, but you didn't hear it from me. I like to give him shit, keep him on his toes." She winks at me, making me laugh.

"Noted," I playfully salute.

"You know, we're actually in desperate need of a new bartender if you're looking for a job." Ruby says, raising a brow. "I mean, I have no idea what you normally do, but if you can mix a drink it's steady cash flow and the tips are really great." She shrugs, wiping down the bar top. .

"Well, I'm not really that experienced," I admit, spinning my shot glass around..

"Oh, that's not true! You told me you made *everyone's* drinks at parties in college." Leah chimes in. She's not wrong. When we would go to parties I was at the drink table for the majority of the night. Not sure if it's something to brag about, but I got pretty good at it.

"But that's not enough to be a bartender... is it?" I turn to Ruby in question.

"Works for me." She says taking me by surprise.

"Wait, really?" I rear back, not hiding the absolute shock in my voice. I thought for sure there would at least be an interview, maybe she'd ask me to make a drink to show that I actually knew how. I don't know, something. Instead, she starts digging behind the bar for something as she keeps talking.

"Look, the last guy we had back here didn't know Jack Daniels from Jack Black." She sets an application on the bar and slides it towards me. I look at it, then back up at her with a blank stare.

"I'm the hiring manager so this is just a formality, but the job is yours..." She trails off.

"Shane. Shane Thompson." I eagerly say, offering my hand.

"Ruby Ranes," she shakes my hand. "Anyways, the job's yours if you want it." She smiles before going to grab more glasses.

I look at my friends who are watching with curious stares. "What do you guys think? Should I do it?" I scrunch up my nose, needing confirmation.

"Hell yes. Why do you think we always put you in charge of drinks on girls' night? You make them the best!" Taylor encourages. I look at Leah and Lauren who both shrug and shake their heads in agreement.

"Screw it, guess I'm a bartender," I toss my hands in the air before grabbing a pen from my bag to fill out the application. "Another, Ruby!" I call out, requesting another shot. When I get a raised brow from Taylor I roll my eyes and turn to face her fully.

"Taylor, I caught my boyfriend with his face between his assistants' thighs on our anniversary and I got turned down for a job at a Color Me Mine. *Color. Me. Mine.* I am doing another fucking shot." I turn to grab the shot Ruby had already poured for me before disappearing and notice two men – two gorgeous, tattoo-covered, Viking gods– *and a dog*– standing behind the bar now, staring at me.

The guy with dark brown hair, deep blue eyes, and muscles I would gladly curl up and die in, was none other than the one who spilled coffee on me earlier today. He snickers then walks to the other end of the bar to talk to customers, the dog following behind. The other guy, the one with copper brown hair, forest green eyes, and a bright smile looks at the four of us and says, "sounds like we need another round, what are we drinking, ladies?" he claps his hands together eagerly.

"Can you make a key lime martini?" Taylor asks, her most flirtatious voice in action.

The guy leans in a little closer to her, "You got it, darlin'." He winks at Taylor and gets to work making her drink. She watches him move around the bar and grabs my arm dramatically.

"I think I'm in love," she holds her free hand up to her chest, all goo-goo-eyed at the bartender.

"Well, he clearly meets all of the qualifications." I tease, tossing back my tequila shot, but my eyes never leave the man who stands at the other end of the bar.

Of course, he works here too.

Ruby makes her way back up front and I wave the application to show her I'm done filling it out, and she smiles before walking over to me.

"Oh, perfect. Hey, Max. Come meet the new bartender I just hired." She calls out, and what do you know, the beautiful, coffee spilling, Viking is my new boss. Awesome.

"Max, this is Shane Thompson. Shane, Max Mullins." She introduces us as I roll my lips together, then smile up at him extending my hand out.

"Pleasure to meet you, Max," I offer my sweetest voice. He quirks a brow and takes my hand. "You too." He grunts, offering the saddest excuse for a smile.

First impression, not great.

Second impression, also not great.

"Can you start tomorrow?" Ruby is moving behind the bar not missing a beat.

"Um, yeah. What time?" I ask, bringing my attention to her and away from Max's eyes.

"4 o'clock. I'll start you off with the night shift, once you get that down everything else is cake." She waves her hand across her face.

"I'll be here." I smile at her. She stops and glances down at my hand, which is embarrassingly still gripped with Max's.

"Max, she might need her hand back." Ruby teases. Max glares at her as he releases my hand. "Welcome to the team, Shane. See you tomorrow." He turns to walk away.

Oh, goody. Max will be here. Maybe he'll bring his dog because *she* seems wonderful.

Chapter 5

RILEY, Tucker, and I finally made our way out of my office to grab ourselves a drink, when I got behind the bar the first sight I was greeted with was the same face I hadn't been able to get out of my head all day. Who was this girl? And why was she showing up everywhere today? I overheard her telling her friend that she was taking another shot due to an ex's infidelity and being jobless. Checks out to me, I'd be drinking too.

She turned to grab the shot Ruby poured her and her eyes locked with mine. I snickered at the comment she'd made before making my way to the other end of the bar. Tucker, however, stayed behind to flirt with the redhead. When Ruby noticed me back there she called me over.

"Hey Max, come meet the bartender I just hired," she says before introducing us.

Well, that answers my *why is she showing up everywhere* question I guess. I nod and start walking in the direction of the girl seated at the far end of the bar.

"Pleasure to meet you, Max." She offers her hand, with a sweet smile.

"You too." I take the hand she extends into mine, and I feel a wave of heat in my chest. *What the hell is this?*

Ruby buzzes behind the bar like she always does, rambling about something to Shane, and I can't stop staring at her. Her smile lights up the whole damn room and I can't figure out how someone who was two tequila shots into grieving her relationship and being turned down for some crappy job, seems so… *happy.*

"Max, she might need her hand back." Ruby teases. I glare at her and retract my hand, as Ruby makes a hasty exit from the bar to the dining room floor.

"Welcome to the team, Shane. See you tomorrow." I turn to walk back to my office, but her sweet voice stops me.

"Your dog is beautiful, does she like people?" Shane asks, hopping down from her barstool. She bends down to pet her before receiving an answer.

Riley can be a little judgemental at times, she likes people she's known for a while, but she can be kind of wary of newcomers. Before I can tell her any of this though, she reaches her hand out to her. To my absolute surprise, Riley walks right over, wagging her tail and brushing up against her.

"Riley typically doesn't like new people, but it seems that's not the case with you," I fold my arms over my chest as Riley is now rolled over letting her pet her belly. *What the hell, Riles?*

"What a sweet girl you are." Shane praises, as she pets Riley's belly. When she stands to head toward the ladies' room, I can't help but smile. It seems like I'm not the only one who got a warm feeling about the new hire since Riley is now following her down the hallway.

"What's got you smiling like that?" Ruby bumps my arm with her shoulder.

Where the hell did she come from?

The grin dropped from my face as quickly as it got there. "I have no idea what you're talking about," I deny as I pour myself a drink.

"Oh please, Mr. Grumpy Puss. *Nothing* makes you smile." She looks around the bar as if she'll find the reason. "Spill." She narrows her gaze at me. I'm not playing her games today.

There wasn't even anything to share, besides the fact that the woman she just hired as a bartender, at *my* bar, is the only thing I have been able to think about since the moment I met her.

"I smile plenty," I plaster on a big, fake smile, and reach to ruffle her hair but she pulls back before I can.

"I will literally cut your fingers off, Maxwell. Do not try me." She threatens, holding up her index finger as a warning. I lift my arms in surrender and back away from the bar. I go back to my office for the rest of the evening, wondering how the hell I am going to keep my head straight with this little ray of sunshine working in my bar.

THE NEXT DAY

When I got home from work last night, I found myself unable to think of anything other than Shane. Which was annoying as shit. I'm not a relationship guy, never have been, and never planned to be. After losing as much as I have, it just makes sense not to willingly let anyone else become significant in my life. Not feeling anything is better than setting myself up for pain in the future. I had been successful in my mission until quite literally, running into Shane. For the first time in a long time, I felt something...new.

The fire that lit inside of me when I saw her blue eyes, so wild and fierce, had me wanting to know every thought that ran through the mind behind them. Then the radiant smile that beamed across her beautiful face had me wanting to hear every sweet thing that ever came out of her mouth.

Not to mention the way she seemed so unbothered by the disaster happening in her life, left me completely dumbfounded. I was marching into uncharted territory thinking about her the way I was, but I was never one to back away from a challenge. Which is what I fully expected her to be. I'm hoping she stays busy with Ruby training her tonight so I can fucking focus.

I'm in the middle of said thought process when Tucker walks in and takes a seat on his usual barstool. "Barkeep!" he shouts, slamming his fist on the bar top. Bringing my attention to him, and away from Shane, who is watching Ruby show her how to use the terminal behind the bar. He knows I hate when he calls me that, but that will never stop Tucker.

"Don't call me that." I raise my brow at him. I grab a glass to make his usual drink, which is the same as mine, whiskey on the rocks.

"Well, maybe you can lighten up a little tonight. We are celebrating." He grabs his glass and motions for me to pour myself one. I look at him curiously but go ahead with the pour.

"Alright, what are we celebrating?" I hold my drink up next to his, waiting for his response.

"Guess who just signed the contract to build the new youth center downtown?" he wags his eyebrows. I think about fucking with him and saying Greer's Contracting, the company he is always up against for jobs. But I don't want to kill whatever high he is riding right now from getting this job so I decided against it.

"You?" I tip my glass toward him.

"Hell, yeah man." He clinks his glass with mine and downs his drink.

"Congratulations, brother. I know you worked hard to lock that one down." I follow his lead and tip my drink back.

"Man, I can't believe it. This one was tough, but they signed today." He runs a hand through his hair. "I thought for sure they'd go with Greer's." He shakes his head and a smile comes across his face. Tucker is one of the hardest-working guys I've ever met. He's poured his heart and soul, and every spare minute he has, into building this company from the ground up. No pun intended.

"You deserve it, man. You've worked your ass off to get where you are. They made the right choice." I clap him on the shoulder and grab two beers before walking around the bar. "Rack 'em. Drinks on me tonight man." I walk over to the pool tables and grab a cue. He sets it up and I let him break.

"That's the girl from last night, right?" Tucker nods his head toward Shane. I take my shot, sinking balls in 3 different pockets.

"Yeah, Ruby hired her as the new bartender," I answer, making my way around the table.

"Oh yeah? I sure as shit hope she's better than the last idiot that y'all had back there." He jokes and takes a pull from his beer.

"Apparently she has a little bit of experience, but Ruby is gonna train her to make sure she really knows what she's doing," I say on a scratch. I stand up and grab my beer, as Tucker walks up to the table for his shot.

"Never seen her around here before last night, you think she's new in town?" his eyes cut over to me as he aims.

"Not sure, but uh, as it turns out, she's the girl I walked into yesterday morning," I look back over at her, noticing she has moved down the bar and is talking to Lenny and a couple of his guys who come in here regularly. She smiles at them and laughs at something they say. Her laugh carries through the loud bar and it is the cutest fucking laugh I've ever heard.

For someone who's spent 36 years completely unconnected when it comes to romantic relationships, this girl has me questioning my decisions in that area, and I've only known her for two days. Tucker looks at me, then back over at Shane and laughs before taking another shot.

"What are the fucking chances?" he asks, rhetorically.

And isn't that the question of the hour?

What are the fucking chances?

Chapter 6

Shane

"Oh, my god. Wait, wait, wait." Lauren laughs as she tries not to spill her wine everywhere.

"So he walked right into you. *Blamed you.* Then winked at you?" she recaps.

"Yes," I nod in confirmation.

"Then you snag a killer bartending job, without so much as an interview, and it turns out he is your new boss?" Leah adds flipping her finger back and forth.

"And he's smoking hot." Taylor chimes in with a wag of her brow.

"All correct." I reach for my wine, and sit back on the couch with my throw pillow tucked in my lap.

"I can't believe you didn't tell us this while we were still at the bar. Your life just got interesting as hell," Lauren says as she shoves a whole cracker in her mouth.

"More like, complicated as hell." I fall back and groan, covering my face with the pillow I have been cradling. "You know I'm swearing off all men anyways, so this shouldn't even be a problem." I shrug, tucking the pillow back under my arms.

Taylor and Lauren start laughing at my unconvincing proclamation. "I'm so glad this is amusing to you two." I throw the pillow at the two of them, and it lands perfectly between them, knocking the cheese out of Taylor's hand and hitting Lauren in the face. Now Leah and I are the ones laughing. We'd decided to have another girls' night after my first-night bartending so I could fill them in on how it went. They insisted on more details about my *"sexy new boss"*, and margaritas, so here we are.

"I still can't believe it's called Chattahoochies. What kind of name is that?" Lauren laughs, trying not to spill her margarita everywhere.

"I don't know, I am so curious to find out though. It's very original." I make a mental note to ask Ruby or Max the next time I work because I just don't think you name a bar something so unique without there being a story behind it.

We spend the rest of the night re-watching *Pretty Little Liars* and discussing how obviously suspicious they act and how we could have done it better. Man, I missed this.

It's only my second shift at the bar but I feel like I'm starting to get the lay of the land. Ruby is amazing at training me because she is unbelievably patient. Which I was sure to tell her around the third time the POS froze after me using it today. POS may usually stand for *point of sale*, but today it's acting more like a *PIECE. OF. SHIT.*

"Have I mentioned how grateful I am for you and your endless patience with me?" I lower my head down and stepped back from the terminal.

"When you have a 3-year-old son, patient is all you can afford to be my friend." She smirks at me as she gets the screen working again. I walk over to the shelf and pull down bottles to start making drinks for the order I had just entered when the phone on the wall starts to ring.

"Got it," Ruby calls out. "Chattahoochies, what's your poison?" she answers the phone differently every time and I get a kick out of some of the lines she goes with. "Are you sure?" her voice sounds panicked so I turn to face her. "Okay, yeah. I'll tell Max and I'll be on my way. Bye." She hangs up the phone and I walk over to where she is standing.

"Hey, is everything okay?" The look of concern on her face is answer enough.

"Hendrix is really sick. The sitter said he spiked a fever and just threw up, I gotta go." Hendrix is Ruby's three-year-old son and from what she's told me, her whole entire world. She's a single mom and works this job to support the two of them. I already admire her for her strength *and* patience and I've known her for a whopping three days.

"Of course. You go take care of Hendrix, we'll be fine here." She looks at me, worried, and then looks around the bar.

"Ruby," I snap twice to get her attention. "Really, things will be fine here. Hendrix needs you more than we do right now. Go." She sighs but gives me a nod.

"Thanks, Shane. Do you mind letting Max know that I had to go?" she takes her apron off and sets it on the counter.

"Marco can help you run drinks on the floor when he isn't bussing." She is already grabbing her keys and heading for the door when I respond.

"Yes, I will tell Max, and I'll grab Marco when I need him. Now get out of here." I wave her off and smile. It isn't too slammed at the moment, so I don't see a reason to hunt down Max, I will just let him know Ruby left the next time I see him.

About ten minutes pass with me behind the bar solo, before Max comes out of his office. Lucky for me only two tables have ordered drinks that Marco has run for me, so I have been able to man the bar with no problem.

"Why the hell are you back here by yourself? It's your second night. You're not ready to be running solo." Max demands as he looks around the bar. His voice is deep and irritated and sexy as hell.

"Where's Ruby?" I turn to face him, trying to look as confident in myself as possible.

"Ruby had to leave early tonight. Hendrix is sick." I answer matter of factly. I am notably smaller than Max, but I am not against fighting him if he copped an attitude over Ruby leaving to take care of her kid.

"Oh shit," he muttered. "Alright. What do we got?" Well, that answer surprises me. Most bosses would show some sort of frustration over people needing to leave early if it left them in a pinch. Especially a pinch with a new hire. He seems much more understanding though. He comes around the back of the bar and throws a towel over his shoulder. Which isn't normally something to get excited over, but I suddenly wanted to be that towel.

Oh my god, get it together Shane.

Wait, why is he back here?

"What are you doing?" I stop myself from pouring the latest drink order to ask him.

"Well, last time I checked this is *my* bar, and I'm not leaving your rookie ass back here alone all night." He snaps.

I look around the bar and notice we are starting to get absolutely slammed. *Damn, that was fast.* Every table on the floor is filling up and there are only a few bar stools left open. I guess he has a point. Two sets of hands are definitely needed behind the bar tonight.

"Get some more glasses from the kitchen and let the guys know to be ready for the rush, I'm calling Heather in." He commands as he reaches for his phone. He is annoying and hot. That's probably a red flag on my part.

I go to the back and grab a tray of glasses and give the guys a heads-up about the rush that is about to come through. I head back out to the bar, but when I go to push the door open it hits something and slams back into me, making me drop the tray of glasses on the floor. Glass shatters everywhere. Completely embarrassed, I look up to see that I pushed the door directly into Max.

"Fuck." His voice is deep and laced with anger as he takes in the mess.

"I am so sorry," I say. "I didn't see you there..."

"Are you forming a new annoying habit or something? Go get the broom from the back and pay attention to your surroundings next time." He bites out through his teeth. I nod my head and tears start to well in my eyes. I hate crying in front of people, so I am more than happy to take a few minutes to regroup while I walk to the back to get the broom. I have had a pretty shitty week, and the fact that I'm making a fool of myself in front of my new boss, again, isn't helping.

I mean, I did just break like *a lot* of glasses, but still. After composing myself and grabbing the broom, as I was so kindly told to do, I head back to sweep up my mess. Max grabs my arm and it feels like electricity is shooting through my veins. My head spins around and I narrow my gaze at him.

"Can I help you with something?" I shake my head with attitude, hoping it covers the embarrassment.

"I'll do this. Go finish those drinks." His tone is still firm, but a *smidge* nicer than when he told me to go get the broom.

Hello, whiplash. Have you met Max?

"Okay." I pull my arm away from him and force a smile. I finish the drinks and walk over to the POS. And wouldn't you freaking know it, the damn thing freezes. Again.

"Fuck, me," I mutter under my breath.

"Careful what you wish for," a deep voice says from right over my shoulder. My eyes are wide when I turn to see Max standing there. "What's the problem," he nods to the screen. Like he didn't just say what I *know* he just said.

"Uh, the *piece of shit* froze up." I shake my head trying to find some clarity. I'm not going to tell him that this thing has an agenda against me and that this is the fourth time this has happened, *today*.

"Jesus. Is nothing safe in your presence?" he huffs, as he leans in to fix it. "There. You've got to type in the code from each ticket. It's not the same number every time," he explains before rushing to the other end of the bar.

When things finally start to slow down a little, and Max and I only have a couple of customers at the bar, he comes over to where I am standing at the terminal looking over my shoulder. His chest is almost touching my back and I swear I can feel the heat from his presence.

"Thank you," I say, still entering items from my current ticket. "For helping me figure this thing out." I look over my shoulder and his gaze immediately locks with mine.

"No problem. Ruby did the same thing for the first two weeks. She was too scared to ask me what was wrong." He chuckles. I laugh and turn back around.

"Well, two days isn't as bad as two weeks, I suppose." I finish entering my ticket and close out the screen. I make my way to where my customer just left the bar, taking his dirty glass and tip money from the bar top.

"I, uh.. I'm sorry for snapping at you about the glasses." His brow is furrowed and his jaw tight. A grumpy apology, that's a new one.

"Oh, it's fine. I would have been pissed if I were you too." I wave my hand dismissively, trying not to sound as defeated as I feel.

"I've realized that you may be having a shitty week, and I'm sure you don't need an asshole boss to add to the list of things going wrong." He looks at me from the corner of his eye.

"Me? Having a bad week? Noooo. My boyfriend cheating cause I wasn't a good enough girlfriend and galleries not hiring me because I'm not a good enough artist, make for the best - week - ever." I say with sarcasm dripping in every word. I huff out a sad laugh and look back at Max, but he does *not* seem amused.

"Don't ever think for a second you weren't good enough for some guy. He sounds like an asshole if you ask me." He's standing there with his arms crossed over his chest, looking as serious and pissed off as usual, then he nods to the crowd of people and begins to move behind the bar again. "We have customers." He walks ahead to someone who just took a seat at the end of the bar near the jukebox, as Heather brings up a drink ticket from a couple who just sat down at a booth. I can't help but stand here wondering why he seemed so mad about what I said.

The rest of the night was confusing at best. The frustration in his voice when he would speak to me at times was a complete contrast to the heat I felt every time he would brush against me, or how he seemed concerned about why I was having a bad week.

There is no denying I think this man is sexy as sin, never mind the fact I'm trying to swear off men completely. At one point our bodies literally slammed into each other and I thought for sure it would be my second and *last* night working here. But he just growled and moved me out of the way and we were back to business as usual.

Then the comment he made to me, *"Careful what you wish for."* I mean what the hell is that about? I am so exhausted all I can think about is a hot shower and crawling into bed. And maybe a certain boss that makes my whole body tingle. But I'm trying to ignore that one.

NORMALLY I LIKE WORKING behind the bar when we're slammed. I love talking with the customers and hearing all of their wild stories. But working back here with Shane proved to be more difficult than I'd imagined. Between all the broken glasses, her giving the bar terminal a seizure, and the fact that her body literally slammed into mine, my focus was shit. It was only her second night behind the bar, and she was clearly having a majorly shitty week, so I tried to cut her some slack. Hearing her talk about being cheated on, had been surprising, but hearing her say she felt it was because she wasn't good enough, pissed me the hell off.

I won't lie, I kind of enjoyed watching her in her little frenzy. She would brush the loose strands of blonde hair behind her ear when she would go to enter orders on the terminal, and her nose would scrunch anytime she was confused about something she needed to enter. After I figured out she had been punching the wrong code in, causing it to freeze up, she was able to use it without having to tell me every time we got a new order.

When she would rush past me hints of lavender would flood my senses and I can't say I minded it. By the end of the night, we were all beat. When I finally locked the doors and switched off the "OPEN" light, I walked behind the bar to pour myself a whiskey. Shane leaned over the counter, burying her face in her arms.

"Oh my god, how do you do this all the time?" she groans. I look over and the view of her ass in her black jeans has me choking on my drink. I cough a few times and she shoots up and comes to pat me on the back. I wave her off when I finally have my faculties back under control and clear my throat.

"You get the hang of it after a while," I say, pouring myself another glass. Maybe this time I won't almost choke to death, now that her ass isn't positioned directly in my face.

"You want anything?" I ask her, my voice hoarse from the coughing fit.

"Um, sure. I'll just have a beer." She starts wiping down the bar as I pop the top of her beer and go to hand it to her. When she reaches for it her fingers trail over mine and it sends a chill down my spine. Marco and Heather have already gone home for the night and the guys from the kitchen just finished up.

"So, I have to know something." She says, pulling her drink closer to her.

"What's that?" I wondered.

"Where did you come up with the name for the bar? It's very… unique." She says, glancing over at me with curious eyes. I let out a sigh and lean back on the counter.

"When I was in the Navy, my buddy Red had the hardest fucking time saying some of the simplest words." I snickered at the thought of him.

"One day we were all shooting the shit and he was telling us about these fancy new Chattahoochie boards." I look over at her and she furrows her brow, a clear sign she has no idea where this was going.

"After a further explanation of the cheeses, crackers, different meats, and sometimes fruits that came on these boards, we realized..."

"Charcuterie! He was trying to say charcuterie?" she laughs. The corners of my mouth turn up in a grin and I nod in response. Shane lets out a belly laugh, and it's quickly becoming my new favorite sound. "That is the greatest thing I have ever heard. He sounds like a class act." She says as she brings her beer back up to her lips.

"Yeah, he really was," I whisper to myself. Shane's voice drowns out my own as she says goodbye to Jackie.

"See you tomorrow, boss," Jackie shouts as he walks out the back door.

"See ya, Jack." I smile and wave at him.

Jackie is one of my day one staff members, along with Ruby. He started as a dishwasher when I first opened, and has worked his way up to a cook. One of my best cooks, actually. He is a damn trooper during rush hours and he never let us get in the red. I don't think we could function the way we do without Jack on our team.

"Wow." A soft voice says. My attention is drawn away from the door, and back over to Shane. She sits on the bar now and is staring at me curiously.

"What?" I furrow my brow. Wondering why she's looking at me the way that she is.

"You've got a great smile." She mentions quietly, smiling as she brings her beer back up to her lips. Those plump, pink lips of hers are currently driving me mad. The thought of what they would feel like wrapped around me instead of that bottle has me struggling to focus on anything else.

"Thank you," I clear my throat. "Yours ain't so bad either, Sunshine," I reply and look up at her taking a few steps to close the distance between us.

"Sunshine?" she questions. I look at her mouth and she swallows hard.

"Mhm.."

She looks confused and excited at the close proximity between us.

Even sitting on the counter behind the bar she falls a couple of inches shorter than me. With her head cocked to the side and her gaze narrowed on me, I can't seem to look at anything but her. Her eyes are on my lips then trail up and meet my own.

"Why…" she starts to ask her question as I lean closer, towering over her just slightly. I place my hands on each side of her, my fore-arms brushing against her hips. I bring my lips close to her ear.

"Maybe someday I'll tell you," I say, my voice deep and direct.

I lean back just enough to watch her face. Her chest rises and falls more quickly now. Her eyes shoot from my lips and back up. She opens her mouth to say something just as my phone goes off. She turns her head as I pull my phone out of my pocket; a message from Tucker.

> TUCKER
>
> Wanna pack up your dick and come unlock this door?

I look up to see Tucker standing outside the front door of the bar.

"Fuck me," I mutter under my breath. I'm never hearing the end of this. My eyes snap back up from my phone when I hear the softest voice say,

"Careful what you wish for." When my eyes meet hers it's like they're burning a hole right through me. I take a step back and clear my throat.

"You should get going." I open the door to the kitchen, gesturing for her to leave. She glances over her shoulder to see Tucker standing outside the bar window. He gives her a shit-eating grin and waves, so. Fucking. Big. *Good God, Tucker.*

She turns back around and I notice the flush to her cheeks, just as she hops down and grabs her jacket. "Right. Um. See you tomorrow." She says in a hurry.

"You're not working tomorrow," I say, watching her in her little frenzy again. She stops and looks up at me.

"Oh, well I'll see you – later." She looks between my eyes and then hurries out the door.

I walk over to let Tucker in the front door, threatening him as I do. "Not a fucking word," I say, my voice firm.

"Yeah, fucking, right my dude." He says in a much too enthusiastic tone. He is grinning ear to ear and it makes me wish I could take back the last five minutes of this night. "Are you fucking the new bartender?" he asks as he sits down on a barstool. I spin around to face him, my jaw now clenched.

"No." I bite out and he lifts his hands defensively.

"Alright. alright. Down, boy. What's the deal then?"

"No deal, Tuck. We were just closing the bar."

"Mhm.." He looks at me with a smug look. I sigh and further explain,

"Ruby had to leave to get Hendrix, so I was stuck helping her rookie ass tonight." I wasn't sure who I was trying to convince that what just happened was nothing, Tucker, or myself.

"You're so full of shit, Maxwell." He smiles wide as he chews on some peanuts. If there's one thing I hate more than Tucker calling me *barkeep,* it's when he uses my full name.

"I swear to god, Tucker, call me that again and I'm throwing your ass out." I finish getting the receipts sorted and hand him a beer.

"Wait, why are you even here?" I ask, pulling my head back. Just realizing that I wasn't expecting him to show up tonight.

"Ah, yes. The reason for my untimely interruption," he lifts his brow and dusts his hands off. "I need to borrow your truck this weekend. Tank is back and needs some help moving stuff to his new place. The bronco just doesn't have enough space for all his shit." He rolls his eyes, even though I know it's just for show. There isn't anything he wouldn't do for Tank.

"Yeah man, of course." I agree.

His younger brother, Tank, just got out of the service and moved back home. He is five years younger than Tucker and Me and has been serving for the last five years. He suffered a minor back injury during duty this past year and was honorably discharged. I knew he wasn't handling it well, and that Tucker was really worried about him.

I had mentioned that if he needed a job, I would hire him at the bar. Tank has far too much pride to take a job working for his older brother, but he and I have always gotten along so I figured the bar would be an easy job for him to take without feeling like a charity case. If anyone understood the need of having something to keep your mind busy after getting out of the service, it was me.

"Let him know I'm looking forward to having him working here as well." I glance up and Tucker gives me a nod.

"Will do, thanks again, brother." He says as I toss the receipts down on the counter.

"Why don't you come back to grab my spare keys real quick so you can pick up the truck this weekend whenever you need it."

"You sure man?" he asks, standing from his barstool.

"Yeah. I've got my bike, and since *I'm* not stuck helping move shit around town, I'm set." It's been forever since I've gotten on my bike. I usually take Riley with me wherever I can, so the truck is always my first option. It may be a nice change of pace to cruise a little this weekend.

SHANE

I got out back and hopped in my Jeep. My head was absolutely buzzing, and it was not from the half of a beer that I drank. No, I believe this buzzing would be from the fact that my insanely sexy, frustrating, hot, and cold boss just had me caged in on the counter, whispering in my ear, and giving me a nickname that made my stomach flip.

What the hell is wrong with me?

The fact that he calls me sunshine then basically kicks me out of the bar seems a little like a contradiction. Who doesn't want to be around sunshine? Is he a vampire? Is he that weird guy from *Benchwarmers* that's allergic to the sun? Or wait, was that guy just afraid of the sun?

Either way, whatever is going on, has my head spinning. It shouldn't matter though, right? I have sworn off men. I don't trust men. Men are trash.

I need a second opinion. When I go to text Taylor to tell her what the hell just happened, and get some unhinged, crazy girl advice, I realize – I don't have my phone. I kept it in my pocket all night, so my guess is, it fell out while I was getting all hot and bothered on the bar counter. Now I have to go back in there, where I was so hastily rushed out. Fantastic.

I walk back through the kitchen and out the door to the bar. Very carefully so as not to hit anyone this time. But the bar is completely empty. I assume Max is outside talking to whoever was out there before because the receipts from the night are still on the counter and the front door is unlocked.

I look around the bar counter for my phone, but I don't see it. I am about to give up when I barely spot it on the floor. It looks like it got kicked under the bar, so now I have to lie on the ground and reach my arm on the nasty floor to retrieve it. Would it be too dramatic to abandon this mission and just buy a new phone? Since I'm not exactly flush with cash I decide to just suck it up and reach for it. I hear the front door fly open just as my fingertips fail to reach my phone by a hair.

"Ugh, hey boss, do we happen to have a little grabber arm around here or something? I can't reach my phone." I jump to my feet, awaiting his answer. Which I assume will be no. How many people keep a grabbing stick around a bar? All of a sudden I am face to face with someone in a black ski mask.

Before I can move or scream he's grabbing my arm, turning me to face away from him, and shoving something into my back. Which I can only assume is a weapon. He tells me to empty the register, but when I look at it, the register drawer is gone. I assume Max took it back to his office before starting on the receipts for the night.

Speaking of Max, where the *hell* is he right now?

I answer the robber, my heart racing against my chest.

"We don't have one." I spit out. He grabs my arms tighter.

"Don't fucking lie to me, princess. Get me the fucking drawer." He grits out through his teeth. My heart is hammering against my chest, and tears begin to form in my eyes because I suddenly don't see myself getting out of this situation. I try to answer but I can't find the words. I already told the truth so I'm not sure what lies I should tell that could possibly make this situation less hostile.

"I — I.." *Say something Shane, dammit.*

Before I have the chance to come up with a lie, he spins me around and slaps me across the face, causing me to fall across the bar, knocking some glasses onto the floor. I hold my face and feel the tears I didn't know were falling.

"Did I fucking stutter? Where is it!" He shouts, holding a gun up to my face. Before my mind can process what's happening, two large bodies rush in. I look up to find the guy who had been outside the bar earlier, now throwing punches at the robber.

Isn't that the martini guy?

The guy in the ski mask lands a punch and Max's friend steps back, but there's still control in his movements. When he starts to walk back over to even the score, the robber grabs my beer bottle from earlier and breaks it on the bar top. He swings it so fast I would have missed it, had I blinked.

"Fuck!" the friend shouts. I jolt from the sound, and when my eyes open again, Max is behind the robber, pulling his arms behind his back. He pushes him to the ground and holds him there.

"Tuck, man, talk to me. You good?" he asks. His voice is so steady, like the things that are happening are some minor convenience and not something that is insanely traumatizing.

"Yeah man, fucker cut me pretty deep though." This guy sounds just as calm as Max. Me, however, my eyes are wildly darting between the two of them. My breath is coming so fast now, I think I am two seconds away from a full-blown panic attack, and my face stings from where I was slapped.

"Shane, can you call the police?" I look at Max but my body doesn't move. I see his eyes move to his friend and he nods his head in my direction. My eyes follow his gaze and the guy is coming around the back of the bar. He picks up a bar towel, holding it firmly on his cut hand.

"Shane, my name is Tucker, great to meet you." He grins and then winces.

"Do you think you can grab the phone and call the police? I need to keep this here." He motions to the towel placed on his hand. "And Max needs to keep *that* from moving until they get here." He nods to where Max has the guy pinned to the ground.

His voice is so kind, steady, and comforting. My breaths finally start to slow, ever so slightly, as he holds my gaze. I shake my head and pick the phone up off the wall to call 911.

"WHAT THE HELL WAS THAT?" Tucker asks, startled. We are back in my office getting the keys to my truck and talking about where Tank will be living and when he can start at the bar when we hear glass breaking out in the bar. I know Shane already left, so I'm not sure who would be in there. Then I remember I didn't lock the front door when Tucker came in.

"I don't know, but I'm not gonna wait to find out." I say, hastily making my way towards my office door. When I open it I hear someone shouting and I look up to see Shane standing behind the bar with someone holding a gun to her.

At a closer glance I can tell it is a fake, but I've already started seeing red. One thing about having Tucker as a friend, there is always an unspoken understanding between us, about almost everything. I head straight for Shane and he goes straight for the guy in a ski mask.

I look Shane over and check for anywhere she might be hurt. Her eyes are filled with tears, and so distant from everything that was happening.

"Shane. Are you hurt?" I study her but she never says a word. She watches as Tucker and this masked robber trade punches. I'm about to try again when I hear a bottle break.

"Fuck!" Tucker yells. Shane's body jerks, her eyes now more present at the moment, but I am up and over to help detain the guy before I can check on her again.

"Tuck, talk to me, you good?" I ask, never taking my eyes off Shane.

"Yeah man, fucker cut me pretty deep though." Shane's eyes start darting all around the room, and I nod Tuck over to talk to her. I can't very well do it while holding this piece of shit in his place. When all I want to do is go make sure she is okay.

After Tucker manages to get Shane to calm down a little bit and call the police; they are there in a matter of minutes. I hand him over and give my statement as quickly as fucking possible so I can finally go see if she is okay. I grab some ice, wrap it in a towel, and hold it to her face, brushing her blonde hair away from her tear-stained cheeks.

"How are you?" I ask. I know it's probably a dumb question, but I need to hear her sweet voice answer me. I need to hear her say she is okay. Her eyes still hold a look of vacancy behind them. She begins shaking her head as her ocean-blue eyes, now accompanied by red, look up at me. Everything inside of me breaks, seeing how scared she is.

"How did you stay so calm?" she asks, her voice hoarse. I take a deep breath in, changing the position of the ice on her face and wiping the dripping water from her cheek.

"It's just kind of instinct at this point," I answer vaguely. She nods her head and hugs her arms closer to her body; I want nothing more than to replace her arms with my own, and hold her until she feels safe again.

"Because of your time as a Navy SEAL?" I nod my head in response.

"After 12 years it becomes second nature to run towards danger and protect others." I shrug. I don't mean for it to sound like no big deal. It's actually a very big deal to me, but it's also true that it feels like second nature. The response from Tucker and me tonight was just normal for us.

"Thank you." She says, her voice barely a whisper. I look at her in confusion.

"For what?" I ask, unsure why she feels the need to thank me for something like that.

"Well, you probably just saved my life, Max. That's a big deal to me. You showed up and protected me – and while I'm sure you would have done it for anyone. Thank you anyways." She's right. I would have done that for anyone. It's also in my nature to protect those who can't protect themselves.

What she doesn't know is I wouldn't have seen red for anyone else, I wouldn't want to comfort anyone else the way I want to comfort her right now. I wouldn't have had the mind to rip that fuckers arms straight off of his body for slapping anyone else. Only her.

"You're welcome, Sunshine. You'll always be safe around me." I assure her as I drop the towel of melted ice into the sink.

"As much as I hate the thought of you having to drive yourself home after this, I should really get Tucker to the hospital to get stitched up. Are you sure you're okay? Is there anyone we can call to come pick you up?" she looks at the clock, as it's past midnight at this point, and shakes her head.

"No, I'll be fine. He definitely needs to get stitched up soon." She goes to walk away then turns back to face me.

"If you take him to the ER off of Church Street, my friend Taylor is an ER nurse there, she's great. She'll recognize you both." She grins and her cheeks begin to flush.

"Thanks, will do." I reply, waving as she walks through the kitchen and out the back door. Everything inside of me hates that I'm not driving her home.

When we get to the Emergency Room, Tucker has a fresh bar towel wrapped around his sliced hand. I look around trying to figure out which nurse is Taylor. It would have been smart of me to get a description, or a last name even. I walk up to the front desk and notice the older lady sitting there, typing away on the computer.

"Excuse me, I am looking for a nurse named Taylor, is she here?" Before the lady can answer, a fiery redhead walks up beside me, holding a chart in her hand.

"Who's asking?" she says loudly, side-eyeing me while still holding the paper from the chart open.

"You Taylor?" I ask, standing straight from the desk to face her. When I'm completely facing her a look of realization comes across her face.

"Oh, hey. You're Shane's boss, right?" she closes the chart and her body language shifts.

"Yeah, I'm Max, my friend has a deep cut in his hand and needs stitches." She looks behind me and sees Tucker holding the towel to his hand.

"Oh, martini man. Sure, yeah. Bring him on over, I'll get him fixed up." Her voice is so cheery now as we walk over to a triage area with Tucker.

"So how's my girl doing at work? Busting her ass I'm sure." She says so confidently.

"Yeah, she's doing alright," I answer vaguely. Not sure it's my place to tell her about the broken glasses, the frozen terminal, or, oh yeah, the fact that she was just held at gunpoint, *even though it turned out to be a fake,* and slapped across the face by some idiot.

"Probably a little shaken up after tonight though, I'm sure." Tucker pipes up. So, I guess it's *Tucker's* place to tell her then.

"What do you mean?" her brows furrow as she stops prepping the tray she'll be working from to stitch up Tuck's hand. I shoot him a warning look and he shrugs apologetically. I turn back to face Taylor who is staring daggers into my soul now.

"Why is she shaken up, Max?" she demands, her voice hard and cold.

"We had an attempted robbery tonight, she was the one behind the bar when the guy came in and he held a fake gun to her and slapped her around. She's not hurt, but she seemed pretty shaken by it." If looks could kill I'd be headed to the morgue.

"And you just fucking *left her*? Where is she? Did she call Leah or Lauren?" Taylor asks. She starts frantically scrolling through her phone, trying to text Shane or one of the other two people she just mentioned, but her hands are shaking and she can't seem to steady them.

"I asked her if she was okay to get home, and she said yes. I asked if we could call someone and she said no. So I brought Tucker here to get stitches and she went home I guess."

"Which, could I maybe get someone a little calmer to do my stitches?" Tucker chimes in.

"Of course she didn't call anyone else. It's almost one o'clock in the morning and Shane will never burden someone else for her own benefit, even when she needs it the most. It's one of the infuriating and endearing things that makes her who she is. But she shouldn't be alone right now." Taylor states, slightly calmer than she was before, but still very much stressed out.

"Look, I know you have to be here, mostly because my friend really does need stitches." I glance over at Tucker and he wears the biggest, most obnoxious smile on his face. Taylor's cheeks flush when she looks his way. "If you would like, I can drive by after I take him home and check on her." I offer. Taylor stares at me through squinted eyes, mulling the idea over. She finally takes a deep breath and agrees.

"As much as I would love to leave and do it myself, I really can't tonight. We are so understaffed it's ridiculous. I'll give you our address and you can drive by and check on her. I'm gonna text and check on her really quick first." She fires off a text and sets her phone down, turning back to Tucker. She takes a deep breath and smiles.

"Okay, mister. Let's take a look." She washes her hands and puts on her gloves, then gets started cleaning Tucker's wound. He was right, that shit is pretty deep. A few minutes later Taylor's phone chimes and she glances over.

"It's from Shane, do you mind checking it since –" she holds up her hands that are hard at work on Tuckers. I pick up the phone, hold it to her face to unlock it, and we both freeze.

"What's your address?" I bite out.

"155 Third Street. It's a blue house with white trim." She says quickly. I set her phone back down and look over at Tucker.

"I'm gonna call Tank and have him come pick you up. I'll see you tomorrow, brother." I clap him on the shoulder and he nods his head. Then I'm out the door and headed to Shane.

Chapter 9

Shane

The whole drive home from the bar my hands were shaking. I did my best to take deep breaths to fight off the panic attack that threatened to make its appearance. I tried to think of anything other than the events that just occurred, but every time I would close my eyes, it all came rushing back. I had pulled into the driveway just as my breaths started coming in so rapidly that I felt like I *couldn't* breathe. I texted Taylor to tell her it was happening. I haven't had a panic attack since my first year in college, I had hoped I would never have to experience another one.

I hold my phone in a shaky hand as tears start to fill my eyes and a lump forms in my throat. The sobs start coming rapidly, as the tears begin to stream down my face. The weight of my anxiety has me feeling like I am seconds away from throwing up, and since I seem to be immobile, I imagine it will land directly in my lap. I check my phone again, through blurry vision, with no new notifications. *Why isn't she texting me back?* Before I know it my door is being swung open. I throw my phone and scream, still unable to see clearly through my tears.

"Shane, Shane! It's okay, it's me. It's Max. You're okay." Max's deep voice washes over me and I blink a few times to clear my vision. He pulls me out of my Jeep, and into an embrace.

"Shh, I got you." His grip around me is tight and secure. He places his chin on the top of my head as my body shakes against his. I let the sobs take over my body to rid myself of them, before starting to try and regain control of myself.

"You're okay. I'm here. You're safe." I still haven't been able to muster a single word after throwing my phone at him. But my breaths are starting to slow down and I feel a wave of calmness wash over me. This is probably the fastest I have ever come down from a panic attack after it started.

I stand here in Max's arms until I am breathing normally again, he never once loosens his grip on me or stops telling me that I'm safe. I move my head to look up at him and he finally lets me loose a little bit.

"How did you know where to find me?" I ask, my voice raspy from the screaming and sobbing.

"I was with Tucker and Taylor when you texted her. She gave me your address so I could come to you." I feel a warmth wash over my body. I can't believe he was so willing to rush over here to be with me in the middle of what's charting as one of my worst panic attacks.

"I can't believe you did that," I say, looking down at my feet. Max sighs, catching my attention. I look back up at him and he's got his deep blue eyes locked with mine immediately.

"To be honest, I hated that you came home alone in the first place." I feel my cheeks heat at his comment. He must notice too because he quickly adds to his statement. "I just knew you were shaken up and I wanted to make sure you made it home okay." I nod in response.

I knew he didn't mean he actually wanted to come *home* with me.

However, after being held by him, having his strong arms and the warmth of his body against mine, I would toss the down comforter out for him any day.

"Well, thank you for showing up. I haven't had a panic attack since I started college, this was probably one of the worst ones I've ever had." I admit. He looks at me with concern on his face, but he doesn't press me for more information. Instead, he changes the subject.

"Meet me at the gym tomorrow. 10 AM." He commands. It's so sexy I don't mind that it wasn't a question.

"Um. Why?" I question, quirking a brow at him. He stares back at me and without words tells me not to ask questions, to just do as I'm told. And fuck it, after the way he showed up for me tonight, I will.

"What gym?" I ask instead, hoping for a verbal response since I am not actually in his head to retrieve the answer for myself. This question makes him smile and I want to remember Max's smile forever.

"Hall's Gym. Three doors down from where we met." He turns to walk away and a grin spreads across my face.

"I'll take an iced vanilla latte. Preferably *in* a cup." I tease. He gives me a warning look as he opens the door to his truck.

"Get your ass in the house. I'll see you in the morning," he smirks.

I turn to walk to the house, and Max doesn't leave the drive until I am safely inside. The panic attack from earlier is long gone now, as my head reels with thoughts of Max. I swore to myself not even a week ago that I was done with men. That they were all trash, not trustworthy and not worth my time. Now I sit here thinking about how the safest I've ever felt was during one of the shittiest nights I've had since I graduated high school – and it's all because of Max. I can confidently say if anyone will change my mind about men, it'll be Max.

MAX

It's our first week of self-defense training, and not once have I shown up without her iced coffee. My own little way of trying to make up for the first time we met. Shane is incredibly strong. She's quick on her feet and dedicated to getting better, so she's picking it up pretty quickly.

I was shocked when she actually showed up the day after I told her to meet me here. I saw the way that night shook her, seeing that fear wash over her face killed me, so I hope she will be more confident knowing she's equipped to take care of herself.

We are just finishing up a session and while my pride in her progress is skyrocketing, something else is trying to as well. Watching her train every day in her little sports bra and tight ass leggings is giving my dick a mind of its own. Things are about to get worse apparently because we both decided to fit in a regular workout after today's training.

Now I get to sit here in an almost empty gym, watching her run and squat and every other damn thing that keeps her body looking as heavenly as it does.

She's got a line running down the center of her stomach where the definition of her abs dares to show. Her waist is shaped like an hourglass, curving down to her hips that sit right above the most perfectly defined ass I've ever seen. Looking the way she does should be illegal.

Her long blonde ponytail whips back and forth as she runs on the treadmill. She pumps her arms and breathes so effortlessly, while everything bounces to the rhythm of her footsteps.

Goddammit, I have got to get out of here.

I walk to the back to start my usual full-body workout, leaving her to her treadmill up front. I manage to do a focused leg and chest before moving on to do my bench press. I'm doing my damn best to keep my mind preoccupied, and my eyes anywhere but on her.

I put my headphones on and start loading weights onto the bar.

When I'm finally done I lay back on the bench and ready my hands to start lifting. When my eyes lift above my head I am met with a navy blue workout set sculpted to perfection and a blonde ponytail.

"Jesus, fuck." I breathe out.

"Sorry to startle you. I tried to make myself known, but I'm guessing those headphones are pretty loud." Shane holds up her hands and smiles at me. I take them down and look back at her.

"Uh, yeah. Kinda." I stare at her waiting to see what she wants.

"Oh, right. I was saying, do you need a spot?" she asks, pointing to the weight bar. I can't help but laugh.

"Are you sure you can handle this much weight?" I ask, looking at the bar holding 280 pounds.

"No, but I figure two sets of hands are better than one if it gets too heavy, right?" she playfully shrugs. This girl earns every bit of the nickname I've assigned to her.

"Sure, you can spot me."

She smiles and claps her hands making me second-guess my decision. Shane stands there spotting me, daring to drag my focus to her body with each passing second. When I get to the last of my set, I start pushing for a couple more. She doesn't say anything but she walks around to the front of the bench where my feet are set on each side. I don't have time to worry about where she's going because these last few reps are kicking my ass and I am struggling.

I hadn't taken into account the workout I had gotten by sparring with her before I started this, so my arms were already tired. Right as I am about to lose the drive to finish this set, I shit you not, Shane sits down on me. Ass and dick perfectly aligned.

My arms lock, shooting the bar up and back into place and my head snaps up to look at her. She sits there, staring at me like she has no idea what she's done.

"What the hell are you doing?" I ask. My heart rate is growing — as well as a muscle I hadn't planned to work out today.

"I read that this helps with adrenaline to finish a set. It looked like you needed the encouragement." She answers as she puts her hands on her hips.

"Were you done?" she asks, pointing to where I have placed the bar back in its stand already.

"I wasn't, but I am now. Because if you stay sitting where you are much longer we're going to have a change of conversation." She looks at where she's sitting and her cheeks flush.

"Alrighty, then I'm just gonna hop up." She says and kicks her leg around the bench to stand up.

I sit up quickly trying to hide the growing erection in my gym shorts.

"I'm starving. You want to go grab some food?" I ask as I pick up my water bottle from the ground.

"Yeah, sure. But I have to shower first. I can't eat when I stink." She hugs her arms close to her as if to hide whatever stink it is she thinks she has. She still smells like lavender and sunshine to me.

"I could use a shower too, I'll meet you back out here in ten and then we can go." I grab my gym bag and head to the shower.

While I'm standing in the shower the only thing I can manage to think about is Shane. Her tight little body stripped down in a shower only one wall away. I still have a *hard* reminder of her perfect ass set directly on top of me. I decided to take care of this problem before going to try and have a meal with the culprit. When I walk out and look around I don't see Shane yet, so I grab my phone and see a text from Tucker.

TUCKER

Hey man. Finishing up a job. Wanna grab a bite?

ME

Just finished workouts with Shane. We were about to go eat. Wanna tag along?

TUCKER

You sure I won't be interrupting? 😏

ME

You're an idiot. You're welcome to come.

TUCKER

Alright. Where at?

ME

Spurs Diner, down the street from the gym.

When Shane comes out of the shower I can't help but stare. The woman just worked out for an hour, not a trace of makeup on her, and soaking wet hair. She's a fucking vision. She walks over to me and smiles.

"Much better! You ready to go?" she asks as she finishes putting her jacket on.

"Yeah, I told Tucker he could join us, I hope that's okay," I ask.

"Oh, yeah. Of course." A look of disappointment flashes across her face when she answers. It was so quickly replaced by her smile that I would have missed it had I not been looking for it. But I was looking.

"Alright, let's go then." I place my hand on the small of her back to lead her out the door.

We pull up to the diner at the same time as Tucker.

"Look at us all punctual and shit," Tucker says as we all come around to the front of our parked cars. I give him a hug then back up beside Shane. Before I can do the awkward re-introduction since she's technically met him twice already, she jumps in and does it herself.

"Hi Tucker, it's great to see you again. How is your hand?" she asks as she gives him a hug. Why the fuck does Tucker get a hug? *She was literally sitting on your dick half an hour ago, asshole. Lighten up.*

"It's doing much better, thanks for asking." Tucker looks over at me and raises a brow, bringing my thoughts back to the conversation happening. "I'm glad you and I get to officially meet without police, blood, and slight trauma present." He jokes with her.

"Yeah yeah, it'll be great. Can we go eat now?" I ask. My stomach is about a minute and a half away from trying to snack on one of my ribs.

"Yes, please! I'm starving." Shane pipes up.

When the woman who is seating us leads us over to a booth, we all three stand there for a second trying to figure out who will sit where. Seeing as how Tucker and I on one side would be a squeeze, and there is no way in hell I am letting Tucker sit next to her, I motion for her to slide in on the side facing the door and I slid in right behind her.

When I glance over at Tucker he gives me a knowing look. I roll my eyes at him and pick up a menu, he quickly directs his attention over to Shane.

"So, Shane. How have you been doing since the last time I saw you?" he asks. What a kind way to ask someone if they've gotten over being scared to death and bitch slapped by a robber.

The waitress comes over and pours us all a glass of water and we order. Shane ordering a cheeseburger and fries surprises me. I am used to girls with dainty, non-existent appetites. This woman can eat.

"I've been okay. I was a bit shaken up at first, but having boss man here train me is making me feel more confident. Safer." She says hiking her thumb over her shoulder towards me.

"Ah yes, the training. How *is* that going?" he smugly asks. I narrow my eyes at him as I lift my glass of water to my lips.

"It's going well. We had a really *hard* session today." Shane bumps my knee with hers and I spit out my water. Tucker bellows a laugh and Shane gasps before she lets out a giggle.

"You two are so not allowed to be friends," I say looking between the two of them.

My wide eyes land on Shane and she gives me a smirk and tilts her shoulder.

"You really thought I wouldn't notice?" she whispers as Tucker reaches for some napkins.

"Maybe, but I didn't expect you to tell *him*." I can't believe she just said that.

"Good luck trying to stop us." Tucker winks at Shane from across the table and I want to reach across the table and punch him in the forehead.

Stop winking at my girl.

Mmm…that was unexpected.

"Yeah, I think this is a friendship destined for great things," Shane responds as she lifts her glass to Tuckers.

"Hear hear!" Tucker responds as they clink their glasses together. I shake my head and grin. I actually like that Tucker and Shane get along. She's starting to overlap in more areas of my life, and I can't say that I mind it.

WHEN I first offered to train Shane, I thought I was doing it to make sure she was equipped to handle herself in dangerous situations. Call it the former SEAL in me that was used to training guys regularly. I am starting to realize though, I may have just wanted another reason to be around her outside of work. Now I find myself hoping she's never in a dangerous situation, or that if she ever is, that I'm right there to protect her myself.

I've never been a relationship guy, anything I started with a woman was usually over before sunrise. I preferred things that way. I didn't have to worry about hurting them, or forming an attachment and losing them. Not to mention, I'd never even met a woman who captured my attention in such a way that I wanted to spend more than a single night with them.

Until Shane.

We are both working behind the bar today while Ruby is out to see

Hendrix perform in his Pre-K Christmas recital. School is about to let out for the holidays, and for some reason three year olds are very busy this time of year. So that left us behind the bar and Heather on the floor.

"I am so sore, I can't lift my arms. If anyone orders top shelf, that's all you, boss." Shane says as she rolls her head around.

"Oh come on, we didn't even go that hard." I tease. We most definitely pushed it in the gym yesterday.

"Says you." She quips.

She leans across the bar to slide a guest their drink and the way her cut Chattahoochies shirt lifts up, showing the small of her back is driving me mad.

You'd think I would be immune to the effects of seeing her gorgeous tan skin since we spend so much time together in the gym, but no. Here I am, eyes gliding from her back to her ass and wanting to slide my hands into her back pockets.

My eyes snap up when she turns to face me, but it seems I've been caught. She quirks a brow at me and her mouth forms a little o as if she's about to say something. Before she can, Heather comes up to interrupt.

Thank god.

"Hey Shane, a table is requesting you," Heather says, leaning over the bar.

"Really, why?" Shane asks.

"If I had to guess," Heather starts, glancing back over her shoulder. "One of them probably thinks you're hot. And I mean, I don't blame them." She says jokingly, making Shane laugh. That contagious, beautiful laugh of hers. I, however, don't want to laugh. I want to tell Heather to wait on them herself and keep Shane planted behind the bar with me.

I look over to Shane who is picking at the skin around her thumb, something I've noticed she does when she's anxious.

"If you don't want to serve them, you don't have to. You are on bar duty today, so Heather can just keep the table." I say, facing Shane. I cross my arms, waiting for her to respond. She shakes her head and smiles.

"No, it's fine. I don't mind." She makes her way over there and I find myself unable to focus on anything else. She stands at the edge of the table, and one of the guys holds out his hand to shake hers. She shakes his hand and a forced smile appears on her face. When another customer sits at my end of the bar, I am forced to tear my eyes away from her.

Shane appears back behind the bar just as I am closing out tabs for my customers. When I look up, I see Heather back at the table Shane was requested at. Right as I am about to ask her why she'd come back behind the bar, the guy who had taken her hand when she first approached the table, waltzes up to her.

"Hey gorgeous, why'd you leave me lonely over there." He pouts. This guy is clearly drunk, and in the middle of the afternoon.

"Oh, I was needed back behind the bar, but Heather is more than capable of taking care of you." Shane answers him so professionally, with her bright smile intact. Seeing as how I hadn't told her I needed help, I got the unspoken message.

This guy leans over the bar, reaching a hand out for Shane,

"Well, I was hoping I could ask you for your number." He says with a smug grin. I have a mind to punch it right off of his face. As his hand inches closer to Shane, instinctively I step in front of her. Crossing my arms over my chest I look down at this pathetic excuse of a man.

"Well, as she said, she is needed behind the bar. Shane, would you like this... person, to have your number?" I ask, never breaking eye contact with the guy.

"Um, no." She says quietly.

"Why don't you have a seat and I'll have Heather bring you your check." I nod the guy back over to his table.

"What if I'm not done?" he arrogantly asks.

"You are." I bite out. He takes his sweet ass time getting back to his booth. Once he's there I tell Heather they're done and to run them their ticket.

When Heather returns she hands Shane the receipt, "Here ya go, It's still under your name." She sets it down on the counter and I notice a phone number written on it. I involuntarily grunt at the thought and Shane looks up at me.

She rolls her eyes as she picks up the ticket. Turning her attention back to the terminal she keys in the ticket number.

"Some guys just can't tell when you're not interested." She says, sliding the receipt into the drawer. She glances around the bar before facing me again.

"Then again, some don't know when you *are* either." She shrugs her shoulders and brushes past me. Her tone is so casual, but the statement feels loaded.

Have I missed a major fucking sign?

If so, I would be pissed.

This is the first girl that's ever captured my attention the way she does. The only one whose laugh makes me want to be a stand-up comedian, and whose smile lights up a whole damn room. Someone who cares so deeply for others that her own needs go unmet until she knows every other person is taken care of.

She's the one person who's ever made me question every belief I have when it comes to romantic relationships. If there were ever a person I *would* go all in with, it would probably be Shane. But if her comment was just that, a random comment, and I'm reading way into this. I don't wanna risk putting myself out there like that. That's just not a risk I'm willing to take. Not yet.

As Shane and I are getting ready to clock out from the morning shift, Ruby and Marco are coming in for the night shift. We still have about half an hour before our shifts are up when Taylor, and two other dark-haired girls I kind of recognized, come walking through the door.

"Shaney, we're headed to Topgolf, you coming?" Taylor asks, sliding onto a bar stool.

"I can't, my shift isn't over yet." She replies.

"Well just come when you're done! Boss man is welcome to join too." She side-eyes me then looks back over to Shane. Before Shane or myself can get a word in, Tucker comes busting through the door from the kitchen.

"Whoa, looks like a party. What, no tequila shots this time?" he teases, bumping Shane's shoulder, making her smile as she rolls her eyes at him.

"Very funny, martini man." Shane teases back.

"No, really. What are we all doing here?" Tucker asks, as his eyes scan over Shane's friends all lined up at the bar. "And I don't believe we had the pleasure of learning your names the first time you were here." He lays on the charm.

"Oh, Tucker, Max, these are my other two best friends, Leah and Lauren." Shane introduces. Tucker and I both nod and say hello.

"We're going to Topgolf, you joining?" Taylor says, directing her question at Tucker.

"Hell yeah, I'm in. When are we going?" he asks.

"Now! Shane and Max are joining after the end of their shifts, *right?*" Taylor presses.

"Of course. How could we say no, when you don't let us say anything at all." Shane eyes her playfully.

"It's called a strategy babe, always come prepared." Taylor winks at her.

"You don't have to go if you don't want to." Shane looks at me, almost like she's embarrassed by Taylor's brash invite.

"Eh, why the hell not." I grumble, winking at Shane. She smiles, a rose color creeping over her cheeks, and turns back to her friends.

"Okay, Max and I will meet you there," Shane says.

"Great! But, umm I need to take your car, we kind of ubered here." Taylor apologetically grins. Shane rolls her eyes and turns to me as she fishes the keys out of her apron.

"Do you mind if I catch a ride with you there?" she asks.

"Umm, Sure. But –" before I can finish, Taylor snatches the keys from Shane's hands and jumps off her stool.

"Perfect! See you guys in an hour. Let's go Martini Tucker." She waves a hand over her head and Tucker laps it up like a thirsty puppy.

When we finally clock out, I am getting a little more nervous about the fact I didn't get to warn Shane about how we would be getting to Topgolf tonight.

"You ready?" she asks, pulling her long blonde waves out of the sweatshirt she had just thrown over her head.

"Yeah, about that…" I start, as we walk towards the back door.

"Oh come on, don't back out on me now. It's going to be fun." Shane pleads.

"It's not that, I'm actually looking forward to it." I admit.

"Well, then what is it?" she asks, looking at me in confusion. I glance over and she follows my gaze to my motorcycle.

"Is this yours?" she asks.

"Yep."

"And this is how we're supposed to get there?"

"Yeah."

"And this is what you were trying to tell me before Taylor hi-jacked my keys."

"Pretty much," I answer.

"Lovely." She stares at my motorcycle and then looks back up at me.

"Do you trust me?" I ask, handing her the spare helmet. She stands there, thinking about it for a moment before grabbing the helmet from me.

"Yes, actually." She answers, making me smile. I'm not sure why hearing her say she trusts me has me feeling the way I do, but here I am. We get on the bike and I move the kickstand back.

"Hold on tight, Sunshine," I say as I start up the bike. It lets out its beautiful growl and her arms wrap around me.

Why does this feel so damn good?

Chapter 11

Shane

I WAS surprised by how much I actually trusted Max. Getting on the back of a motorcycle with someone is definitely at the top of the list of ways you'll know I trust you. But I always feel safe with Max. Our very first run-in outside the coffee shop was a small speed bump in comparison to the ways he's managed to show up for me since then.

I don't think he even realizes how big the gestures are, either. It just seems like second nature to him, to protect people. Showing up during my panic attack seems a little more intimate, but I guess I still don't know him well enough to strike that from his instincts.

The whole ride to Topgolf was exhilarating. I have never experienced anything quite like it. The speed, the purr of the bike beneath us, the close proximity to Max. I could think of worse places to be than wrapped around his body while he takes us to hang out with our friends. The bike isn't the only thing purring anymore. When we pull up and he cuts the engine, my heart is racing against my chest.

I hop off, allowing him to do the same, he turns and looks down at me with a smile spread across his face.

"Now, that wasn't so bad was it?" Max says, helping to remove my helmet.

"That was absolutely amazing. How long have you been riding?" I ask.

"Mmm, since I was about 18 so almost 20 years." He answers. I forget sometimes about the difference in our age, but it honestly just makes him that much hotter to me. He sets our helmets on the bike seat, and I can't take my eyes off him. He has on dark wash jeans and a heather gray t-shirt, paired with his leather jacket and biker boots. His hair is messy from having his helmet on, then running his fingers through it, but it's freaking *working* for him.

"Maybe I'll give you lessons sometime and you can join Lenny's biker gang." Max jokes. Lenny is one of the regulars at the bar I had the pleasure of meeting my first night working there. He told me if I had a bike I could join their gang and he'd have a special jacket made just for me. He's a total riot and I love when their crew comes in.

"I think I'll stick to riding with you. However, the custom leather jacket is almost worth it." I tease back. A smile flashes across Max's face as we head toward the entrance.

When we start walking up the stairs I hear a vaguely familiar voice call out.

"Hey, Shane!" I turn around and see Luther running up behind us.

"Hey, Luther. What are you doing here?" I ask. Max's body stiffens beside me as his gaze zeroes in on Luther.

"I'm not late am I?" He asks, ignoring my previous question. I suppose Lauren invited him tonight from his latest inquiry.

"No, not at all," I answer, a little confused by his being here.

"And you are?" Max asks, making Luther cut his eyes over to him.

"Oh, gosh sorry. Luther, this is Max, Max this is Luther. He works with Lauren." I introduce them and Luther extends a hand to Max.

"Nice to meet you, Max." Luther smiles.

"Yeah, you too. We better get inside so we don't end up being late, huh?" He nods toward the door. Luther grins and nods in agreement before taking the stairs two at a time.

Max puts a hand on the small of my back to guide me in front of him. The gesture sending shivers down my spine, as well as a wave of comfort.

When we make it inside I look around for the group that came ahead of us. I spot Taylor, Leah, Lauren, and Tucker all sitting at the bar. Tucker looks like such a player surrounded by my beautiful best friends, though all of his attention seems to be turned to one fierce redhead.

"There you guys are!" Leah calls out, waving us over. Luther walks over first, greeting Lauren and then saying hello to everyone else.

"Tucker, this is Luther, we work together," Lauren says, and I notice the look on Luther's face. Making me wonder if maybe they do more than just work together.

"Nice to meet you, man." Tucker shakes his hand and then turns to face me and Max.

"Tank called and said Ruby cut him loose early since the bar was slow tonight, he asked what we were up to, so the party just keeps on growing." He holds his hands out and smiles.

"Fantastic," Max says flatly.

"It'll be fun, and if you end up having an awful time, we can go." I say quietly, smiling up at him. He narrows his gaze at me, before agreeing.

"Deal." He winks at me.

"Oh, we're going to have fun. Let's go" Taylor says, linking her arm with mine. Without even thinking about it, I reach my hand back for Max's. Before I can realize what I'm doing and retract it, he takes my hand in his, and the electricity races straight to my core.

Oh boy, I'm in trouble.

"It shouldn't count, I'm sore!" I argue as everyone boos me after my shot.

"Yeah, yeah. A tale as old as time." Tucker mocks. I stick my tongue out at him and Tank's eyes dart between us.

"Okay, how do you two know each other?" Tank asks.

"Keep up little brother," Tucker ruffles his hair as he stands to take his turn. "These lovely ladies came into the bar to drink away Shane's shitty week. Rubes hired her as a bartender. The place almost got robbed so I heroically punched a robber in the face when he was all up in Shane's, and then we bonded over lunch one day after a *hard* workout she and Max had." Tucker puts all the major pieces of our meetings in a nutshell.

"Did I miss anything?" He asks, pointing his golf club at me and winking.

"No, Tuck. I think that about sums it up." I laugh, taking a drink from my beer.

"Okay, so I say we play the rundown game." Taylor pipes up. Leah, Lauren and I smile.

"What the hell is the rundown game?" Max asks.

"The rundown game is when you give everyone the rundown on your life. Since we have all met at different times and know very little about each other – except for us girls – it'll be a fun way to get the rundown on everyone." Taylor explains. I look at Max and his jaw ticks.

"I'll go first!" Leah says, taking another sip from her drink. Tucker sits back down after making his shot, which none of us were paying attention to.

"I'm Leah Gates. I am 25. I went to UT. I teach Kindergarten. I'm currently working on getting my master's and I am *not* sporty," she glares over at Taylor - who I'm sure dragged her out here tonight. We all laugh at the remark as Taylor rolls her eyes.

"That's how you play," then Lauren, Taylor, and I all say, "thanks for the rundown." and Leah does a little seated bow.

"Alright, I got this," Tucker says, rubbing his hands together.

"I'm Tucker Landry, I am 36 years old, and the more handsome Landry boy," he bumps Tank who puffs out an unimpressed laugh. "I served as a Navy SEAL for almost 12 years. I run my own architect company and I am currently crushing all of you losers at this game." He claps and points to the scoreboard, arrogantly smiling. We all pick up random things to throw at him.

"Okay, my turn," I say.

"I'm Shane Thompson. I am 25. I am an artist, turned bartender. I went to school at California College of the Arts, and recently moved back home when I caught my ex-boyfriend with his face buried between his assistants' thighs. *On* our two-year anniversary." I hold up my beer and Taylor matches my movement.

"Fuck Peter the cheater." She cheers. It makes me bust out laughing when literally *everyone* repeats her *"Fuck Peter the cheater!"* and clinks their drinks together. Everyone except Max, who is staring at me with an unreadable expression. The game keeps going –

Lauren Long. 25. Best real estate agent in Nashville. Was a makeup artist in another life.

Tank Landry. 31. Honorably discharged Marine for a back injury. Could still take his brother in a fight. Seeing what his next step in life will be.

Luther Sims. 27. Second best real estate agent in Nashville. Has a pet turtle. (wtf)

– and comes to a screeching halt when *Taylor Clark. 25. ER nurse,* decides one of her rundown points will be how she's seen an 85-year-old man's penis. Tucker almost choked to death on his drink before she told the car accident blanket story that she'd shared on my first night in town.

"Max, your turn!" Taylor points to him, after finishing her retelling.

"Pass." He responds, a hard expression replacing the amusement from a moment ago. Eyes dart around the group, but no one makes a fuss about it. Max doesn't strike me as the "let me tell you about my life" type, so we continue the playful conversation without another word about it.

After laughing so much my cheeks hurt, we all decide to call it a night. I am happy it seems like Max ended up enjoying the night. He was two points away from beating Tucker which I feel would have been the icing on the cake.

As we are walking to the parking lot, Taylor asks if I want to drive home, but I secretly want to ride with Max again. Which would definitely make people suspicious since I *live* with Taylor. I hesitate when she asks, and my eyes involuntarily find Max. He's already looking at me, so when I turn my head our eyes lock. He must be able to read my mind because he instantly chimes in.

"Actually, she's riding back with me." He responds. Everyone stops and turns as if they're waiting for further explanation. Which never comes.

"Ready, Sunshine?" He asks simply.

"Um, yeah." He grabs my hand and says goodnight. Leaving my friends looking at each other and then back at me. I smile and shrug before turning around to keep up with Max's pace.

I'm so hot for this man right now. No explanations are necessary, he just takes my hand and leads the way.

WHEN I HEARD Shane's rundown tonight two thoughts popped into my head. One was, if I ever see this Pete character, I'm punching him square in the jaw. The second was, I had no idea she was an artist. She definitely strikes me as the creative type, with her radiating positivity and her unique outlook on life. But it's never come up so, how would I know?

We pull up to her house and I cut off the bike. I'd taken the long way back so she could enjoy the ride a little longer. Shane hops off and removes her helmet, running her fingers through her long, blonde waves. I stand up and copy her movements.

"That is literally the coolest feeling. Thank you for bringing me home." She says, smiling up at me.

"I didn't know you were an artist," I say, changing the subject abruptly.

"Yeah…" Her answer drags with sadness.

"Are you not anymore?" I press. She sighs and leans against the motorcycle, looking up at the house.

"That is a complicated answer. I will always be an artist, it's just who I am. I can't just turn it off. But, I am not currently painting. I looked for art-related jobs when I first moved back, but nowhere was hiring. Then Ruby told me about the bartending position which was honestly perfect for the time being.

"So, here I am. Taylor's house is too small for me to set anything up to paint in there, so I am left to shelf my creativity. For now, anyway. My old boss offered to help me find solutions to keep me in San Francisco, working as an assistant curator at his gallery, but it just wasn't in the cards for me at the time." She shrugs, bringing her attention back to me.

I watched her expression carefully as she spoke, seeing the sadness that washed over her when she talked about not being able to paint. The uncertainty when she mentioned staying in San Francisco, which is an idea I'm not a fan of, by the way.

"Sorry, I meant, 'Yes, Max. I am an artist.'" She laughs, backtracking as if she's shared too much.

"Do you ever wish you'd stayed in San Francisco?" I ask, leaning beside her on the motorcycle.

"For any reason other than my job, not at all. I missed being home so much, and being surrounded by my best friends makes me never want to leave again. But I had a really great job, and I was sure Hugh was getting close to displaying one of my pieces." She says, hope straining in her voice.

I look up at the house again and see Taylor's eyes peeking out the blinds, which makes me laugh. This girl is nosy as hell.

"Looks like you better get inside," I say, pointing at the window. When Shane's eyes dart to the open blinds, they instantly snap shut.

"Oh my god, she acts like she's my mother." She laughs. "Thanks again for the ride."

"Anytime." As I swing my leg back over the bike to take a seat, an idea starts brewing concerning tonight's conversations.

"Do you mind getting to the bar a little early for your shift tomorrow?" I ask.

"Yeah, no problem. Is like half an hour early good?" she asks.

"Perfect. See you then." I say. She waves goodbye, but I don't pull away until I know she's safely inside. Then I head straight to the bar.

When Shane got to the bar, I had just finished the project I started working on last night. I had run home and got a few hours of sleep and a shower before coming back up here to finish before she showed up. I round the corner just as she walks through the door from the kitchen.

"Oh, hi!" she says, stopping just before she runs into me.

"Hey, thanks for coming early." I'm starting to get nervous now that she's here. I don't want to overstep in her life, and now I feel like this may seem like a bigger deal than I'd originally thought it'd be. But I guess there's no going back now.

"What's up?" she asks.

"Umm. Okay, so I wanted to show you something. Follow me." We head towards the corner of the bar where my office is. There's a door to the left directly inside my office that leads upstairs to the extra storage space. We walk in and I open the door to the stairs.

"After you." I gesture for her to go ahead of me.

"You do know Taylor will murder you if I don't come back home tonight, right?" she asks, half teasing, half serious. I laugh and nod.

"Oh yes, I am fully aware," I say, motioning for her to follow through on my request to head upstairs.

When we reach the top we are met with a wide open, empty space. It's still a little bit dusty since I didn't exactly have time to deep clean the place after moving the shit ton of boxes out of the way. I flip the switch that turns the overhead lights on, illuminating the large space. The sunbeams are casting a little extra light from the circular window on the east side of the building.

"Whaaat are we doing here?" Shane asks, eyes wild with curiosity. I clear my throat and wipe my hands down my dusty jeans.

"Well. Last night, you mentioned that you didn't have anywhere to paint." I say.

"Right..." she answers warily.

"I wanted to offer you this space." I hold my hands out to the wide-open room we are standing in.

"I mean, it's not much but it's just been housing boxes for the last couple of years and I finally moved those. So now, it will either remain empty, or you can use this as your own little studio. Whatever you want." I offer. She looks around the room, and her eyes glisten from the tears welling inside.

"You're just. Giving me a room above your bar. So I can paint?" she asks.

"Well... Yeah. It's no big deal, I just – wanted you to have some-place to put that creativity to use." I shrug. She turns to face me straight away, her fingers covering her pouty pink lips. She moves them to wipe a tear that has fallen, and I realize...this was a much bigger deal to her than I imagined.

"When I was with Pete, he had plenty of space in his house for me to set up a canvas somewhere to work. Several spaces, actually. But he told me not to because he didn't want me to get paint on anything and ruin it," she scoffs. "A true romantic, that one." Her head dips in embarrassment, but I take a step closer to her, and lift her chin so she's looking right at me. I place my hand around her neck, my thumb feeling her pulse and the rest of my fingers resting at the base of her ponytail.

"Sunshine, you can paint the walls, the floor, the ceiling, or even the window. I don't give a damn. All of this is yours to destroy, I only need one thing from you."

"Anything," she says.

"Don't mention that dickhead ex-boyfriend of yours anymore," I demand.

"Why?" she asks as her eyes go wide.

"Because every time I hear how shitty he was to you, I get the mind to show you how you *should* be treated so that you'll never settle for less. But that's something I can't do right now." I feel her swallow hard beneath my grip.

"Why not?" she asks again, looking at my lips while biting the inside of her own.

"Tell me you won't mention his name again," I repeat. She nods in agreement.

"I won't" her voice is mouse-like.

"Good." I turn to walk downstairs leaving her to enjoy her new space. I stop when I hear her call after me.

"Max," she starts taking steps towards me and wraps her arms around me. I take her small waist in my arms and breathe all of her lavender goodness in.

"Thank you, so much. This really means a lot." She says, pulling away again.

"No problem, Sunshine. Glad you like it." I say, turning to head back down the stairs.

It takes every bit of my self-control not to absolutely ruin every inch of that storage space with her. Everything about her has me feeling things I've never felt, and doing things I've never done. I just won't let myself give into these feelings, or urges, whatever the hell they are. Shit if I don't even know what I'm feeling, I definitely don't need to act on it yet.

Chapter 13

Shane

Max Mullins keeps surprising me in the most unbelievable ways. The first day I met him his eyes held a sadness behind them and everything about him seemed grumpy. But little by little, I'm seeing more to him than grump. He's protective on instinct, he treats his employees well, he loves Tucker and Tank like brothers, and he's dealt with Taylor on multiple occasions and is still standing, so that says a lot. But outside of how he is with everyone else. The way he is with me keeps my stomach fluttering almost constantly.

He rushed to my side during a panic attack, he offered to train me so I would feel safe, he stepped in when a customer got sloppy with me, and now – out of all the little things he's done to make me low-key swoon over him, he gives me a studio space in his bar. Just because I mentioned not having anywhere to paint. I get the feeling I'm not the only one forming some sort of attachment here either. The comment he made when I mentioned Pete has lived in my head rent-free since he said it.

"Because every time I hear how shitty he was to you, I get the mind to show you how you should be treated so that you'll never settle for less. But that's something I can't do right now."

Repeat it about a thousand more times and you'd be where I'm at with it.

He looked sexy as hell that day too. He was still dirty from cleaning the room out, wearing dark jeans, a white t-shirt that hugged him perfectly around his chest and arms, and some sneakers. But the absolute panty dropper was the damn backward baseball hat.

Sexy.

As.

Shit.

I had been spending every second that I could in that little studio upstairs, blasting my music in my headphones and letting my brush strokes express all the things I had been feeling lately. The way my stomach flipped any time I was around Max, the way I would let my mind wander with dirty thoughts about him. How happy I was to be back home and surrounded by my best friends constantly. It was all transferred from the confines of my mind, onto a canvas.

It was now the night before Christmas Eve. Lauren and Leah had just gotten to the house looking like the fierce beings that they are. Lauren wears her short, shoulder-length brown hair in loose waves, her makeup consists of winged liner, and red lipstick on top of an absolutely flawless foundation. She has on black ripped skinny jeans, red stilettos, and a red bodysuit paired with her black jacket.

Leah has her long auburn hair pulled up halfway, with a few pieces framing her face. She wears a dark green sweater dress and tan suede boots that hit her knees, her makeup simple with a light foundation, blush, and mascara. A timeless look for a timeless soul.

Taylor and I, being the procrastinators that we were, still have on our baggy t-shirts and sweatpants while we do our hair and makeup in her master bathroom with Ashnikko bumping on the Bluetooth speaker. Her bathroom has a double vanity so we get ready in here on nights we go out.

We normally do a movie and margaritas for our annual Christmas girls' night, but this year we decided to go out before coming home and getting cozy with the Grinch.

"Any idea what you guys' are wearing yet?" Lauren asks as she fluffs her hair.

"I think I have my outfit picked, it just depends on whether or not it looks as good on me, as it does in my head," I answer as I finish putting curls in my hair. I decided to go easy on the makeup tonight, doing a thin winged liner and nude eye shadow.

"What color are you wearing?" Leah asks.

"White top, denim pants, olive shoes," I tell her while taking one final look in the mirror.

"Then you need this." Lauren hands me a darker brown lip color. I raise a brow at her and she just shakes her head.

"Trust me, Shane. We're making statements tonight. Don't be afraid to stand out." She hands me the lipstick and I put it on. I lean back and examine the result.

"Okay, what kind of makeup wizard are you?" I tease. I honestly didn't think I could ever pull off such a dark lip, but here I am. Doing the dang thing. Lauren has a gift when it comes to knowing what makeup would look good on others.

I get dressed in my long-sleeved, white bodysuit. It's a ribbed material that feels like heaven but has a scoop neck that makes it just sexy enough to wear out dancing. I pair it with my dark skinny jeans and my olive green booties.

It feels so good to not be in my bar tee or usual sweatshirt and leggings combo that I wear when I paint or go out for errands.

Once Taylor and I finish getting dressed we are out the door. Chattahoochies recently made changes that allowed for a dance floor. Once eleven o'clock hits people are packed in and flooding the dance floor. And for my friends that was all they needed to hear. So off dancing, we went.

MAX

I am on closing shift with Ruby tonight, and the bar is starting to pack 'em in. Rubes convinced me to move some tables around in the bar to make a dance floor for the late-night crowd. I fought her on it at first because this is absolutely not that kind of bar, but Ruby is one tough broad to say no to. So now we have a fucking dance floor.

It was flooded with a bachelorette party last night which made it seem ten times louder in here than normal. I move behind the bar to make drinks for some of my regulars when my attention is pulled to the festive bunch that just walked through the door.

Shane, Taylor, Leah, and Lauren are all in variations of white, red, and green. It is a subtle kind of festive, but still making the statement I'm sure they are going for. They sit at one of the booths along the wall and Heather goes over to take their order. I watch Shane laughing with her friends, her radiant smile lighting up the whole damn place.

Jackie calls me back to the kitchen as the delivery guy shows up, so I can receive the last-minute holiday order I'd put in. I needed to replenish things we were almost out of before tomorrow, thank god my delivery guys liked me.

I keep Chattahoochies open on Christmas Eve and Christmas Day, unlike most places around here. I wanted there to be a place open for the people who had nowhere else to go on those days, so I make sure we are stocked for the occasion. No one should be alone on Christmas, even if *I* am the only company they have.

Once I get done checking everything off the invoice I leave Jackie to store the supplies, and I head back out front. I notice Tucker has wandered in and is sitting at his usual stool, I give him a nod before my eyes involuntarily scan the room for Shane. I don't see her or her friends at the table they had been at when I left.

I scan the room a bit more and see them all on the dance floor. I stand there, unable to take my eyes off her. She moves her body like she doesn't care who is around or who is watching. She dances between Taylor and the one with red heels on – Lauren, I think? She tosses her blonde hair behind her, laughing at something one of them has whispered in her ear.

"See something you like, boss?" Ruby taunts from beside me. I shake my head and toss the bar towel over my shoulder.

"I don't know what you're talking about." I deny. Knowing absolutely no one is buying it.

"Haha, busted man." Tucker chimes in obnoxiously. I glare at him in hopes of shutting him up.

"Well, seems you're not the only one." Ruby nods her head over to a group of guys that stand off to the side of the dance floor. I watch them whisper to one another, while their eyes never leave the girl I have also just been staring at. They start walking towards Shane and her friends and my hands fist at my sides. It is the dipshit that got a little too handsy and left his number on Shane's ticket last week.

"Whoa, down boy," Tucker says from his seat. I don't really care what Tucker thinks right now. I don't like this guy or the way he and his little friends are looking at Shane. Or her friends.

"Look, this guy was in here a couple of weeks ago and started getting handsy with Shane, it made her really uncomfortable. I'm just making sure he doesn't cross a line." I explain.

"A line you're about to leap over like a gazelle?" My statement seems to have Tucker honing in on them as well. Though it doesn't keep him from giving me shit about it. I start to move around the bar, keeping a close eye on what is happening as I cross my arms over my chest trying to assess the situation.

All of these guys have spiked hair in various colors and wear button-up shirts and khaki pants. They look like absolute douchebags. When the blonde-headed one leans in to whisper in Shane's ear my jaw clenches.

She leans away from him with an uncomfortable look on her face. I feel a growl come from my chest, but when he grabs her by the arm I can't keep my feet planted if I wanted to. This dude clearly thinks he's going to get some kind of action from her.

I think the fuck not.

Before I know it I am rushing through the dance floor. When I get a little closer I hear Shane's voice.

"Look, can you please just let go." She says, in the sweetest tone. This dickwad does not deserve even an ounce of the kindness she is giving him. I remove his hand from her arm and give him a small shove, making him step back a couple of feet.

"I suggest you take that hand off of her if you want to keep it." I demand, coming between this asshole and Shane. The guy scoffs, turning to his friends with a *what's he gonna do* look on his face. I take a step closer to him, to let him know he is seconds away from finding the fuck out. He waves a hand in front of him as if to dismiss me before he and his friends made a hasty exit from the dance floor. I turn to face Shane and the girls, and they all look a variation of annoyed, intrigued and confused. I nod to her friends then take her by the arm.

"Come with me." I growl. Nodding Tucker over to make sure the other girls are okay.

SHANE

I stand there watching Max come between me, my friends, and the guys from last week who'd requested me to wait on them. The girls and I had been dancing and laughing at the comment Lauren made about how we were being stared at by some creepy accountants in the corner when the very same "creepy accountants" ended up coming over in their sad attempt to hit on us. Max turns around from threatening the guy and grabs me by the arm.

"Come with me." He growls. The way Max has his hand on my

arm is gentle but firm enough to not lose me in the crowd. It is sending heat throughout my entire body, but I am still confused as to why he is currently dragging me across the room.

"Max, what the hell are you doing?" I pointlessly ask, as he ignores me.

I follow his line of sight to Tucker sitting at the bar. He nods, directing him toward my friends, and Tuck nods back before heading to the dance floor.

I look behind me to my friends who are standing there with their eyes wide and mouths hanging open.

When Tucker approaches them he smiles first at Taylor then greets Leah and Lauren as well. So much less aggressive than the way Max had just pulled *me* from the floor.

Before I can protest his barbaric actions, I am being pushed up against a door. My eyes dart around to see where we are, having had my focus on my friends during the brisk trip here. I quickly realize by my surroundings that we are in his office.

"What the hell is your problem?" I ask him. Looking up as he is towering over me.

"I wanted to check on you." He says in his deep, gravely voice.

"So you had to drag me into your office to do that?" I push his chest, trying to put some space between us. "Well I appreciate it, but I'm fine, can I go now?" I say, not hiding my irritation. I cross my arms over my chest, awaiting his response. He looks at me and furrows his brow.

"Sure. Just stay off the dance floor tonight." Was this guy serious right now?

"I'm sorry." I scoff. "I missed the part where I am supposed to just follow your every instruction. I'm not on the clock, so what I do is none of your business." I huff and point my finger to his chest.

He takes a step closer to me, grabbing my wrist to move my finger from his chest, backing me into the door, once again. He puts his hands on either side of my head on the door, caging me in. How do I keep finding myself in this position with him? I look up at him with a fire in my eyes, and a warmth in my chest; sparking a desire for him I haven't felt before.

"That may be true, Sunshine. But I didn't like the way he was looking at you. And I sure as hell don't want anyone else's hands on you. So if you could stay at your table tonight so I don't have to take out some asshole who thinks he can touch you, well that would make my night a whole lot better." He says.

His voice is eerily steady – proving he means every single word. His eyes scan my face, his gaze landing on my lips. When his tongue swipes out to wet his bottom lip I think everything above my neck stops working. Why doesn't he want anyone *else's* hands on me? Does that mean that his hands being on me is okay? He seems adamant about no one else touching me.

"Max," I say, a little more breathy than intended.

"Hmm." He growls in response.

"Do you want to kiss me?" It's bold of me to ask, but I am tired of wondering. The way he is looking at me right now, the way his gaze lands on my lips has me wondering if maybe the idea isn't so crazy.

"No." He snaps back, in that deep, panty-soaking voice. "I want to completely devour you. I want to show you what it feels like to be with a real man. I want to put you first and never make you question your worth. I want to make you feel things you never knew you could feel. I want to show you pleasure so intense you wouldn't dare to even think about another man. Kissing you, Sunshine would just be the beginning." He answers.

I think I forgot how to breathe.

"Then do it," I say, staring into his deep blue eyes.

"I can't." His jaw ticks, showcasing his perfect jawline.

"Why not?" I question in frustration.

"Because once I kiss you, Sunshine, I won't be able to stop. Once I kiss you, you're mine. Once I kiss you, I run the risk of losing you, and I'm not ready to risk that yet." He admits.

My head is absolutely pinning from the events of the last five minutes. I can't believe he just said he wants this too. Not enough to act on it, apparently. Not enough to risk losing me. Which, why does he think he's going to lose me? Where am I going? Maybe outside for now because I need some air.

Before I can say or do anything there's a knock at the door. A gasp escapes my lips but Max doesn't even flinch.

"Yeah?" he calls, his gaze never leaving my face.

"Umm, we're kind of getting slammed out here," Ruby says on the other side of the door. "So if you could get your ass back out here soon, that'd be great." I love this girl. I take a deep breath trying to gather myself.

"I'd better go. You have a bar to run." I say, rolling my lips together.

He doesn't move right away. He looks me over, stopping briefly on the scoop of my bodysuit that is showing off the perfect amount of my cleavage. He lets out a low growl, then finally steps back.

I turn, flipping my hair over my shoulder, and swing the door open. I walk straight to Taylor, Leah, and Lauren, who are sitting back at our table. I am beyond ready to get home and try to steady my heart rate.

"What the hell was that about?" Taylor asks with a brow raised. She looks between me and Max, who's just walked out of his office and is heading straight towards the bar. I look over at him, and he winks at me. *This man.*

All three of the girls turn to face me with their mouths hanging open. Yep. They saw it too.

"That's exactly what I'm trying to figure out," I say as I grab Taylor's hand.

"Let's go." We all grab our things and walk out the door. I don't miss the way Taylor looks back at Tucker and smiles at him. I will be inquiring about that later.

Chapter 14

Shane

AFTER GETTING home from the bar with the girls, we sit there mulling over everything that happened with Max. Taylor mentions how sweet Tucker was to come over and make sure those guys didn't bother them again, and her cheeks get rose-red when she talks about him. But for the most part, the conversation stays on what was happening between Max and me.

"That is so hot," Taylor says as she grabs a handful of popcorn.

"Let's break this down though," Lauren says. She's always the one to get to the bottom of things. Especially when it has to do with men.

"Okay…" I say as I sip my margarita.

"So he's a super grumpy boss, then just gives you a place to paint, then tells you it's taking all of his self-control not to ravish you right there in his office?" Lauren says.

"I mean… I feel like we're missing some details, but yeah?" I say back.

"Sounds like a certain tatted boss man has some pent-up feelings for you," Leah says.

"No shit, Sherlock. We're past *that* realization." Taylor mouths off. "Now we just have to figure out why he's holding out on our girl, and where the hell he thinks she's gonna run off to."

"Yeah, that part confused me. Why does he think he's going to lose me?" I wonder aloud. We all came up with about a hundred different scenarios, but the answer was clear. The only way I'd know what he meant by that, was if he told me himself. And who knows if that will ever happen. We finished the night off with girl talk and laughter while our movie played silently in the background.

CHRISTMAS DAY

Not having any family to spend the holidays with always had Taylor inviting me, nay, trying to drag me to Colorado to spend Christmas with her family. I opted out this year, just like every other year. *Maybe when it doesn't hurt so much to spend the Holidays without them.*

Plus, she had to catch a flight at the ass crack of dawn on the 24th and I had no intentions of going to the airport on Christmas Eve. As much as I love Taylor and her family, I would just rather be alone this time of year.

Most years I go out and see if any homeless shelters needed volunteers or I spend my time at the children's hospital, reading or passing out gifts. My mom was always doing things like that for others. She had a heart of gold, wanting to give back whenever and wherever she could. There wasn't a soul on the planet she wouldn't help.

My whole life I've hoped to be more like her every single day. So, I am currently on my way out to read and pass out Christmas gifts at the children's hospital downtown. I called a few days ago seeing if they could use any more volunteers and they'd eagerly agreed. I wore my sweatshirt that had a reindeer wearing sunglasses on it, always a crowd favorite with the kids, and paired it with skinny jeans and my favorite gray boots.

When I arrived, the hospital was full of Christmas cheer. The kids all wore Santa hats, reindeer ears, or elf hats. They would smile ear to ear as they saw the volunteers coming down the hall with the red bags full of gifts for them.

The parents are always so grateful and tear up as they thanked us for helping make Christmas special for their kids. When my time there came to an end, my cheeks actually hurt from smiling so much. It always filled my heart to be there with the kids, to know I was helping bring a smile or a hint of joy to someone when they were in a less-than-desirable situation.

On my way home I passed by the bar and noticed that it was open. I could have sworn I didn't see anyone on the schedule for these two days though. I pull into a parking space out front and walk inside. To my surprise, it's actually pretty crowded in here.

There are a few older men sitting at the booths, and I notice they're wearing veterans' ball caps. A few stragglers sit at the bar, who look like they wandered in off the street, and Lenny and some of his guys are in their matching Drengr MC leather jackets playing pool. I look around, but I don't see Ruby, Heather, or Marco anywhere.

When I make it up to the bar one of the men sitting a couple of stools down turns to face me.

"It's a Christmas miracle that someone as beautiful as you would walk in here." He says in a raspy voice. When he grins at me he looks so genuine and kind, through the torn and tattered clothes and the way his hair and beard seem unkempt, I see none of it when he smiles. I smile back at him, but before I can say anything in return a voice behind the bar interrupts my thoughts.

"I don't call her Sunshine for nothing." I look up and Max is bringing food from the kitchen. He winks at me as he sets the plate down in front of the man.

"Sunshine." The man repeats softly. "Yep. It's perfect."

Right then I hear a dog bark. I look around and see Riley curled up in a booth.

"Hey girl!" I call and she jumps down and over to me. I start to pet her head and she is eating it up. This dog is an attention whore and I love her for it. The man at the bar glances over and chimes in.

"Oh, is that yours?" he asks, looking over at Max. He smiles when he looks over at her.

"Yes sir, Riley there was in the service with me, she's my girl." He turns to wash his hands at the bar sink, and I look over at her and smile.

"Lucky girl." I think to myself. Only, I didn't think it to myself. I said it. Out loud. Probably not even in a whisper. Heat rises to my cheeks faster than Riley ran over to me when I called her. I turn to look at him, hoping by some chance, he didn't hear me.

No such luck.

He is staring right at me, smirking as he dries his hands. Completely embarrassed, I try to change the subject as quickly as humanly possible.

"So, um, I didn't know we were open today. I didn't see anyone on the schedule." He was now staring directly at my chest and if it were possible for my face to get any redder, it would have. I look down and notice my rather festive sweatshirt and can't help but laugh.

"Oh, yeah. It's pretty popular with the kids." His attention comes slowly back to my face.

"Kids?" he lifts an eyebrow in question.

"Oh, yeah. I volunteered at the children's hospital today. I like to go read and help pass out toys on Christmas." I shrug. The smile that had been plastered to my face all night, reappears as I think about the joy I saw in those kids tonight.

I look up to see Max staring at me, his face growing softer as he watches mine.

"So, you didn't answer my question," I say as I fold my arms across my chest.

"Technically, you didn't ask a question. You made a statement." He says, giving me an arrogant grin.

"Okay, fine. Could you use some help since we're open and I'm here?" I offer. He stops what he is doing and studies me for a minute. He stands back and grabs my apron from under the bar.

"I think these fellas would really like that." He nods at the man at the bar, who promptly turns and smiles at me again, which makes me giggle.

We spend the rest of the night taking turns behind the bar and on the floor. Lenny tried to convince me to join Drengr again, but I told him I would stick to the casual ride every now and then. I couldn't believe Max had been doing this by himself until I got here.

When it was finally time to close he goes and locks the front door and turns off the open sign. I finish closing out the receipts from the night and shut down the computer.

"So, do you always run the bar alone on Christmas?" I ask. He nods as he stacks chairs on top of the tables.

"Ever since I opened." He answers.

"How come?" my curiosity peaks.

"Well, I wanted there to be someplace open on Christmas for those who didn't have anywhere to go. Whether they're homeless, without family, or just hungry and avoiding the family they do have. I like to be open for them" he answers with a warmth to his tone. "If you're wondering why I do it alone, aside from Jackie of course, that is because everyone else has people to spend Christmas with and I don't want to take them away from their families by asking them to work." He finishes stacking chairs and makes his way behind the bar.

"Well, I think that's really nice of you," I say with a smile. He nods and continues to work. I walk over and sit in the booth next to Riley. She wags her tail and sets her head in my lap when I go to pet her.

"So a service dog, huh?" I ask, smiling down at her. "I can't believe I didn't know that. How did you end up lucky enough to bring her home with you?" I turn my head to face Max, while still petting Riley between the ears.

"They usually let the dogs stay with their handlers, depending on how long they've served. I got her the last four of my twelve years in, and after the things we went through together, they knew she wouldn't go with anyone else. So, when I got out, so did she." He answers. He never looks over at me though, he just keeps working.

"Did you enjoy your time in the Navy?" I ask. He stops and looks over at me, making me feel a little silly for asking. Heat rises to my cheeks quickly.

"I'm sorry, is that a dumb question? I know it must be a hard thing to do, I just wondered…" he saves me from further embarrassment and cuts me off.

"I know what you meant. Yeah, I mean the shit we did was important and the guys on my team became like brothers to me. We had some good times through it all, but the loss isn't something you ever get over." He looks spaced out as he talks about it.

He stands behind the bar now, pouring himself a glass of whiskey.

"Is that why you and Tucker are so close?" I stand from my place at the booth with Riley, and walk over to the bar closer to Max.

"Uh, yeah. Tucker and I have been friends since middle school actually." He smiles. "I was getting picked on, bullied really, and Tucker saw it one day and stepped in. Having Tank to look after at such a young age, made his protective instincts higher than most. That day those instincts kicked in for me. Been friends ever since." He says, bringing his glass to his lips.

"Wow, and you guys ended up serving together?" I ask.

"Yeah, I spent two years in college after high school, but it was the most boring shit I had ever endured. I decided one day that I wanted to enlist and do something more with my life. Something that mattered. When I told Tuck he shocked the shit out of me and said he was enlisting with me." He shakes his head, the corners of his lips turning up.

"That's amazing. What about your friend Red? The guy who says 'Chattahoochies' were you guys friends before or did you meet him later on?" I was smiling, looking up at the neon sign above the bar that had the name on it. When I look back at Max his expression is harder now. No trace of a smile left from before.

"No, we met him after we enlisted." He clips. I'm not sure what nerve I've struck, but I think maybe it was best that my questions end here.

"You want a beer?" he asks, walking to the fridge.

"Um, yeah. Thanks." I force a smile, but his expression never changes.

I definitely struck a nerve.

WHEN SHANE ASKED me about Red, everything in my body went cold for the first time since meeting her. It wasn't like the wound was fresh, but that doesn't mean re-opening it doesn't still hurt. I only open it and air it out once a year, and that day wasn't today. Even though I felt the urge to tell her everything – about Red, about my life, the reason I wouldn't just kiss her and finally make her mine. I decided to avoid it a little bit longer though. So I offered her a drink and decided to change the subject.

"What about you, Sunshine? Volunteering at a children's hospital on Christmas Day. I'd say that's pretty nice too." I say as I lean against the bar.

"Yeah, It's much better than being alone. Seeing all their sweet faces light up at the presents and hearing their laughs during whatever story is told. It's just the best feeling, you know?" she beams, looking up at me. She has so much joy on her face, I envy that feeling.

"Does your family ever go with you?" I ask.

"Um, no. It's just me." There is a sadness in her tone that piques my curiosity.

"How come?" I press. "Your parents not live around here?"

She takes a deep breath and rolls her head back, looking up at the ceiling. I'm finding myself wanting to know more and more about her. The hurt on her face from my last question makes me wonder if maybe I shouldn't have asked.

She lets out a sigh, and then looks at me, her eyes wet with emotion.

"They passed away the day I graduated high school." My heart aches for her instantly. I know the pain that accompanies loss. The fact that she had to endure it so young, simply isn't fair.

"I'm sorry, we don't have to talk about it if you don't want to," I reassure her. She nods her head a little. I walk over to her and lift her chin, bringing her eyes to meet mine.

"But if you want to talk, if you *need* to talk about it, I am here."

Her lip starts to quiver and she squeezes her eyes shut, causing the tears that fill her eyes to fall freely down her cheeks. I wipe them with the pad of my thumb and she pushes out a breath.

"I'm sorry, I probably look so crazy right now." She says as she turns her head away from me. She takes a couple of steps in the opposite direction, but I follow quickly behind. I grab her arm and bring her attention back to me.

"You don't look crazy. You look like you're in pain. Don't feel like you have to hide that from me though. Not ever." My voice is firm, so she knows I mean it. She nods her head and then takes a deep breath.

"Thank you. It's just really hard to talk about, most people don't understand it so I don't see the point." Her voice is shaky. "What about you? Are you close to your parents?"

"My dad left us when I was too young to remember, but my mom and I were always close," I answer truthfully.

"But not anymore?" she asks. One simple question, followed by one simple admission, drives me to do something I never thought I'd do.

"Will you go somewhere with me?" I ask.

She tilts her head in confusion but nods in agreement anyway. I finish closing down the bar and lock up, then we hop in my truck with Riley. The ride is quiet, and Shane never asks where we are going. It's not a long ride, but when we pull up Shane's head turns to me and her brows pull together. My headlights shine brightly on the sign in front of us.

WILLOWPOINTE CEMETERY.

"Um, not to sound worried or dramatic, but why did you bring me to a cemetery?" Shane asks.

"Come with me." I laugh. I'll let her wonder, just a few minutes longer. She stays unmoving when I open my door, so I bend down to look at her.

"Do you trust me?" I ask.

"Of course." She retorts.

"Let's go then." I nod. Riley jumps out of the truck, then Shane slides out behind her. I shut the driver door and take her hand to lead the way. It makes my whole chest warm just having her hand in mine. We walk for a few minutes before coming to a stop.

I shine the flashlight that I'd held in my jacket pocket to illuminate the writing.

CECELIA MAY MULLINS. BELOVED MOTHER.
1956 - 2012

"Max..." she whispers, her eyes coming up to meet mine.

I can feel the emotion creeping up my throat again. Something I suppress 364 days of the year, when it does make its way out, it comes with vengeance. Which is why I choose to be alone when it does.

Until tonight, apparently.

"I just wanted you to know, I understand the pain of loss. I lost my mom, who was my fucking hero, to cancer ten years ago. Then we lost Red during our last mission six years ago. They died on the same day, just years apart. That shit hurt, and it's affected me more than most people know. It's why I don't let people in. I have lost too much in life to set myself up for it again." I explain, hoping she realizes how much I am admitting to her through the words.

Shane studies me. But she doesn't ask about their deaths. She doesn't press me for more information. She just looks at me with those caring eyes, understanding that I just let her into a part of my life that not many others get to see. She takes a deep breath, looking down at my mom's headstone. Then she tells me the story:

"It was just me and my parents growing up. I didn't have any siblings or anything, so we were always really close. On the day of my high school graduation, I asked my parents if I could go to an after-graduation party. Some of the other kids in our class wanted to have one last hoorah before we all went off to different colleges. Taylor and I were going to ride together, and I would meet my parents for dinner later on. We were going to be planning our summer trip to San Francisco that night. I was going to be attending college there in the fall, so we wanted to go see where we would hang out when they would come to visit me, and they wanted me to get better acquainted with the area before I officially moved there.

"When my mom texted me that night telling me they were heading to the restaurant I said my goodbyes to all of my friends and headed to meet them. On my way there I got stuck in traffic for like 30 minutes. A tanker truck had flipped over on the highway, so only one lane was open for traffic. I called my mom to let her know I would be late, but she didn't answer so I left her a voicemail.

"When I finally got up to where the truck had flipped, I realized it hadn't just flipped, but had flipped onto another vehicle. I soon understood why my mom hadn't answered the phone. It was their car the truck had flipped onto." Tears pour down her face, but she never once tries to wipe them. I remain silent so she can go on.

"Everything that happened next was a slow-motioned blur. Before I knew it I was sprinting from my Jeep over to the caution tape surrounding the scene. I was screaming, trying to let the police know that those were my parents and I needed to get to them. They needed me and I couldn't get to them. I guess at some point in the midst of it all I called Taylor. She and her parents met me at the hospital, but by the time we got there, it was too late. They were already gone before they ever made it to the emergency room." She blinks and more tears fall.

She sniffles and wipes her face with the sleeve of her sweatshirt. She goes to turn her head away from me again, but before she has the chance, I pull her into me. I know loss and the pain that comes with it. I can recognize when someone is telling a story for the hundredth time, or for the first. From the way she falls limp into my body, with sobs taking over hers, I know. She's never told this story to anyone.

I run my hand along the back of her wavy, blonde hair bringing my lips to the top of her head.

"I'm so sorry that you endured such a great loss at such a young age." She lets out one final sob and I stand there holding her tight to me while she lets herself feel it all.

She takes a deep breath in, and I loosen my grip on her slightly, not wanting to let her go, or push her away. I want her to know I'll be here until she doesn't need me to be anymore. She leans back to look at my face, her ocean eyes shining from the tears, accompanied by the puffy redness from her grief.

"Thank you, Max." She says, her voice raspy from crying. She leans her head back into my chest, and we stand there. For as long as she needs.

Chapter 16

Shane

I TOOK A DEEP BREATH IN, breathing in *him*. He smelled woodsy with traces of leather and vanilla. I felt peaceful, calm, and safe, standing there, in the middle of a cemetery, with Max holding me. This was the second time his embrace calmed every nerve in my body so effortlessly, and I loved it. When his grip softened, not completely releasing me, I looked up at his face.

I stood there noticing all the depth there is to this man. He'd seemed like such a grump the first day I met him outside that coffee shop. But in this moment I can't help but think about how he has cared for me, on several occasions, noting the way I felt comfortable enough to open up to him about my parents, something I've *never* done in the seven years they've been gone.

The way he looks happiest with Riley, and the fact that he opens his bar to those who have nowhere else to go on the holidays, but lets his employees off to be with their families. The way he makes sure my friends are taken care of when creepy assholes show up at the bar. How he just keeps showing up and doing things for me that no one else does. I think he cares about more people than he's willing to admit.

The next week I spent as much time as I could painting. When I wasn't working at the bar or working out with Max and Tucker, who had become a regular in our sessions, I was in front of a canvas. Painting has always been my outlet. I channel everything I am feeling into my paintings, letting my emotions take the lead. I used it a lot to cope after my parents died. It's a good thing I was going to college to major in art, otherwise, I'm not sure that I would have actually gone.

This week's paintings are variations of heat, grief, desire, and safety. Things with Max felt so complicated on the one hand, with his grumpiness, aversion to feelings and basically telling me he wants me but won't take me for fear he'll lose me. On the other hand, they were simple for all the same reasons. I had suffered a great loss in life, but I never once thought shutting out my feelings would be the way to go.

I kept living my life, open to the possibility of love, even if it meant I'd end up hurt in the end. That's just part of life, isn't it? With no pain, there can be no love. Whereas Max has suffered great losses as well, only instead of coping with his pain, it seems he pushes it away. Building up walls around his heart fearing that if someone gets in, he'll lose them and end up hurt again.

I feel lucky that he was comfortable enough to open up to me, even as little as it was, about losing his mom and Red. I still have so many questions – I want to know so much more. I am hopeful that one day he will let me in completely. That I will be the one lucky enough to help him through the pain and show him that there can be life and love after loss. But I also don't want to lose the friendship we are developing by pushing him. My desire for him will have to lay dormant until he is ready to take that step, if he ever was.

These canvases didn't stand a fucking chance right now.

I have my headphones in and an empty bottle of water in my hand as I stand back, examining the piece I just finished. My phone alerts me through my headphones that I have messages coming in.

TAYLOR

are we still going to the bar for NYE? ••

LAUREN

oh please say we are, I need to see how sexy boss acts around Shaney. 😂

My whole body tingles when I remember the way it felt as he held me and when he'd told me he wanted me.

LEAH

Maybe he'll just take you right there on the pool tables and call it done. 🎱 🔥 😏

My best friends are assholes.

ME

You guys are insane. 😌

Having three best friends around all the time was a blessing and a curse because, for one, they know everything, but also, they know *everything*. I have kept them all well-informed when it comes to Max. From his protecting me the night of the robbery to how he comforted me on Christmas when I opened up to him about my parents. Which I think shocked them all the most because they're all well aware of the fact that it's a topic I *never* talk about.

Taylor had gotten back in town three days ago from visiting her family for Christmas and insisted we have girls' night to discuss my life. The woman has to be a robot. She partied with us on the 23rd, caught a flight on the 24th, and was back home on the 27th hosting girls' night. Now she's ready to party it up again tomorrow? Couldn't be me.

ME

> But yes, I mean I'm working so I have to be there and I wanna spend NYE together, even if I'm serving your fine asses while in my uniform. 🐻 & honestly IDK what's going on with Max…

I set my phone on the small table by the easel and walk down to the kitchen to refill my water bottle, my headphones still playing loudly in my ears. It is almost 10 AM so no one will be opening the bar for at least another hour so I have plenty of time to pack up and slip out before they come in. It isn't a secret that I paint here, I just prefer leaving before it gets busy. People tend to ask a lot of questions about what I'm working on and I usually just like to keep it to myself. Though I do kind of want to show *one* person what I've been working on today.

When I walk back through the kitchen door that leads out to the bar, I just about jump out of my skin. Max is standing there in all his sexiness, wearing a navy blue hoodie, light wash jeans, and a backward baseball cap again, holding an iced coffee. Only, Max doesn't drink iced coffee. I move my headphones down from my ears and place them around my neck.

"Sorry, I called your name but I'm guessing you didn't hear me." He says, pointing to the headphones on my neck.

"Yeah, the noise canceling part is definitely intact." I quip. "Is uh, that for me?" I nod to the iced coffee in his hand and smile.

"Um, yeah. I stopped to get one before Tucker and I head to the range and pulled around back to see if you were here painting. I figured you might be and thought you could use some caffeine." He answers, handing me the coffee.

He had become familiar with my order ever since I teased him about bringing me one the day he told me to meet him at the gym. I didn't actually expect him to, but he brought me one that day, and every gym day since then. Today was unexpected though.

"Thanks, I will never say no to coffee." I take a sip. *Perfection.*

"Anyways, I'll get going so you can get back to it." He says, turning to walk out the door.

"Actually," I call after him, making him turn back around. "Can I show you something?" I point towards the door that leads to the studio.

"Sure." He nods, following behind me. When we get to the studio I make my way over to set my coffee on the table by my phone. When I turn to face Max, he is looking around the space, taking in the dozens of canvases I have painted since he let me start using the space.

"Sorry, it's a bit of a mess. When I get inspired I just kind of toss one to the side and start with the new inspiration." I explain.

He walks over to me, standing in front of the canvas I had been working on this morning. The one inspired by Max's afflictions with his own feelings. I watch his face as his eyes roam over the piece. I always wondered if people who weren't artists could see the depth and meaning behind paintings the way that we could. It seems as though something is resonating with him as he reaches out to touch the paint.

"Oh, umm. This one is still wet." I warn a little too late. He looks down and there is red paint on his fingertip. He smirks and wipes it on the tip of my nose.

"This is incredible, Sunshine." He says, motioning towards the painting.

"I um - I made this one for you." I shyly tell him. He glances over at me, looking surprised.

"For me? Why?" he asks.

I look around the open space, surrounded by paintings that were inspired by the feelings I have experienced since I got back to Nashville. I think about how a lot of them are because of Max. I hate the idea that he's built up a wall, not allowing himself to experience love for fear of pain. I figure now is as good a time as any to tell him the truth about why I painted this piece for him.

"When you took me to the cemetery, you let me into a part of your world that I get the feeling you don't let anyone else into." I start.

"That would be correct." He confirms.

"Well, when I told you about what happened to my parents, I let you into a part of my world that I don't talk about with anyone. Not even Taylor, Leah, or Lauren. I haven't spoken about that day with anyone since it happened." I admit. He just nods to let me know he's listening.

"We've both suffered great losses, and while I will never pretend to know what it's like to lose someone who is like a brother to a battle that he was supposed to come back from, I also won't pretend my loss hurt any less than yours. You said your mom was your hero. My parents were mine, too. I was an only child, and we did everything together. I was supposed to celebrate graduating high school with them, and explore a new city with them. I was supposed to call them every night and tell them how school was going, and tell them about all the places I couldn't wait to take them when they'd visit me. I was robbed of those experiences the day I lost them.

"There were plenty of days I didn't want to keep going. I didn't want to experience a life where I didn't get to celebrate the big moments with my parents. But I remembered something my mom always told me. When I was young and I had the fear every child has of losing their parents, she would tell me,

'Shane, parents are never meant to outlive their children. While it may hurt to think about living a life without me, just know – that's what I want for you someday. In the future, when you're chasing your dreams I hope I'm right there chasing them with you, but I may not be able to continue the journey with you. But you're going to go on. You're going to keep chasing those dreams, living your life, and experiencing love, and hurt, and excitement and disappointment. Because without those things, life wouldn't be worth living, and you, my girl – are going to live a life worth living over and over again.'

That played in my mind again and again, until one day I got out a canvas, and painted all the pain I had felt from losing them. I let myself feel all the pain, the grief, the anger, I took it out on a canvas. And you know what happened?"

"What happened, Sunshine?" Max says tightly.

"I finally felt like I could breathe again. I reflected on the pain and the hurt, to be able to move forward. Once I did I was able to remember all the good times, the life lessons, the jokes, and the memories I know they would want me to hold onto. One day, it just got easier to share things with them in my heart, even when I wished I was telling them over the phone. I didn't stop living my life, because even with pain and loss and grief, life is something worth living. I still have Taylor, Leah, Lauren, and now Tucker apparently," I laugh out, making Max laugh too. "And you, hopefully. Maybe you'll never let yourself give in to the feelings you have for me, that's your decision to make. But I won't pretend mine don't exist. I really like you Max, and I hope one day you'll let me in completely. But if all I ever get to be is your friend, I'll count myself lucky. I just don't want you to miss out on an epic love because you're afraid." I take his face in my hands, the scruff from his perfectly chiseled jaw tickling my palms.

"You don't want to love someone as fucked up as me, Sunshine." He says. His voice is gruff and tears well in his eyes.

"I'm not scared to love you, Max. I'm scared you'll never give me the chance to." I admit. My phone dings three times in a row as Max's goes off too. I walk over to the stool and pick up my phone.

> TAYLOR
>
> I'm not going to argue, But I don't believe you. He's so into you.
>
> LAUREN

She must be showing a house because she only sends strictly emoji texts when she's really busy.

LEAH

See you in 20 Shaney.

I'm supposed to be meeting Leah at the gym in 20 minutes. Shit.

"Umm... I gotta go." I sigh, not wanting to leave this conversation unfinished.

"Yeah, Tucker's actually outside waiting for me." He clears his throat and takes a step toward me. He plants a kiss on my forehead and then turns to head down the stairs. I have no idea what he's thinking right now, and it's going to drive me absolutely crazy. Once he's gone, I pick up my phone and text Leah back.

ME

I just have to change and I'll be on my way!

Thanks to the fan I set up in here, the painting is already almost done. I grab my gym bag from the corner and put on my light blue workout leggings and matching sports bra, I pair them with my favorite white workout sneakers and throw my paint sweatshirt back on. I had been wearing my hair in a messy bun on top of my head and wrapped a bandana around it to act as a headband. So I left it alone. When I walk back over to the painting I touch a few spots to make sure it's dried. I grab it off the easel and pick up my bag, throwing it over my shoulder to head downstairs.

When I get down to Max's office, I set the painting on the small table behind his desk chair and grab a post-it from his desk. I scrawl on it and post it on the painting before heading out to meet Leah.

Chapter 17

Max

THIS WOMAN WAS GOING to completely break me, and I am becoming more and more willing to let her. She was right, about everything. She let herself feel the worst things in life so that she can welcome the good things. I wanted that. I wanted her joy, her goodness, her pure sunshine to completely overtake me. I was more than ready to make this girl mine. Thanks to Tucker and whoever was on the other end of her phone notifications, today wasn't that day. But it sure as shit would be soon.

"What the hell took you so long in there, man? You finally make a move?" Tucker pesters. I run my hand over my face, trying to hide the smile creeping up.

"Oh shit, you did, didn't you?" Tucker exclaims.

"No, you fucking golden retriever, I didn't. Will you just drive?" I say holding my hand out towards the road.

"What the fuck, Maxwell. Have you seriously not realized yet how mad you are for that girl?" he asks, clearly irritated by me.

"Can we please just go?" I plead.

We head to the range and my mind stay on one thing the whole time. I think about everything that's happened in my life since I met Shane a few weeks ago. The day I met her, those ocean-blue eyes completely captivated me. Her smile and fiery attitude pulled me in within minutes. When I learned Ruby had hired her at the bar I was curious to see how long it would take for the things I'd felt right off the bat about her to fade. Most of my female interests lasted a day, maybe two. But every time I am around her, I only want more.

When I saw her in danger I felt violent, when I saw her getting hit on I felt jealous. When I see her smile I feel warm. When I feel her touch I'm at ease. There's nothing about her that is a fleeting feeling. I am still scared shitless to let myself give in to her. I am still the guy who's lost too much. But I'm finally starting to see that Shane Thompson is worth the risk.

NEW YEARS EVE

The bar has somehow become a hot spot for people to spend New Year's Eve, and it is absolutely fucking packed in here. We have everyone who is on staff working and we are still having to send people away at the door so we don't break the fire code. People are coming in with the craziest outfits on. Sequin pants, feathered tops, light-up cowboy hats. It looks like Big Bird got a hold of a bedazzler. But the person who holds my attention all night is wearing a simple Chattahoochies t-shirt and jeans that fit so tight they looks painted on.

Shane Thompson has something about her that sends me into overdrive. I've had to fight like hell to treat her the same way I treat every other employee on staff at the bar. If I'm being honest, I'm not sure I've ever actually accomplished that. We've had moments here and there when it would be just the two of us and my guard was down. I can say with complete certainty, she's the only one to ever make it happen, and she doesn't even know it.

Shane takes a chance to go dance with her friends during a minor lull, and I can't peel my eyes away from her. Ruby is behind the bar, Heather and Marco are running food and drinks on the floor and Shane is going wherever she is needed tonight. Once I notice Ruby is starting to get slammed again I take it upon myself to let Shane know she needs to help. I walk over to her and lean my head down, bringing my lips to her ear.

"Ruby is starting to get slammed, why don't you go help her out?" I was trying to be sure that she could hear me, but by the look on her face, I'm assuming it came across as harsher than I intended.

"Yeah, of course." She looks over at the bar and then turns to tell her friends she'll catch up with them later. She walks past me and over to the bar. When I turn back around Taylor, Leah, and Lauren are staring at me with smirks on their faces. I gave a look as if to say *What?*

"Be good to our girl," Taylor says, winking at me before dragging her friends further into the dance floor. Well, that's not what I was expecting. I turn back around to face the bar and Shane works it like she's been doing it her whole life. You would have never guessed her second night here was a total shit show, but she's come a long way since then.

The smile on her face when she talks to guests or when Ruby whispers something to her could light up a room. The same way it did when she helped me out on Christmas Day. I swear every straggler and biker that came in here that night fell in love with her. They weren't the only ones. I shake off the thought before walking over to greet Tucker.

"Happy New Year, brother," he says before bringing me in for a hug. I clap his back and pull back.

"Almost there, man." I look around the bar, which is packed in tight. There are people dancing and shooting pool, obnoxious laughter booming at the other end of the bar, and one couple in the corner booth by the door that is fighting.

I don't think they'll be making it into the New Year together.

I'll keep my eye on that. I haven't seen the place packed like this since the first week we opened. Whoever made this the hot spot tonight, did the job well.

"It's wild in here tonight, my guy," Tucker says as his head spins around taking in the place. "I know. I'm surprised you made it in unscathed." I laughed.

"I'm gonna make the rounds. See if I can get into some trouble." Tucker wags his brows. I give him a nod and watch as Taylor turns her gaze to Tucker. Interesting pair they would make. *Damn troublemakers.* I look up at the clock and it is ten minutes until midnight, and the only thing I can think of is getting Shane alone when that clock strikes.

I walk around the bar talking to customers for a few minutes. Some that I've known since the day we opened, and some are first-timers trying to figure out what exactly this place is. I'm starting to wonder that myself. This damn dance floor has to go. I send the couple that had been fighting outside, as they became more than I want to tolerate tonight. It is cold as shit out there but they are going at it and I have a no-bullshit policy here. So out to freeze their asses off they go. When I make it back behind the bar it is time for the ball to drop.

Ruby turns the TVs to the same channel so anyone who cares to watch the stupid thing, can. People start packing in at the center of what now acts as the dance floor for the final countdown. Noise-makers and confetti poppers are being passed out frantically. I'm not even sure where the hell those came from, but I am beyond glad I'm not the one that has to clean this shit off the floor later. I scan the room looking for Shane, and as luck would have it she is coming through the kitchen door, heading back behind the bar.

She starts to walk toward her friends, but I intercepted her before she makes it too far. I grab her arm and her head spins around to look at me. I leaned in, bringing my lips just to her ear. "Come with me," I say firmly. She looks at me confused but gives me a nod in agreement. I walk her back to my office, where Riley lays curled up on the couch.

"Yeah, boss?" she asks, crossing her arms. She doesn't look mad, just curious as to why I have brought her back here. People start counting down the ball drop.

"10...9...8..."

"Say you're not meeting anyone at midnight." I demand. She starts to turn my favorite shade of pink as I run my fingers up her arm. She pulls in a breath and looks up at me.

"Just you, " her voice is barely a whisper. I look down just as she pulls in her bottom lip with her teeth.

Goddammit, she's killing me.

"Good answer." I smirk at her. I put both of my hands around her neck, pulling her closer to me, I graze her lips with mine and she lets out a little gasp. Not a second later my lips are crashing into hers.

"5...4...3..." people keep shouting.

She pulls away and scans my face briefly. I already miss having her soft lips on mine, but I don't have to miss them for long. She pulls me back in, even harder this time. She wraps her arms around my neck and I bend to lift her. I wrap her legs around my middle and spin around to put her back against the wall.

"...1 — *HAPPY NEW YEAR!*" the crowd erupts in the other room.

She parts her lips and my tongue slips in. I explore her mouth with my tongue and my hands cup her ass to keep her secured against me. She bites down gently on my bottom lip and I let out a deep growl. This woman is going to make me lose my damn mind.

She smiles against my mouth and her fingers tangle in my hair. My lips leave hers to kiss her neck – the smell of lavender coming from her is intoxicating, and it is my new favorite scent. I nip at her ear and she lets out a soft moan, which has my dick springing to life against my zipper. He'll have to calm the hell down, for now.

I kiss her lips once more before I place her feet back on the ground. She looks at me with satisfaction in her eyes. She bites her bottom lip again and the urge to move it with my own lips is strong. She stands so close to me that our bodies never lose contact.

"Was that just your way of saying Happy New Year, or..." she asks, making me laugh.

"No, Sunshine. That was me saying *thank you.*" I reply, holding her body against mine.

"For what?" she furrows her brow in confusion.

"For the painting. For letting me into the hard parts of your world. For listening when I shared hard parts of mine. For showing me there's a different way to view life with loss than to try and avoid it at all costs. Thank you, for just being you." I kiss the tip of her nose, making the blush on her cheeks darken.

"You're welcome." She says gently, reaching up to kiss me again. It's soft and sweet, just like everything else about her.

I run my fingers through her hair again when a banging sounds on the door.

"Yo, if you're done giving evaluations in there, I could really use some help behind the bar. It's fucking New Year's for christ's sake!" Ruby yells. Shane's eyes go wide and her hand flies up to cover her mouth.

"Coming, Rubes." I call out. Then I lean down bringing my lips to Shane's ear.

"Soon you will be too," I nip at her ear then lean back and wink at her. Her mouth drops open as I lean down to pet Riley.

"Good girl, hold down the fort, I'll be back in a bit. Come on Sunshine, let's go," I nod towards the door. When she walks past me I slap her ass and she looks back at me, rosy cheeks in full bloom.

That kiss was like nothing I have ever experienced before. As I head back towards the bar all I can think about is when I'll get to taste her again.

Chapter 18

Shane

"Excuse me, ma'am, what the shit just happened back there?" Taylor asks, her eyes wild with excitement.

"Why does Sexy Boss look so happy?" Lauren raises a brow and smirks.

"Don't even *try* to tell us it's work-related, because I already know that's bullshit." Leah giggles and takes a sip from her drink. I stand there with my heart feeling like it is going to beat out of my chest. My mouth hangs open but I can't even tell them what happened.

"I…he, um." I run my fingers through my hair, smiling and trying to calm the hell down. How do I put into words that I'd just had a kiss that rocked my world harder than anything in the two whole two years I was with Pete ever did? Before I have a chance to try and form words into a sentence, I hear Ruby's voice.

"Shane! Slammed. Let's go." Ruby yells her short commands as she shakes a drink in her hands. I look between all three of my friends who are waiting anxiously for my answer.

"Agh, I have to get back to work," I say, throwing my hands in the air. They all look like I just punched their favorite childhood pet in the face.

"I promise I will fill you all in as soon as my shift is over." I hold my hands over my heart as a promise.

"You fucking better," Taylor says as she kisses my cheek. "Because you look like you just got your world rocked and I will *not* be deprived of details." She raises a brow at me.

"Okay, bathroom break then dance floor," Leah says leading them toward the hallway.

I walk behind the bar to help Ruby handle the masses. She wasn't kidding, I think there are more people here now than before the ball dropped. I glance around, discreetly looking for Max, but he is nowhere to be found. I take a deep breath and try to shake off the last few minutes so I can focus.

I do my best not to think about what just happened. I need to focus on work and the customers. Not the earth-shattering kiss that made me forget that there's ever *not* been Max in my life. Clearly, I'm not doing a great job at the whole *not* thinking about it thing, seeing as how Tucker is sitting in front of me now waving his hands like he's trying to land a plane.

"Hellooooo, earth to the barkeep!" Tucker shouts at me. I shake my head and laugh.

"Oh my god Tucker, chill out." I say looking around to see people turning to face us. I feel my cheeks warm instantly at the attention.

"Woman, don't tell me to chill. I have been sitting here trying to get your attention for a minute and a half, where's your mind wandered off to?" he asks playfully. I'm unsure how to answer, but my eyes involuntarily dart to Max's office door when I see it open.

Tucker follows my gaze but doesn't say anything about it.

"*Anyhow*, now that I have your attention, barely," he says dramatically, making me roll my eyes. "Whiskey, rocks." I nod and start making his drink. "And, I wanted to ask you something." He says leaning a little closer over the bar. I lift a brow and look at him curiously.

"Uh-huh?" he looks around the dining room and bar and then back at me.

"Do you think your friend Taylor would give me her number?" There's no sense of playfulness in his voice, which is so out of character for him. He's serious and he's...nervous? I have never seen this man look this way before. I think about it for a minute, remembering how she looked at him the night we came dancing. She was also the one who stitched him up after the attempted robbery. Maybe there was a little something going on that I didn't know about.

Which made me feel like an asshole of a friend for *not* knowing, having been so caught up in my own shit lately. I make a mental note to reinstate weekly girls' nights as we had in high school, only now instead of studying and talking about boys, we can drink and talk about boys. I slide him his drink and smile at him.

"Tucker, she would eat you alive." I laughed at the thought. I have only recently gotten to know Tucker and he seems so sweet and playful. Taylor is wild, fierce, and sassy like none other.

"Oh, don't you worry about me Shaney, I bite back." He gives me a wink before looking over at her. I follow his gaze to my gorgeous best friend. She looks over to see us both staring at her. She furrows her brow and puckers her lips at me as if to say *whatchu looking at?* Then when she notices Tucker looking, she smiles and tosses her bright red hair over her shoulder before turning away.

"Go for it," I say to Tucker. Taylor seems to be flirting with him, and I think they'd be cute together. The wit between the two of them would be unmatched, but if I'm wrong then I'm wrong. He'll never know if he doesn't try. He finishes his whiskey and knocks on the bar.

"Say no more." He says, running a hand through his copper-brown hair.

He is definitely Taylor's type, though I know she's talked lately about not getting into anything serious so she can focus on work. He's well over six-foot tall. Maybe six-foot five, if I had to guess. His hair is cut similarly to Max's in the way it's shorter around the sides and longer on top, maybe old Navy habits die hard? It's light brown but with strong hints of red throughout. He's got a five o'clock shadow that's a much lighter red and bright green eyes. Muscular like Max too from working out regularly. Oh yes, my best friend will surely eat him alive.

I watch as he approaches Taylor and the girl looks a mixture between intrigued and in charge. I would expect nothing less. Leah and Lauren make their way to the dance floor together while the two of them talk. I stand there smiling at the interaction because I know how much my best friend works and she deserves to have some fun. I turn around to start hustling with Ruby again, and almost instantly my thoughts are back on Max, his office, and that kiss.

Tucker was a good distraction for a few minutes, but I'm not sure there's anything that could distract me long enough to make me forget what happened tonight.

I WALKED BACK to my office minutes after I went to help with the rush. I figured I probably shouldn't be walking around my bar with a hard-on for God and everybody to see. I think spending some time in the office with Riley will help me to chill the fuck out. That girl is more intoxicating than anything or anyone else I had ever encountered, and believe me there isn't much I haven't experienced.

The way she bit her bottom lip like she knew what was coming. How she tangled her fingers in my hair and how she felt wrapped around me while I held her against that wall. I don't think I'll ever look at another woman the way I look at her.

My Sunshine.

I slip out of the office long enough to grab myself a drink and notice her talking to Tucker at the bar. I like that they get along so well. They are annoying when together sometimes but in the best way. I like the idea that my best friend likes her. He has started coming to the gym with us more often and the two of them bicker like siblings. I go back to the office quickly, not wanting to leave Riley alone much longer. I bring her with me to the bar more often than not, but I especially want her here tonight knowing there will be fireworks going off all night, I know she will be stressed.

The two of us always stick together during stressful events, and I know that will never change, no matter what else in my life does. Riley is my partner and she'll be with me till the end. Once the bar is closed, I make my way back out of the office.

Ruby went home as soon as she finished up her part of closing, which consists of register count and bottle check. Heather and Marco left after bussing the tables in the dining room, and the kitchen staff is finishing up with the dishes now. Shane is wiping down the bar when I walk out of the office and make my way over to her.

"Hey there," I say as I lean against the wall.

"Hi." She smiles at me, already turning that perfect shade of pink.

"I need to talk to you for a minute,"

"Okay, what's up?" She lays the towel down on the bar and turns to face me.

"We aren't going to be training this week," I say, watching as confusion fills her face.

"Okayyy, how come?" She gives me a puzzled look.

"I have to go to Texas for the week."

"Texas?" she repeats back to me.

"Yeah, I have to check on some of my rental properties," I explain.

"You have *rental properties*?" I laugh at her remark. She's so full of questions, as always. Her nose scrunches up in confusion and I fucking love it.

"I'm full of surprises, Sunshine. Yes, I have a few rental properties and the ones in Texas need some attention, so I had planned to go this week to make sure everything is alright." I tell her, walking over to wrap her in my arms. She juts her bottom lip out in a pout.

"Well, alright then. I guess I will see you in a week." She smiles, but it's a sad smile. Not to sound like an asshole, but I kind of love that she's sad I'm going. Maybe she'll miss me as much as I know I'm gonna miss her. Suddenly Riley comes barrelling out of the office.

Shane looks over at her and smiles.

"Hey, girl! Are you having fun ringing in the New Year?" she asks in that soft sweet voice, bending down to call Riley over to her.

"Yeah, I figured it would be best if we stuck together tonight, with all the fireworks going on," I say, clearing my throat. She looks at me with concern in her eyes. This woman cares so much for everyone around her, it's making me want to pull her in and kiss her all over again.

"Are you okay though?" she asks. I look over at Riley and smile.

"I've come a long way since I first got out," I answer truthfully. "I had a good distraction tonight." I say, directing my smile toward her.

She stands to face me and runs a hand along my arm sending heat through my whole body.

"I'm glad to hear that, and it's so good that you have each other." She says softly. Before I know it, there's a warmth on my cheek from Shane's kiss. "Goodnight, Max." She starts to walk away, but before she gets too far, I pull her back to me. I wrap my hand around her neck and my lips are met with hers once again. The softness of her lips glides over mine, causing the desire in me to build even more. She stands on her toes to try and reach me better, so I pick her up, walking over to set her on the pool table. I slide my hands into the pockets of her jeans, as I've imagined doing so many times before, as she wraps her arms around my neck pulling me into her.

I swipe my tongue against her lips and she lets me in once again. When I spread her legs to move in closer to her she lets out a little gasp that makes me smile. I pull back to look at her face and she bites her bottom lip again.

Before I can lean back in for more, the kitchen door flies open. Shane jumps at the sound and we both look over. Jackie stands in the doorway with a big ass grin on his face.

"Night, boss." He nods to me, then directs his attention to Shane. "Night, Shane." He winks at her and then holds up his hand as he walks back through the kitchen to leave. Shane buries her face in her hands and laughs.

"Oh, my God. Poor Jackie." I grip her thighs in my hands and shake her a little to get her to look at me.

"Oh, please. That's probably the most action Jackie has seen in over a decade." I tease. Jackie is good people, he never married and always minds his own damn business, which I respect like hell. Shane laughs and rolls her eyes as her phone dings. She picks it up to check it and looks back at me, pulling in her bottom lip with her teeth.

"I should go, Taylor is being all *mama bear* on me about getting home because of how crazy people act on New Years." She says with the corner of her lips turning down.

"Can I give you a ride?" I question, making her smile.

"Um, aren't you headed out of town?" she asks, bringing a frown across her face.

"Yeah, I guess you're right. Give me your phone." I instruct, holding my hand out for it. She hands me her phone and I glance up at her and smile while putting my number in it.

"Here." I hand her the phone back and she looks down at it and smiles. Then she furrows her brow.

"How have I worked for you and been going to the gym with you for a month and not had your number?" She asks, holding her phone up.

"I guess because we have a standing gym time and you're the best employee and you never call out." I tease, kissing the tip of her nose. She scrunches it up and then hops off the pool table.

"I better get going." She says as she grabs her jacket from the wall.

"Let me know when you've made it home. Taylor isn't the only one worried about you."

"Yes, Max." She says sweetly. I walk over to her, no longer caring if I invade her space. Not that I'd ever really let it stop me before.

"I'm serious Sunshine. I know how long it takes you to get home from here, and if I don't hear from you in 20 minutes, I will show up at your door to make sure you're in one piece." My forehead is now touching hers and she looks up at me.

"I will. Pinky swear." She smiles and holds her pinky up. I quirk a brow but wrap my pinky around hers and I kiss her lips one last time before she walks through the kitchen doors to leave. I take in a deep breath, letting the warmth of emotion travel through my body, then grab the broom to start sweeping all this goddamn confetti up, which I swore I wouldn't be doing tonight. *Dammit.*

Chapter 20

WHEN I GET HOME from the bar on New Year's Eve, Taylor, Lauren, and Leah are all waiting eagerly to hear what happened in Max's office and how the night ended.

"SHUT THE HELL UP!" Lauren yells.

"YES, BITCH! OH MY GOD!" Taylor joins in.

"Oh good, the crazies are riled up," Leah says watching our other two best friends go absolutely batshit crazy.

"I know. I still can't catch my breath. I mean, I had picked up some heat between us here and there, and I mean you guys even saw him wink at me before Christmas." I say looking for confirmation. They all nod in agreement.

"But, now…" my face is as red as a tomato, I can guarantee it.

My best friends all let out loud shrieks, and I am right there with them.

I had sworn when I first got to Nashville that I was done with men. That they weren't deemed trustworthy and would just end up hurting me in the end.

But after meeting Max, I'm certain this is where I was supposed to end up all along. He's had my trust since the first night we worked together, and has earned it over and over again since then. He's strong and brave, kind and protective. He's everything I want to be around.

I'd been holding out hope that one day something would happen between us, but I was okay with only being his friend if that was all he could ever manage to be. When I'm around him my whole body tingles, and when he kissed me tonight, I completely lost myself in the way he made me feel.

Max left for a week the day after New Year's Day, to check on his *properties*. That still floors me. How much else do I still not know about him? He's been texting me constantly since he's been gone though, which has me rushing to my phone every time it goes off.

MAX

Texas is really gloomy without you, Sunshine.

MAX

Nothing smells like lavender here.

MAX

Don't take any more of Heather's tables while I'm gone.

That one makes me chuckle. This man is 800 miles away and still makes me blush.

I asked Tucker if he still wanted to hit the gym with me and Leah while Max was out of town and he was eager to join. I send Max a selfie of Tucker and me at the gym. His arm swung around my shoulder and we both made goofy faces with our tongues sticking out. Tucker truly feels like the older brother I've never had, and this photo captures that feeling perfectly.

ME

Tucker is much nicer during sparring than you are.

MAX

Attackers aren't nice Sunshine, that's why we train the way we do. I'll make it up to you soon.

Tuckers' phone goes off right after mine and he bellows out a laugh. Before showing me his phone screen.

MAX

Get your fucking arm off my girl.

TUCKER

Calm down old man. We're all friends here.

MAX

I may be old but I'll still break your arm.

"What kind of drug did you coat your lips with Shane, damn." Tucker teases. I roll my eyes in response and head for the treadmill. Some may call Max's reaction a red flag, I call it hot as fuck.

Hearing Max's bike pull up at the bar has me feeling like a kid on Christmas morning. My stomach is doing somersaults and excitement is building in my throat. Like, I actually feel the need to scream. I choose instead to drink some water to try and calm the hell down.

I am working the day shift this week so Tank can train on nights with Ruby, we're just closing out from the lunch rush when Max comes through the door.

His eyes instantly find me and he smiles. Oh my god, I almost forgot how sexy he is. He's wearing a baby-blue t-shirt, black jeans, biker boots, and his leather jacket. His dark brown hair is a mess from his helmet and his deep blue eyes lock on mine. He glances around and notices the lull then walks over and grabs my hand.

"She'll be right back." He tells Heather who is standing behind the bar with me. Pulling me back to his office and closing the door behind us. He spins me around, pressing my back against the door, kissing me senseless.

"Hi," he says against my lips, before pressing his full, warm lips back into mine.

His hands wrap around my neck and into my hair, while my own wrap around his abdomen. I want to koala wrap myself around him and never leave this office. He pulls back a little bit pressing his forehead to mine.

"Damn, I missed you, Sunshine," he says, kissing the tip of my nose.

"I missed you too. You just kiss a girl and leave her for a week, what's that about?" I tease.

"I am never leaving you for that long again." He says reassuringly. I pull my head back and scrunch my nose.

"Actually..." I drag out. He lifts his brow in disapproval.

"Yes?" he asks.

"I am going to San Francisco for a week," I roll my lips together, waiting for his response.

"San Francisco." He says, his tone hard. "What for?"

"My old boss, Hugh, invited me to an event *The Gallery* is hosting."

"Oh, for a whole week?" he asks, still seeming uneasy at the idea.

"Well, the event is only one night, but he booked me a hotel for the week so I thought I would go to some of my old favorite places. Maybe go to the beach and paint a bit." I explain, "I actually have two tickets to the event, and I was going to see if... Well if it's not too fast or anything, I was hoping maybe you'd go with me." My heart is racing inside my chest. I have no idea if this is entirely too fast, or if he has absolutely no interest in going with me. I just figured it would be a fun trip with him, he could see where I used to live, and meet Hugh.

"When do you leave?" he asks.

"Umm. Tomorrow." I nervously smile. He lets out a sigh and pulls me closer.

"I would love to go with you, Sunshine. Unfortunately, I can't." The smile I formed at the beginning of his sentence, drops at the end of it. I poke my lip out in a pout.

"Oh, yeah. That's okay." I wave a hand dismissively.

"Tucker and I help with training classes for the new Navy Recruits coming up, and one of them is joining to be a SEAL. They're week-long classes and they start the day after tomorrow."

Oh, that's a pretty legit reason for not going.

"Well, I think it's really cool that you guys do that. Those guys are lucky to have you both helping train them." I smile, wrapping my arms around his neck.

"Speaking of training, I hear I'm too hard on you?" Max teases, picking me up and wrapping my legs around him.

"Yes! I didn't realize how crazy you trained me until I went to the gym with Tucker!" I laugh in agreement.

"Well, I told you I'd make it up to you," he says, setting me down on his desk.

"You did." I agree, staring back at him.

"So, be a good girl, lay back, and let me." He commands, leaning in to kiss me as he lowers me back onto his desk.

He begins feathering kisses down my neck to my collarbone, sending shivers down my spine. He runs his hands under my shirt, his warm fingers grabbing onto my waist. When they move down to the button of my jeans I bite my lip in anticipation of what's to come. I have been fantasizing about this for weeks, I am more than ready for Max to have me, in whatever way he wants.

He undoes the buttons from my favorite flare jeans, sliding them down my legs before discarding them on the couch. He pulls my panties down next and I'm thankful I wore a cute pair today. Not that

I think he'd mind by the way he's looking at me right now. When he slides them over my sneakers I move my feet to kick them off, but he stops me before I can.

"Oh you're keeping the fucking sneakers on," he insists. So I do.

He runs his hands all the way up my thighs until his fingertips reach my hips. He licks and kisses my thighs inching his way closer and closer to where I want him the most. I take in a deep breath when his tongue runs along my clit.

"So fucking sweet," he growls, making my cheeks blush instantly. He brings his tongue back to my pussy, licking me up and down in perfect rhythm. When he licks circles around my clit, I can't help but let out a soft moan. As if he knows exactly what I need, he slides one finger inside me, followed soon by another. His fingers and tongue work perfectly together until I am full-on panting. I grip his hair and my hips grind in rhythm with him.

"Max," I moan. I'm aware of the people still in the bar on the other side of the door, I just don't seem to care at this moment.

"That's it, baby, let everyone out there know who's making you feel this good." He says, lifting his mouth from me only long enough to urge me on. His tongue soon rejoins his fingers, bringing me to the edge of my orgasm. He finds his pace again quickly and I am completely gone. My back arches off the desk, my fingers gripping his hair tighter.

"Oh, Max. I'm coming," I moan breathlessly.

He doesn't stop his mouth or his fingers until my body relaxes. He slides his fingers out, and stands to his feet, wiping my arousal from his beard. I never knew that could turn me on so much, but his devilish smile right after has me needing to clench my thighs together. He walks toward me and grips my chin, bringing my gaze up to him.

"You taste like heaven," he leans in, planting a gentle kiss on my lips. He brushes his nose against mine before he walks to the couch to grab my jeans. He walks them over and begins sliding them back on my legs.

"Um, Max? I think you're forgetting a step." I say, eyeing my panties on the chair.

"Nope. I'm keeping those." He says, standing me up to continue pulling my jeans over my ass. "I have to have some part of you with me when you leave for San Francisco." He says.

"Well, what part of you do I get to take with me?" I ask playfully.

He stares at me a moment and narrows his gaze. He rolls his lips together and hums as he thinks, making me giggle. "Here," he walks around pulling something from his desk drawer. He walks over and puts a chain with his dog tags in my hand. I look up at him, completely stunned.

"Your dog tags? I can't take these." I say, trying to hand them back.

"Why not?" he asks, puzzled. Like it's not something insanely sentimental and personal.

"Be-because you have my *underwear.*" I blurt out, making him laugh.

"Yes, I do. And I'm very happy about that. I still don't see the problem." He teases.

"I have like 40 pairs of underwear. I'm pretty sure you only have one of these, what if something happens to them? What if I lose them? I would never forgive myself." I frantically try to hand them back to him.

"First, I feel like 40 pairs of underwear is way too many. Second, I want you to take them. Yes, they're important to me, but so are you. I know you'll keep them safe. I trust you, Sunshine. Have a little faith in yourself." He folds my hand over the dog tags, letting me know he won't be taking them. He kisses my forehead and steps back, sliding my panties into his pocket.

"Now, you have to get to work, and I have to get home to see Riles." He slaps my ass, sending me out the door.

When we walk out of the office, heads turn in our direction and it feels like eyes are burning into my soul. I look at Max wide-eyed, remembering that his office is *not* soundproof. He shrugs and wraps his arm around my shoulders, walking me over to the bar. He glances around the room at everyone, then looks back down at me.

"Catch you later, Sunshine." He kisses me soft and sweet, then looks back around the bar.

"Now can we move on?" he announces.

The crowd has become mostly regulars – bikers, vets, and a few wanderers. There's more of a mix around the holidays, but now that they've passed it's back to all familiar faces. They hoot and holler, acting like a bunch of loons, which makes me laugh. Lenny looks at me and holds his hand to his heart as if I've somehow hurt him.

"I'd be a terrible second wife, Len. Don't be too heartbroken over me." I explain, making him laugh instead.

I spend the rest of my shift alarmingly aware that I have no underwear on. Every time I think of *why* I don't, it has me squeezing my thighs together.

When I clock out and head home to pack for my trip I text Lauren to see if she can ditch the office for a week. She's got the most flexible schedule out of all of us, plus it's been ages since the two of us did anything together.

ME

You feel like a girls' trip to SanFran with me for an art event this week?

LAUREN

Hell to the YES! When do we leave?

ME

Get packing babe, we leave at 8 AM tomorrow.

Chapter 21

THAT LAST MESSAGE has me blushing. Why the hell am I 2,000 miles away from him right now?

"I will never get over how freaking fabulous this place is," Lauren says as she spins around the hotel room Hugh got for us. It is definitely somewhere I would never be able to afford on my own. The suite has a king size bed, a full kitchen and a balcony with the most beautiful view of the city. The marble in the kitchen and the massive flat screen tv mounted above the dresser was enough to tell me this place cost a pretty penny. Don't even get me started on the rooftop restaurant and pool.

We spent the first few days visiting all our old hangouts from when the girls would come visit me in college. We walked on the boardwalk, rented bikes, grabbed fro-yo, and went shopping. Then we spent a couple of days holed up in the hotel room just watching movies. I didn't realize how much I'd missed San Francisco, but my desire to move back here was fading more and more every day. I have new things in my life that make me excited now. However, I really do miss working in an art environment, specifically my position at *The Gallery*. I am hoping I will get my fix during the event tonight.

Hugh is absolutely loaded and loves me like family so he spared no expense for my trip back out here this week. It's only been two months since I've seen him, yet it feels like it's been a lifetime.

"Yeah, Hugh has deep pockets, but you'd never guess it when you meet him. He's so kind and down to earth. Truly one of a kind in our line of work." I finally respond as I plop down on the bed.

"Listen to you, *our line of work*. Sounding like a true artist." Lauren says proudly. I reach for my phone but no more messages from Max have come through. I toss it down beside me and sigh. "I'm sure whatever Sexy Boss is doing, he's thinking of your fine ass. Don't you worry." Lauren reassures, as she plops down beside me.

"You're probably right. I am so freaking glad you came with me, Lu." I say, resting my head on her shoulder.

"So, What time is the event tonight?" Lauren asks.

"Seven o'clock," I answer, flipping my head to look at the clock that reads **2:30 pm.**

"Okay, I am going to the gym to get a workout in. Wanna come?" she says hopping back up from the bed. I narrow my gaze letting her know there's no chance in hell.

"Message received." She lifts her hands defensively and walks out of the room.

I grab the remote and flip through about a hundred channels with nothing good on before getting my ass out of bed to shower before the event tonight. Traveling and walking down memory lane this week has me completely worn out. I grab my phone from the bed before heading to the bathroom.

The bathroom here is absolutely massive. It has an ivory stand-alone tub sitting outside of the center wall of a shower that could *probably* house the Lord's supper table. It's completely black marble from floor to ceiling and has a freaking rain shower.

A hot bubble bath seems a bit more appealing than a shower today, the less standing, the better. I grab my phone and get the courage to be bold, sending Max a sudsy selfie. I'm completely covered in bubbles, but he'll get the idea.

After I hit send I set my phone on the little table outside of the tub; I sit there and soak for what feels like an hour. Once my water gets tempered, I hop out wrapping my plush hotel robe around me, shuffle back in the room, and fall into bed. I don't wake up until two and a half hours later, when the hotel room door slams, jolting my body into an upright position. My hands involuntarily fall into a karate chop position.

"Calm down, Jackie Chan." Lauren laughs. I look at the clock to see it's now five-thirty at night, and Lauren is still in her workout clothes.

"Jesus Christ, Lauren!" I say, holding my chest dramatically. "Next time leave the door on the hinges when you come in."

She rolls her eyes and kicks her shoes off.

"Always so dramatic, Shaney." She smiles, beaming with a sickeningly gorgeous post-workout glow.

"Where have you been, anyway? If you say you worked out for two whole hours, I'm leaving your ass here when I go back to Nashville." I fall back onto the bed trying to slow my heart rate.

"Relax, I took some breaks." She playfully glares at me through the mirror. She's acting suspicious but I'm not in the mood to pry.

"Shower quick, you're in charge of this tonight," I say, circling my face with my index finger.

"Shut up, are you serious?" Lauren squeals, running over to hug me. She presses our cheeks together and I push her face away with my hand.

"Yes, but some of us already showered, you sweaty robot, so get off of me." I wipe my face dramatically, laughing as she skips off to the bathroom. I walk over to pick up my phone before drying my hair, and I see a text from Max.

MAX

You're killing me woman.

My cheeks flush at his response. Even two thousand miles away, he finds ways to make me feel warm and giddy. Something I don't think ever happened with Pete, even in the closest proximity. I bite my lip and toss my phone on the bed. Taking a deep breath, I try to focus on the task at hand – getting ready in under an hour. Fantastic.

The Gallery looks breathtaking tonight. It's always been one of my favorite places in San Francisco. It's white everywhere you look, but not in a sterile way. Hugh opted for warm lights in all of the more relaxed areas, to give it a more intimate ambiance, only using more vivid lights around the paintings.

There are white sofas and armchairs to the left and right as soon as you walk in, with glass coffee tables in the middle, and white roses cover every single surface in here. They're hanging from the ceiling, some are in giant planters in the entryway, and full bouquets are in glass vases on every cocktail table.

Waiters are in every corner passing out champagne, and the paintings being auctioned are in glass displays that make them look like they're floating. The event is a silent auction on new-release paintings for the California Wildfire Prevention Foundation. Philanthropy is just another thing to add to the long list of reasons I love and miss working for Hugh.

"You ladies look lovely this evening." The smooth swagger of his voice is impossible not to recognize. I quickly turn around and face Hugh.

"You're one to talk," I say, motioning a hand up and down Hugh's body.

He's wearing a black Hugo Boss suit with gold cufflinks, a white dress shirt, and a black bow tie. The pants of his suit are cropped, in his signature style. His dress shirt fits tightly across his chest and the suit jacket hugs his arms perfectly showing off the definition beneath.

He wears black Burberry loafers and a black and gold Versace watch to match. The simplest of outfits, still putting everyone else here to shame. His salt and pepper hair and beard are immaculately cut and styled, with his hair slicked back for the occasion.

"Ah well, you're too kind, Shane. We sure do miss having you here." Hugh says, leaning in to give me a hug. I graze his cheek with a kiss, before stepping back in line with Lauren.

"Hugh, this is Lauren, Lauren this is the infamous Hugh Burgess." I take the chance to introduce them.

"Pleasure to meet you, Love," Hugh says, winking at Lauren.

Umm... Okay.

I look over at Lauren, not missing the way her cheeks turn pink at his actions.

"Pleasure to finally meet you," Lauren says back.

"Well if you'll excuse me, I am going to make the rounds. Enjoy your evening. Shane, don't leave without saying goodbye." Hugh says as he backs away.

"I won't," I smile and wave as he turns away from us.

I turn to face Lauren, who is a lovely shade of red.

"Your face matches your dress, *Love*," I tease, addressing the way Hugh just winked at her *and* gave her a nickname. Her floor-length red satin dress does nothing to hide what a bombshell she is. It hugs her body from her chest down to her hips, where it falls more loosely as it flows to the floor. The off-the-shoulder sleeves on it are the freaking cherry on top. She looks absolutely stunning.

"Let's get some champagne, shall we." She raises a brow,

completely deflecting the conversation concerning Hugh. I narrow my gaze at her, letting her know this conversation is *not* over. We finally come across a waiter and grab some champagne before making our way around the gallery.

I don't bid on anything, seeing as how I have no money and no place to even display such gorgeous pieces of art, but I admire the hell out of each and every piece. When I make my way to the very back wall there is one piece of art that stops me in my tracks. I would recognize it anywhere, seeing as it's one of mine. The piece I couldn't find when I left a couple of months back. The piece that brought me back to life.

"I thought it was time." His smooth voice says from behind me. I spin around, my eyes wet with emotion. Hugh stands there, looking like the proud mentor that he is.

"How did you –" I say, pointing at the painting. My voice catches on the lump in my throat, stopping my words from coming out.

"You left it here, on your last day. It must have gotten left in a different room when we moved things around a while back. When I found it I thought about calling you, letting you know it got left behind and that I would be more than happy to send it to you." I turn to face the painting again, wiping a tear that falls.

"But then I thought about it a little longer… This is one of the most compelling pieces I have ever seen from such a young artist, Shane. I remember when you told me the inspiration behind it. I thought it was time the world saw it. Or at least the part of the world that walks through here today. I do hope that is alright with you." Hugh says as he walks up closer to the painting.

This was the first piece I painted after my parents passed away. It's a depiction of what I felt, of what I went through that first year. The bright yellow and vibrant sienna is soon overtaken by gloomy shades of brown before they deepen into the deepest black. Representation of the black hole I was drowning in as I started college, unable to share this new journey with them as I had always planned to.

The black soon begins to fade into a dark gray, then lighter gray, before hints of deep sapphire seep into the azure blue. Until the colors can compare to the clearest waters in the ocean. I found my way back out through the art I always shared with them. I was no longer drowning in my grief. I found a way to swim through it.

"Thank you, Hugh." I hug him and wipe a tear from my eye. "Excuse me," I say as I make my way to the bathroom to freshen up.

I look in the floor-length mirror, brushing my hair back out of my face. I smooth out the tulle from my dress and cock my head to the side, examining my look for the night.

A few weeks ago Lauren helped me pick out the most perfect gold dress for tonight. It has a corset-designed top that has silk rose details in it and bubble tulle sleeves. The bodice stops at my waist where the full tulle skirt drops, stopping just a few inches above my knees. She paired it with matching gold stilettos that I would have never picked out myself. But when it comes to fashion, you don't argue with Lauren. Even if I look like a walking ray of sunshine.

Sunshine.

Thoughts of Max flood my head as I stand here in the bathroom, tapping concealer under my eyes where mascara has slightly smeared. I wrapped his dog tags around my wrist to wear like a bracelet tonight. Even though Lauren told me it clashed, I didn't care. I open my clutch to drop the concealer back in when my phone dings with a text notification.

MAX

Don't go running off with any rich art buffs tonight.

ME

Grumpy bar owners are more my speed. 😉

I take a deep breath and look in the mirror one last time before heading back out to the gallery. When I walk out, I find Lauren looking at the piece I painted, proudly displayed at the auction.

"I am so proud of you, Shaney," Lauren says, tears welling in her eyes.

"Stop it, I just finished crying, don't you dare make me start again," I say, hugging her tight. We both sniffle, trying to reel our emotions back in. I love how supportive all of my friends are. They know the pain I went through and how hard I fought to get here. This is a big moment for me and I am so glad Lauren was here to share it with me.

"You wanna get out of here and *really* celebrate?" she asks, wagging her eyebrows. I give her a curious look, intrigued at what kind of trouble she wants to get into.

"Let's do it," I agree, setting my champagne glass on the tray as the waiter walks past us.

"Wait, wait," Lauren stops me, grabbing my arm. "Stand over there." She waves her hand in the direction of my painting.

"What, no!" I whisper back, glancing around the room. It's one thing to have your painting displayed, but isn't it kind of vain to pose in front of it?

"Oh my god, no one is over here right now, just do it." She commands, pushing me over in front of the painting. Maybe it isn't vain, maybe it is. But I'm choosing not to care. This is something I should be proud of.

Reminding myself never to argue with Lauren, I stand in front of the display. I cross my feet at the ankles and look over at the painting, *my* painting, that's about to be finding a new home after tonight. It's a bittersweet feeling. This painting means so much to me, it's such a powerful statement of how I went through such a dark time in my life, drowning in grief, but I made it out the other side. Before I know it Lauren is locking her arm through mine, and we are heading out the door.

"What did I tell you about leaving before saying goodbye." His tone all tease, Hugh walks over to Lauren and me by the door.

"Sorry, Hugh. We got swept up in plans to celebrate." I smile at him apologetically.

"You're forgiven. Go celebrate, but be safe. Shane, I would like to speak with you again, sometime soon. Contact me when you're back in Nashville will you?" he asks in a more serious tone. I give him a nod, letting him know I will, while wondering what on earth about.

Tonight isn't the night for questions though, tonight is a night to celebrate. Because I just had my very first piece of art displayed in a gallery. This is surreal.

I ABSOLUTELY HATED LEAVING for Texas the day after I finally kissed Shane for the first time. I decided after one day of being gone that I wouldn't leave for that long again unless absolutely necessary. At least, not without taking her with me. Then after getting back, I find out she has to leave for San Francisco for an art event, and I hate that she's out there without me. Lots of douchey rich guys, trying to sweep her off her feet talking about paintings, thinking they have a chance.

Like hell they do.

I thought maybe I wouldn't miss her as much as I have, but here I am, using the social media account I never thought I'd touch to look her up. I find Shane's page, seeing an update from 20 minutes ago at the event they're attending.

My Sunshine.

She looks absolutely stunning in her gold dress and high heels. Her wavy hair is pulled back in a ponytail with loose wavy pieces framing her face. I feel warmth in my chest when I notice she's wrapped my dog tags around her wrist like a bracelet. She's a fucking vision, and she's got my name wrapped around her wrist, and somehow everything about that feels right. She stands next to a painting hanging in a glass display, and she's looking up at it so intently.

The painting is absolutely breathtaking. On the left are variations of yellow and orange, then it gets really dark in the center with browns, blacks, and dark gray, then on the other side the dark blues turn lighter until it looks like ocean water. I zoom in and am almost knocked on my ass when I see the plaque under it. It's hers. *She* painted it? Why didn't she tell me she would have a painting on display?

When I swipe to the next photo my jaw clenches. She's standing next to a guy with salt and pepper hair but doesn't look much older than me. His arm is around her waist and they're both smiling ear to ear. I click on the tag and see the name, *Hugh Burgess*. The owner of the gallery and the boss she hated leaving. I try to calm my jealous streak down as Tucker walks up and slaps me on the head with his towel.

"Shit, Tucker," I mumble, rubbing the back of my neck.

"We're supposed to be working out here Max, not stalking your girlfriend." He jokes, looking over my shoulder at the Instagram page I am stopped on. We had an early end to classes with the new Navy recruits today, so we decided to hit the gym before calling it quits.

"I'm coming," I say, locking my phone and dropping it into my gym bag.

"So what's going on with you two?" Tucker asks, taking the weights off the weight rack. The way this guy manages to be so involved in my personal life is unreal.

"Do you not have anything else to talk about right now?" I shake my head, grabbing my own weights.

"Nope. You've been different lately man. I wanna know what's up."

"Different how?" I glance at him through the gym mirror.

"I can't describe it, man. You just - look for her."

That's the dumbest fucking explanation I could have gotten.

"I look for her?" I stand to face him, my face surely letting him know how dumb I think that sounds.

"Yeah, like. You're happier when she's around, and not your own twisted version of happy, but *actually* happy. You look for her when she's not around." He continues his reps while I stand there processing.

Shit. Maybe it wasn't that dumb.

Tucker knows me better than anyone so I'm sure the recent change in my attitude is obvious. I drop my weights back on the rack, placing my hands on my hips and staring at my feet. I didn't quite know what to expect with Shane when we started getting closer, but now that I've had a taste of what it's like to be with her, she's it for me.

I remember her mentioning after Topgolf that she missed her job back in San Francisco. With her being out there tonight, I selfishly hope she doesn't realize how much she still misses it. She may come back all *'Thanks for a good time, but I'm off to California again.'* And I'm not sure I could handle that, because I find myself caring more about her with every passing day. I guess Tucker is right, she makes me fucking happy. A feeling I haven't experienced in a very long time.

"She looks for you too, man. Her face lights up the second you walk through the door. " He claps my shoulder before walking over to the pull-up bar. And dammit if I don't love hearing that.

When Shane walked into work today it took everything in me not to immediately drag her back to my office, just like I'd done when I got back from Texas. She is wearing a denim mini skirt and black sneakers with her Chattahoochies t-shirt today. Taking my eyes off her legs is damn near impossible.

Shane and I are getting the dining room set up and the registers ready while Marco and Heather sit at a booth rolling silverware. The glances she's giving me have my dick springing to life, just from the way her ocean eyes watch me while we work around the bar. The scent of lavender is finally present again, surrounding me everywhere I turn. God, I missed her.

I make my way back to my office for a few minutes while Shane does the bottle count. When I think she may be done, I get up to open the office door and step outside calling her over.

"Shane," I nod my head to the office, and she immediately leaves her task behind the bar to make her way over. When she stops in front of me I motion for her to walk in and I follow closely behind, before shutting the door. She turns around to face me, but before she can get a word out, my hand is in her hair, the other on her hip, and my lips are on hers.

Fucking finally.

She doesn't even hesitate to kiss me back, bringing her hands up to hold my face. I back her up until her ass hits my desk, then I lift her at her thighs and place her on top of it. I let my hands stay on the back of her thighs, enjoying the warmth of her skin against mine. I squeeze them tight before letting my hands travel up toward the hem of her skirt. She leans back and my lips make their way to her neck.

Lavender.

"Did you miss me, Max?" she says breathlessly. I let out a growl, and bring my lips back up to hers. They barely graze along them when I whisper,

"More than you know, Sunshine." I nip at her bottom lip and she smiles.

She grabs my shirt pulling me closer and our lips are together again. She slips her tongue into my mouth and scoots her hips closer to me making her skirt raise even higher on her legs. One more scoot from her and she'll feel just how excited I am that she's back. She slides closer once more, and I am already about to lose my damn mind.

A deep rumble sounds in my chest and she pulls back slightly to smile. Her eyes flutter open and our blue eyes lock.

"I missed you too, Max." Her voice is soft and sweet.

I lean down and kiss her again, inching my hands up her legs a little more, getting closer and closer to her pussy. Her hips slide toward me like she's eager for my touch. I smile against her lips. "Getting eager there, Sunshine?" I tease. Hell, I'm eager for her too. The tent in my boxers is proof of that.

"Yes," she breathes out, moving her hips once again. I trail my fingers along her clit, and she pulls in a quick breath. I move the thin black fabric out of the way, running a finger along the pool of wetness.

"So fucking wet for me." She lets out a moan and I slowly slide a finger in, working in and out of her before sliding in another. When she goes to let out another one of her beautiful sounds of approval, I take it captive with my own mouth.

My tongue swipes her lips, and she parts them letting me in, as my fingers continue to explore her. I can feel the tension building in her body so I begin to work her clit and she fucking whimpers. I can feel her right on the edge of her orgasm, when I pull my fingers away, licking her arousal from them.

"What are you doing?" she asks in an aggravated pout.

"You're not coming unless it's on my face," I growl, raising a brow at her. "Do you know how much it's killed me, not being able to taste you for the past week?" I ask, running my hand along her golden locks. She shakes her head, but no audible response leaves her lips.

"It's been fucking torture," I tell her, grabbing a handful of her hair.

"I'm sorry," she whispers, trying to look away. I place my hand on her neck, bringing her gaze back to me, brushing my thumb across her cheekbone.

"Don't be sorry, Sunshine. You're here now, and you're not leaving this office until I've tasted every part of you." She bites her lip, driving me fucking mad.

"Now get on your back, and come on my face." Her cheeks grow red again and I love that she reacts to me this way, that heat rises to her face from just the thought of my head between her legs. She rolls her lips, staring up at me doe eyed.

"Tell me how much you want it, Sunshine. Tell me how badly you want me to taste you." I command.

"Please taste me, Max. It's all I've thought about all week. Please." I smirk at her and brush her bottom lip with my thumb.

"Good girl."

My hands move underneath her skirt and my fingers slide under the band of her panties. She lifts her ass and I yank them down in one swift motion. I kiss her once more before dropping to my knees for her. She spreads her legs for me without hesitation, and I about come apart right then and there. I sit there, admiring the incredible creature in front of me. So wet and ready for me to taste her.

I kiss along her thighs, making my way up to her sweet little pussy. I swipe my tongue across my bottom lip before I indulge. My tongue runs along her entrance and I hear her suck in a breath. I move slowly at first, savoring every drop of her, but when she runs her fingers through my hair, all caution is thrown to the wind.

I grab her thighs, pulling her closer to me. Working my tongue around her puffy lips and up to her clit, before dipping my tongue inside her, making her moan once again.

I keep working her with my tongue as my hands slide up her body. Pushing past her shirt I feel the warmth of her smooth, toned abdomen. I inch my hands up further, cupping her firm breasts in my hands. I feel a low growl in my throat as my fingers make contact with her perky nipples, her lace bra doing nothing to hide their peakedness. I move my tongue along her most sensitive area, pinching her nipples as she whispers my name.

"Max." God I love hearing my name on her lips, so needy for me.

Knowing exactly what she wants, I slide my hand back down her body, slipping two fingers inside her once again. Working them in and out as my tongue moves in circles on her clit. She grips my hair in her tiny hands, grinding her hips in sync with my movements.

"That's it, come for me, baby." I keep my rhythm steady, making her body quiver with pleasure. Her back arches as she goes over the edge, saying my name even louder this time.

"Max!" it comes out as a plea. I wait for her to ride out every last bit of her orgasm and her hand releases its grip on my hair before I remove my fingers and stand to my feet. I lick every last drop of her pleasure from my fingers once more as she watches me, her tongue swiping out to wet her bottom lip as I do.

"You're gonna drive me fucking mad, you know that?" I lean in and kiss her slowly before reaching over and grabbing her underwear from my desk.

"I should send your ass home for coming to work in that skirt, wearing this sad excuse for underwear." I raise a brow at her, holding her black thong up on my finger.

"Who said I'll be wearing them?" she crosses her arms over her chest.

"There's no chance in hell you won't be," I say firmly. She rears back at my statement.

"I'm not taking a chance of someone else getting a glimpse at what's mine. And I don't feel like taking someone out in my own bar if they do. Now, put them back on, before I do it for you." I command. She takes her underwear, sliding them ever so teasingly back onto her body. She holds her hands out in a *ta-da* motion. I grip her chin bringing her lips right up to mine.

"Good girl." I kiss her gently and send her out to work. When what I really want to do is see how many different ways we can fuck up this office.

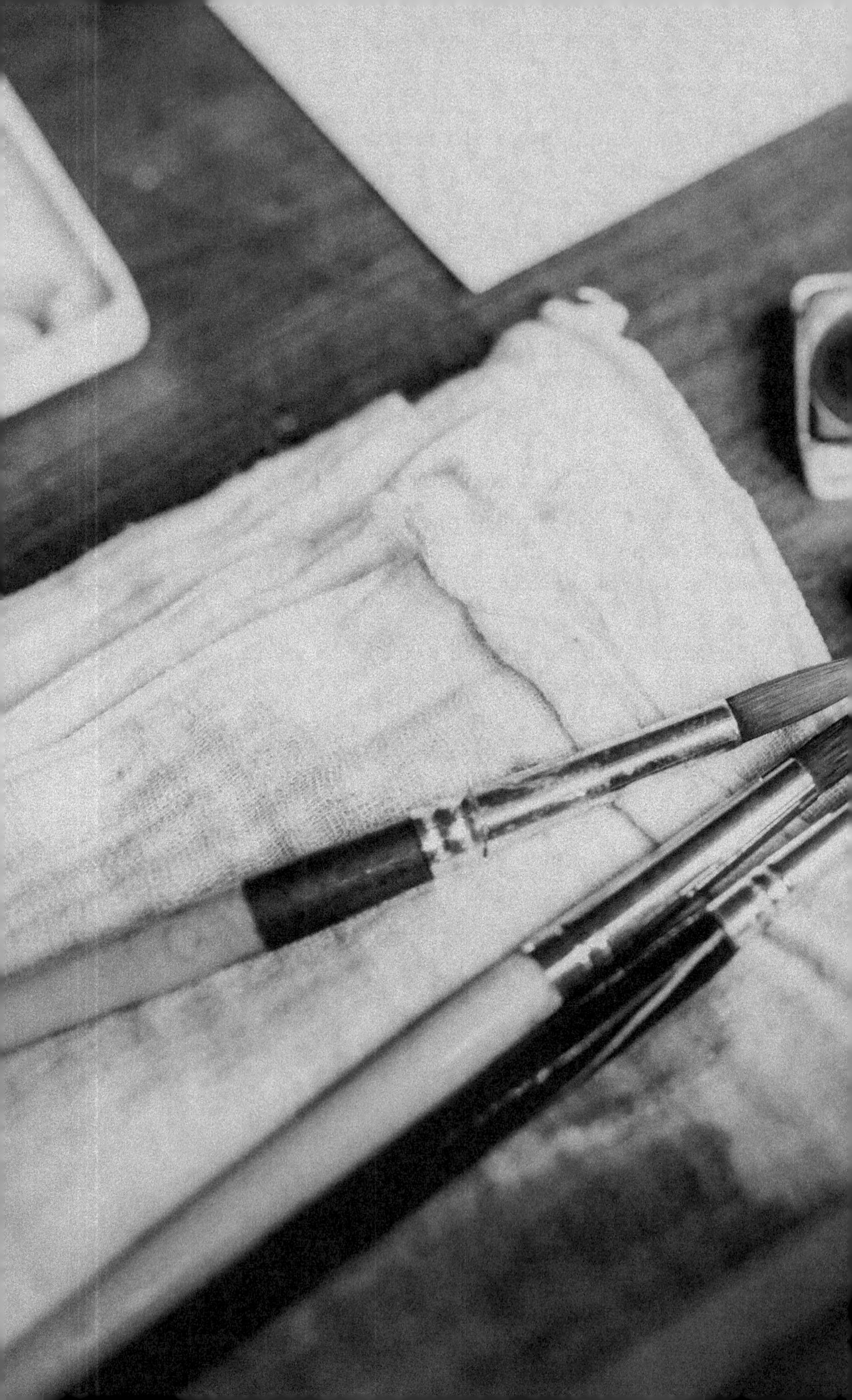

Chapter 23

Shane

RETURNING to work after my boss just gave me the best orgasm of my life is not an ideal situation. I go red in the face every time I think about it. Heather asked me once if I was having an allergic reaction to something then busted out laughing at how wide my eyes got. I have gotten pretty close to everyone on staff at the bar and I truly look forward to coming to work. I am so glad to be back in Nashville with my friends, old and new, and Max of course.

I thought of nothing but him while I was in San Francisco this past week, and there's a possibility my bubble bath was a little more relaxing than I had originally planned for it to be. After sending him my bathtub selfie I couldn't get him out of my head. I was hot and bothered thinking about him and since he was back in Nashville, well... You get the point.

Since I opened today, that means Ruby is closing with Max. I am honestly sad to go when my shift ends because this job is super fun.

Especially when I get to stare at Max all night. But I am also super excited because tonight is girls' night. We've made it a regular event ever since I got back and it has become one of the highlights of my weeks.

If you've ever watched the *Harry Potter* series, then you might be familiar with a mandrake, and the sound they make. Imagine that sound coming from three grown-ass females when I told them about my recent trip to Max's office.

"You lucky little bitch!" Taylor yells at me.

"That's so hot, Shaney. That man is sinfully sexy." Lauren never holds anything back in her thoughts, and I love her for it.

"I mean, it's not pool table sex, but… it's fine I guess." Leah teases. My face is hot with excitement as I dish all the dirty details with my best friends.

"So are you guys like a thing now, or what?" Taylor asks, dipping a tortilla chip into the queso that is on the coffee table… In a scent burner? What the hell Taylor? Wait, that's actually kind of genius.

"Hello, woman! Edge of our seats here!" Lauren snaps her fingers in my face, bringing me back to the conversation.

"I don't know, honestly. I mean, we text back and forth all the time, he told me he missed me and not to run off with a rich art buff, and we've been stealing any moment we can when we are together. But I mean nothing *official* has been said." I shrug. Uncertainty is not something I'm particularly crazy about, but as long as I'm with Max in some capacity, I'm happy.

"Well, as long as you're happy and getting yours, who needs labels." Lauren offers, forking her chicken, cheese, and rice into her mouth.

"So, I feel like I'm the only one ever talking about their personal life. Someone else give me *something*, please." I plead, grabbing my margarita from the coffee table.

"Max's friend, Tucker, asked me for my number," Taylor says quietly. Taylor never says anything quietly, so the whole room falls silent for a moment and my mouth drops open.

"When?" I ask, turning to fully face her.

"Well…" she picks up her margarita glass and takes a slow drink. My eyes grow wide with anticipation.

"SPIT IT OUT," I wave my hand rushing her along. I remember when he asked me about her on New Year's but that was weeks ago, if it happened then why is she just bringing it up now?

"New Year's Eve," she finally admits. The whole living room is quiet except for Michael Scott, from *The Office*, yelling on the TV.

"Ummmm. Way to hold the hell out on us!" Leah finally says. Taylor never takes her eyes off me though.

"Did you give it to him?" Lauren asks. Taylor's eyes dart down to her lap and back up at me, her ivory skin starting to turn pink at her cheeks. The corners of my mouth turn up and a smile spreads across my face.

"So, you and Tucker then?" I ask as I playfully bump her arm. She breathes a sigh of relief and giggles.

"Maybe, I don't know. I mean we're just kind of friends right now, I have *kinda* been seeing someone else at work off and on." She says scrunching her nose.

"WHAT!" Leah, Lauren and I shout.

"Why are we just now hearing about this?" I ask, completely shocked that she hasn't told us this sooner I'm not sure I would have told Tucker to go for it had I known.

"I don't know. Things have just been so busy and stuff since you got back. Plus it's nothing serious, you know me." She rolls her eyes dismissively.

"Taylor, we are best friends. It doesn't matter what's happening in my life, or if the guy you're seeing is serious or not, you share these things with us. Always!" I grab her hand to get her full attention. She smiles softly at me and nods. I hate that she felt like she couldn't tell us this, but thank god for girls' night so we could find out now.

"Bitch, did you give him the number or not?" Lauren asks impatiently.

"Yes," is all she says in response.

"Well freaking finally someone else has something to talk about besides me. No offense." I glance at Leah and Lauren, who start laughing and talking about how the "meat market" has been less than impressive as of late. Which has me and Taylor busting out laughing right along with them. We are reminiscing on some of Taylor's high school crushes and how absolutely questionable they were when my phone dings. I pick it up from the couch cushion and swipe open the message from Max.

> **MAX**
>
> Closing with Ruby sucks. She won't stop asking why I'm smiling.

> **ME**
>
> Well, why are you smiling, Max?

> **MAX**
>
> Thinking about what I had for lunch today.

> **ME**
>
> The burger Jackie made you? He does make the best.

> **MAX**
>
> I was thinking of the appetizer I had. It was a little more blonde, and a lot more wet.

My face goes completely red at his text message. I bite my thumbnail as I think of how to reply. Taylor leans over and reads my texts without me even noticing until she's right in my ear.

"Damn babe, that's hot as hell. " I flinch and hold my phone to my chest.

"Ma'am. This is a private conversation." I tease, knowing I was probably about to tell them about it anyways. Then I get an idea of how to respond.

ME

Wait until you see the main course.

MAX

You're killing me, woman.

ME

See you in the morning

Happy with my response, I focus my attention back on my girls. Tomorrow Max and I start back at the gym, and I honestly can't wait. I have gotten so used to it being a part of my routine. A little over a month ago, I was wondering when I would get to make my way back to San Francisco, now I can't imagine leaving Nashville. Which is something I never thought I would say.

Chapter 24

RUBY WOULD NOT LEAVE my ass alone last night while we were at work. I couldn't help but smile every time I thought about Shane lying back on my desk. The look in her eyes, the way she told me how bad she wanted me to taste her, *the taste of her.* I was going crazy all night. I finally escaped her questioning when we got slammed and the rest of the night she never brought it up. Shane is on her way to meet me at the gym now, and I can't wait to see her. Stolen moments with her aren't going to be enough for me for much longer, but I just don't know where her head is at when it comes to us. We never really talked about what this is – the thing happening between us, we've just let it happen.

I see her perfect body in her light blue workout shorts and an over-sized sweatshirt that probably has a matching sports bra underneath like it always does. Her blonde ponytail whips back and forth as she makes her way down the sidewalk and into the gym. I lean down, picking up a coffee cup, before handing it to her.

Iced vanilla latte.

I have brought her one to every workout we've had since we started. It always makes her smile, and I'd do anything to see Shane smile.

"My hero." She takes a long pull from the cup and dramatically *AHHs* after. "We stayed up way later than we should have last night. So I may be dead weight today." She takes another long sip of her coffee before setting it down.

"We could have pushed the time." I offer, grabbing my own coffee and finishing it off.

"That's okay, I actually have somewhere to go right after this." She says cheerily. I look at her with a raised brow as I scan over the shorts she is wearing. It's bad enough that every asshole in this gym gets to see her perfect ass in them. I will gladly follow her wherever she's going after this to kill anyone else who tries to take a second look.

"Down boy, I have a change of clothes in here." She swings a backpack around that I hadn't noticed she was carrying. The added remark she made is not lost on me though.

"I swear to god, you and Tucker spend way too much time together." I roll my eyes, recognizing his famous *down-boy* comment from any time I get worked up about Shane.

"We do not. Only at the gym and the bar." She argues, crossing her arms over her chest.

"Yeah, and that's too fucking much." I tease back. She's the one that rolls her eyes now. After an hour of sparring, squatting, and strength training, we are both covered in a layer of sweat. "Well, I definitely need a shower." She pants, running the back of her arm over her forehead. I look at her and my eyes travel down her body, taking in every defined curve. Her tan skin is a beautiful contrast against the blue workout set she's wearing today, and her hourglass figure is enough to bring me to my knees right here. When my eyes finally lock with hers she's got a brow lifted in return.

"Like what you see, Maxwell?" she teases, knowing I hate being called my full name. Though, it doesn't sound so bad coming from her lips.

"Every single inch of it." I tell her, closing the distance between us. "Go ahead, I'll see you back out here." I give her a kiss and she heads off toward the showers. Before I can follow suit and head for the men's showers, Jimmy walks up to me.

"Hey there Max, I got kind of a favor to ask you." He says, running his hand along his neck. "Heidi broke down on the freeway and I need to get out there and see what's what. Tommy is out today so I don't have anyone to watch the gym while I'm gone. Would you mind locking up here when you and your girl leave?" He asks, almost seeming embarrassed at the request.

My girl.

It sounds nice coming from someone else and not just playing around in my mind.

Jimmy and Heidi Hall opened Hall's Gym about 8 years ago, and Tucker and I have always been loyal members. We came in every time we were home from a mission, and have been regulars since getting back home permanently. We've formed a sort of friendship-like acquaintance so he knows he can trust me to lock up for him.

"Of course, it's not a problem. You can swing by the bar later to pick up the keys. No rush, just when everything settles down. Hope everything is okay." I assure him. He hands me the spare gym keys and gives me a nod.

"Thanks, Max, I owe you one." He turns out all the lights before walking out, and I head towards the showers. I'm only in there about 5 minutes before I hear Shane's voice out in the hallway. She must be done and wondering why the lights are off and no one else is here.

"Hello?" she calls. "Max, are you still here?" she sounds slightly panicked.

"I'm here, it's alright," I call from the men's showers.

"Why are the lights off, and where is everyone?"

"Jimmy asked me to lock up, he had to go take care of something."

I yell as I turn the water off. "Why don't you come on in here, I'm almost done," I call. She doesn't answer, but a moment later I hear her footsteps in the room. I walk around the corner, catching a glimpse of her in her dark, skin-tight jeans, and a fitted long-sleeve top, paired with her white chuck taylors. I smile as I finish running a towel over my hair. I already have my boxers and blue jeans on, but my tattoo-covered torso is completely exposed.

Her eyes glide over my body like she's taking it all to memory. I take a few steps toward her when I see her biting her lip. Her eyes shoot up, locking with mine as I come to a stop towering over her.

"Like what you see, Sunshine?" I ask, my voice sounding rougher than usual. She lets out a soft moan and nods her head. I lean down, taking her mouth with mine, as one arm wraps around her tiny little waist. She grabs onto my arms with both hands, standing on her toes and pulling herself into me. She begins letting her hands explore my body, running along my biceps and up along my shoulders. Once they've made their way down over my chest and her dainty fingers are tracing over my abs I can't take it anymore. My dick is pressing hard against my jeans, trying to join the fun. I pull her into me a little more, letting her feel the effect she's having on me. She pulls her face from mine, looking down where I'm firmly pressed against her. I grab her by the jaw, turning her face to mine.

"Look at what you're doing to me."

"I can help with that if you'll let me." She smiles up at me mischievously.

This fucking woman.

"Could you now?" I ask, releasing my grip on her jaw.

Her eyes are doe-like as she watches me while lowering to her knees. I take a breath in as I watch her undo the button from my jeans, pulling them and my boxers down, freeing my cock.

Her eyes grow slightly wider seeing my full length, they dart from my cock, back up to my eyes. She grabs a hold of it, her tiny hands stroking it back and forth a few times before she stops.

"Don't fucking tease me, Sunshine," I growl. The look on her face flashes innocence. Piquing my interest.

"Can you…" she starts before her eyes fall away from me, trailing off.

"Can I what?" I question.

"Can you show me how? I've just never… I just never did this with…him." she admits.

"Look at me," I instruct, bringing her ocean-blue eyes back to me. God, she looks so perfect down on her knees for me. "I don't want you thinking about that asshole. I'll show you anything you want to learn, but when you do it, you better be thinking of me. Only me." I command, "because I'm only ever thinking of you, Sunshine. Understand?" she nods her head in response.

Her fingers wrap around my base and I place my hand on top of hers, helping her set a rhythm. When she seems more confident I let her take control. My jaw ticks as she moves up and down so smoothly. She looks up at me with wide eyes, looking for assurance.

"Just like that baby." I encourage her.

"Can I um…" she swipes her tongue along her bottom lip as she eyes my cock.

"Suck it." I finish for her. She smiles timidly, her cheeks growing pink, which makes my dick throb in her hand. "If it gets to be too much, we'll stop." I run my thumb along her bottom lip as she nods her head.

"I understand." She says softly.

"Now, take my cock in that pretty mouth of yours," I tell her. She opens her mouth, taking as much of me as she can. She works one hand at my base as she runs her pouty pink lips up and down my cock, using her tongue to perform some kind of magic as she does.

Holy fuck, nothing has ever felt this good.

"Damn baby, that feels so good." I praise. Because it's fucking true and I know she needs to hear it. If this is her first blow job then she's a natural.

She picks up her pace and my head falls back, I can feel the energy building throughout my whole body. Not only is this the best head I've ever gotten, but you add the fact it's been years since I've been with anyone and my window of holding on is closing. Fast.

"I'm close, baby, just keep doing what you're doing." With that encouragement, she takes me further down her throat, and I'm gone. She takes my full length all the way in three more times before I try to pull away, but she doesn't let me. Her determined eyes lock with mine as she keeps me right there in her mouth, swallowing every bit of my release. When my cock finally stops pulsing on her tongue, I slide myself out and back into my jeans. I pull her up to me and she smiles up at me, a blush washing over her cheeks.

"Was that okay?" she asks timidly.

"You listen to me, don't ever doubt yourself. That was fucking perfect." I kiss her lips, wrapping my hand around her neck and pushing her back against the lockers. Just as I get the mind to return the favor, I hear the gym door open.

"Maxwell, where the hell you at, brother?" Tucker calls out. I let out a frustrated grunt and pull away, looking at Shane.

"I'll take care of you, later." I kiss her on the nose and she scrunches it up the way I love.

"Yeah, in here!" I call. Shane's eyes go wide as if I've forgotten she's in here with me. I shrug to let her know, I don't really care if Tucker knows what just happened. I would happily own up to it. I throw my shirt over my head as he appears in the doorway.

"Well, *excuse* my interruption." He animatedly drawls. I roll my eyes as I throw my duffle bag over my shoulder, putting my other arm around Shane.

"You didn't interrupt anything, Tuck. We are finished here." I wink at Shane, and she immediately blushes. Tucker narrows his gaze and then turns to walk back out into the gym.

"You ready to go?" he asks, bringing Shane's attention up to me.

"Where are you boys off to?" she asks, looking between the two of us.

"Spurs. It's lunchtime girl!" Tucker exclaims. "You joining us?" he opens the door and we all exit the gym. I lock the doors before throwing the keys into my gym bag and heading for the parking lot.

"No, that's okay. You two have fun. I actually have somewhere to be." She says, looking down at her watch.

"Be safe. You'll text me later?" I turn her to face me, admiring the pink hue still set on her cheeks.

"Yes, of course." She smiles, reaching up to kiss me before sliding into her Jeep. I close the door behind her and wave one last time as she pulls away.

I'm so fucking gone for her it's disgusting.

Chapter 25

Shane

T H E W A Y M A X is absolutely primal when we are alone, has me feeling some kind of way about him. We've spent as much time together as we could over the last few weeks, but it's mostly us working at the bar. We had gone to Topgolf again with the same group, minus Luther this time, and it was so different having Max kiss me and put his arm around me, and no one freaking out when we left together on his motorcycle.

I also started volunteering at the local art center a few days a week since they finally had an opening. So I am seeing Max a little less than usual. We grab coffee or lunch during open windows between our busy schedules but I crave more time alone with him.

It feels so natural to do simple things with him. With Valentine's Day approaching I am nervous to ask him if he has any plans for two reasons. One being, I'm not even sure if we are officially "dating" or not. We still haven't talked about it and I don't want to be the one to bring it up. The other reason is I know the date approaching is significant to him, having noticed the date of death on his mom's headstone was *February 13th, 2012.*

I decide I'll be bold and ask him if he wants to spend Friday together anyways. With it being the day after, maybe he'll want to get out and get his mind off of things. He doesn't seem like the kind of guy to make a big fuss over such a holiday but honestly, I just want to spend some time with him outside of the bar to possibly see where things will go. I am ready to take things between us further and I am desperate to know if he is too.

"Hey, Max. You got a minute?" I ask as I walk up beside him at the bar. There is only one couple seated on the other end of the bar and Ruby is on the floor talking to some of the regulars.

"For you, Sunshine, always." He winks at me as he leans against the counter.

"I was wondering what you're doing this Friday?" I roll my lips together anxiously.

"I don't know, you have something in mind?" I feel my cheeks flush and I dip my head tucking my hair behind my ear.

"Well, I thought maybe we could do something. Away from the bar and the gym. Maybe something other than lunch or coffee." I propose. He seems to like the thought at first until I continue my rambling.

"It doesn't have to be Valentine's related or anything. I just thought it would be nice to –" I don't even finish my sentence before he cuts me off.

"I can't." His expression hardens, and his body language follows. Before I know it he's back to working around the bar. *Ouch.*

"Okay…" I say to myself. I start to replay the invitation in my head; wondering when I hit the part where I told him I wanted to murder him and throw his body in the river. My train of thought is put on pause when Ruby makes her way back behind the bar.

"You guys ready for the Rush?" she asks, nodding to the door.

I look over and smile at her, before cutting my gaze over to Max, whose expression hasn't softened. Not even a little bit.

When he walks back to the kitchen during a lull, I make it a point to follow him.

"Max." I call after him.

"Yeah?" His demeanor is still hard from earlier, but I'm hoping to help change that if I can. I stop right in front of him, and run my hand down his arm.

"Look, I don't want you to think I was being insensitive about what this weekend is. I remember the date from her headstone." I say softly, catching his attention. His deep blue eyes finally find mine. "I figured you'd want to be alone that day. I just thought, maybe after you were alone you might want to be… I don't know, with me maybe? Just to just get your mind off of it. I didn't mean to upset you." I explain. He takes a deep breath and pulls me into his arms.

"I know you didn't Sunshine, I just don't know if I can." He kisses me on the top of my head. "I hope you understand." He looks at me with confliction, his jaw ticking away. I shake my head and he walks out the back door. To where, I have no idea? But I make my way back up to the front where I spot Ruby.

"Hey Ruby, you think the boys can handle the bar on Friday night?" I give her a mischievous grin.

"Actually, the bar is closed the whole weekend, but what do you have in mind?" she narrows her gaze.

"Well, me and my girlfriends are going to the black hearts party. You wanna join?"

"Hell yeah, I'm down. Let me make sure I can get a sitter for Hendrix and I'll let you know." She says squeezing my arm before grabbing some empty glasses from the bar top.

THURSDAY - FEBRUARY 13TH

Since the bar is closed this whole weekend, I decided to come paint tonight once I left the art center. I love teaching art there, but there's nothing like having a brush in my own hand, working on pieces that are close to my heart. Max has been heavy on my mind all day today, though I haven't heard from him once. I want to be there for him during his time of grief, but he's made it pretty clear that he'd rather be alone. It's taking everything in me to respect that and not drive to his house to be with him. It's eerily quiet here tonight, but I don't mind the silence. I always let myself get lost in my thoughts, and let my inspirations run rampant in my mind.

I am starting to get hungry and making my way down the stairs to the kitchen, when I hear a loud crash. My mind instantly flashes back to the night the bar almost got robbed. I shakily pull my phone out and out of pure instinct and start calling Max. I am not even sure he'll answer, but I know him well enough that he'd want me to call in this situation. When I hear a phone ringing outside the door, I start to wonder if it was Max I heard down there to begin with.

"Shane, where you at?" Max calls out. Though he doesn't sound like his usual self. I walk through the door that leads from the stairs to Max's office and see Riley curled up on the couch.

"Hey girl," I whisper and her tail begins to wag. "Max?" I call, walking out of his office and into the bar. I see Max behind the bar pouring himself a whiskey.

"There you are." He drunkenly smiles at me.

"Here I am. What are you doing here?" I cross my arms over my chest. Unsure what to think of his new version of him.

"What? A man can't come to his own bar?" he asks, spreading his arms out to their full length. The way his muscles look beneath his tight t-shirt and tattoos has me struggling to focus.

"Of course you can, you just startled me." I say, walking over to him. I lean on the bar top and study him for a minute. I have seen Max have the occasional drink here and there but I have never seen him drunk. I don't think I've ever even seen him buzzed. He's always in control.

"I'm sorry. I didn't know you'd be here." He says sadly.

He stares at the whiskey in his hands but doesn't drink it. Instead tears well up in his eyes before falling down his cheeks on a blink. I have never seen Max cry, or even look… sad; the last time I saw someone look as broken as he does right now, was in my own reflection after my parents died. He takes the whiskey glass and throws it against the wall by the bathrooms, shattering the glass as whiskey runs down the wall. Riley comes running out of the office to Max's side, pawing at his leg. My own tears begin to form as he backs up to the wall, sliding down to sit on the floor. Riley crawls into his lap and his hands rest on her back. I don't know how to help, but I'm sure as hell going to try. I walk over to him, sitting on the floor with my back against the bar.

"Max, It's okay. I'm here – unless you want me to go." I cautiously offer.

"Please, stay." He whispers through his tears. I nod and sit there on the floor with him. I won't move until he does. I won't speak until he's ready. I just want to be here so he knows he's not facing this alone. When he seems a little more sober he finally looks over at me.

"I don't get drunk. I don't cry. I don't lose control. Except for this one day, every year. The one day everything was taken from me – twice. It's the one day I lose control, because I can't control the losses I've suffered. I always spend the day alone, so I don't drag other people through my bullshit. But if I'm being honest, I really didn't want to be alone today. That's why I came here.

"I was really hoping you'd be here painting. Because while I normally spend today thinking about everything I've lost and drowning in my pain, today I couldn't stop thinking about you, Sunshine. And everything I've gained since you came into my life." I'm stunned at his confession. It makes my stomach flip and my heart pound harder inside of my chest.

"Max… you don't have to face this alone. I'm here." I assure him, placing my hand on his leg.

"I know you are," he half smiles. "For the first time, I think this may be the year I come to terms with it all and start moving on. I finally realize that loss is a part of life that I'll never be able to control. That even though I've been hurting for so long, I can still be happy. And I want to be happy. I want to be happy with *you*. If you'll have me." He says, his sad blue eyes locking on mine. He reaches his hand out for mine and when I offer mine back he pulls me into him. I'm now tucked underneath his warm, muscular arm – my safe place.

"Of course I will. I've been waiting on *you* to be ready Max, I've *been* yours." I admit, looking over at him.

His tears make his deep blue eyes shine brighter than I've ever seen them. He reaches over, cradling my face in his massive hands, running his thumb over my cheek. He pulls me into a kiss, then moves me on top of him, my legs resting on either side of his hips. His hands are tangled in my hair, his tongue dipping into my mouth. The electricity from it shoots throughout my entire body. His hands trail from my hair, down my back, landing comfortably on my ass.

I start grinding my hips, as I feel his erection growing. He pulls away and looks up at me, smiling when he sees me bite my lip. He lifts me by my hips, moving me off of his lap, as he stands from the bar floor, pulling me with him. I poke my lip out in a pout, wondering why he's stopping what's happening. As if he knows what I was thinking, he answers before I even ask.

"No pouting baby, I'm not done with you. I'm just getting started." He says, bending to pick me up, my legs wrapping around his middle.

He walks over to the empty pool table, setting my ass on the edge. Kissing me more passionately now than he ever has before. It's full of desire, need, and freedom – he's finally letting himself experience the good in life. I hope he experiences it all. He begins unbuttoning the white dress shirt I often paint in, sliding his hands around my waist once the last button is undone. He slides it off my shoulders, letting it fall to the table.

Max begins moving his kisses from my lips, along my cheek and down my neck, taking in a deep breath when he gets there. He continues his path down my neck, over my collar bone and down to the slopes of my breasts. He stands back just long enough to slide my pink lace bra straps down my arms, rubbing his thumbs along my shoulders. When he reaches back and unhooks my bra, it falls into my lap. I move my hands enough to free myself of my shirt sleeves and bra completely.

"You are the most exquisite thing I've ever laid eyes on." Max breaths out, making me scrunch my nose as my cheeks turn pink. Before I know it he's taking one of my breasts in his mouth, running his tongue along my peaked nipple. He cups my other breast in his hand, taking my nipple between his thumb and index finger, causing my head to fall back with pleasure. A soft moan escapes my lips, which draws a growl from Max. He lifts his lips back to mine, while his hands still explore my breasts.

My hands find the hem of his shirt, lifting it over his head, and discarding it on the table beside me. His body is so unbelievably sexy. His tanned skin is covered in tattoos and the perfect amount of chest hair, and his happy trail is causing an ache of desire between my legs. I run my hands over his perfectly formed abs before reaching for the button of his jeans.

"Not so fast," Max reaches for my wrists, stopping my movement from freeing him from his jeans. "Not until I've tasted you first." He kisses my lips once more, before reaching for the waistband of my leggings. I lift up enough to let them slide over my ass, as he rips them from me completely.

"Dammit, woman. Are you trying to kill me?" he asks upon the realization that I have no panties underneath. I bite at my lip and smile at him.

"Never," I respond playfully. He lets out a grunt before dropping to his knees in front of me. I am sitting on a pool table in the middle of his bar, completely exposed, my blonde waves pulled halfway back by a ribbon, and all I can think of is how long I've waited for this moment.

Max wraps his arms around my thighs, pulling my hips closer to the edge of the table. When his tongue swipes along my pussy I suck in a breath, softly moaning it back out. He runs his tongue up and down, then slides it inside me before coming back up to roll circles on my clit. This man knows what the hell he is doing. I can't even begin to imagine how good it will feel when he's inside of me.

With that thought, I'm already on the edge of my release. I run my fingers through his thick dark hair, his tongue still working my clit, not stopping his movements until my body shakes from the orgasm. He laps up every last bit, before standing up towering over me once again. I look at the erection daring to break through his pants and run my tongue along my lips.

"My turn?" I ask, pleadingly.

"As much as I want that sweet mouth of yours to work its magic on my cock, I can't wait one more minute to be inside you." He bites my bottom lip before unbuttoning his jeans, he drops them and his boxer briefs to the floor.

I take him in, not a single flaw on his body, his massive cock at full attention. I shake my head in agreement and he reaches for his wallet, grabbing a condom from it. My hand lands softly on his wrist to stop him, and his eyes cut back to mine.

"Max, I've never been with anyone without protection, and I'm on the pill. Can we… not?" I ask bashfully, glancing at the condom in his fingertips. There's passion burning behind his eyes.

"Not even with…" he starts, but I shake my head so he doesn't have to finish the thought.

"No. Never." I assure him, shaking my head.

"And you're sure you want to?" His eyes are burning with passion, I can tell he wants this too.

"Please. I only want you, Max. And I want to feel all of you." I beg.

"Dammit, Sunshine, you're going to ruin me." He growls, smiling down at me. He runs his tip along my entrance once before pushing himself completely inside of me.

He wraps my legs around his waist, pumping into me slowly at first to let me adjust to his size. I lean back on my hands on the pool table, grinding my hips in rhythm with his, my tits bouncing with every movement we make. Before I know it he wraps an arm around my waist, lifting me from the table, our bodies never losing contact. I wrap my arms around his neck as his hands move to my thighs just below my ass cheeks. Moving my hips back and forth as he pumps into me, harder and faster.

"Oh my god, Max!" I cry out. The pleasure making my entire body tingle.

"Fuck baby, you feel so good." He says as his jaw flexes. "I'm not gonna last much longer." He tells me.

I can feel my orgasm coming faster with every movement. I lean in and kiss him hard and fast, exactly how I want him to be with me – he obliges. Pumping into me harder and faster, the sound of our bodies colliding filling every corner of the bar. With three more pumps I am completely gone. My head falls back as I scream out his name, bringing him over the edge with me.

"God dammit," Max says as he empties himself inside me.

I feel his release pulsating as I tighten around him. When we've finally come back down from our orgasms, I lean my head back down, his forehead meeting mine as he holds me close in an embrace.

"Say it again, Sunshine." He pants.

"Say what?" I ask a little confused

"Say that you're mine. Say that you don't want anyone else but me." He pleads.

"I'm yours, Max. Only yours." I run my hand along his scruffy jaw. Loving the way it tickles my palm.

He walks over to the bar, our bodies never losing contact, grabbing a bar towel and carrying it in his teeth. I mean, I know I just finished, but he's turning me on all over again. He walks a few more feet into his office, throwing the towel down before laying me down on the couch. When he pulls out, he watches as the remainder of his release falls from me, smiling devilishly at me as he does. I roll my lips together, and my cheeks blush under his gaze.

"I'll be right back." He stands up from the couch, walking back out to the bar area. I just lay here on his office couch, butt ass naked, wondering what the hell he is doing. When he comes back he has all of our clothes in his hands and a glass of water.

"Here you go." He says, handing me the water.

He pulls his boxer briefs back up and plops down on the couch, setting my cup on the table before pulling me on top of him. I lay there at his side, my head resting on his chest listening to his rapid heartbeat slow down. He kisses me on top of my head, running his hand along my arm.

"I'm so fucking glad you were here when I showed up." He says, his voice a low rasp. I look up at him and smile.

"Me too." My stomach growls as soon as it's quiet and my eyes go wide with embarrassment. Max just laughs, his deep, gravely laugh is something I hope I get to hear a lot more of in the future.

"Sounds like we worked you up an appetite." He says, squeezing me to him.

"I guess so," I agree, trying to hide how embarrassed I am by my loud ass stomach.

"Come on, let's eat." He lifts us up off the couch, handing me my clothes.

"Where?" I ask, as I slide my legs back into my leggings.

"Here? I'll make us something." He says assuredly. I stop getting dressed and turn to him.

"You can cook?" The shock in my voice is not hidden at all.

"Yes, I can cook. Like I said before. I'm full of surprises." He winks at me. Buttoning his jeans and throwing his t-shirt back over his head. I finish getting dressed and he takes my hand leading me back out to the kitchen, where he makes me the best burger I've ever had in my life.

I think I'm in love.

Chapter 26

FRIDAY - VALENTINE'S DAY

My friends all shout in excitement, at the same time.

"Well it's about fucking time!" – Taylor

"Hell to the yes, friend." – Lauren

"You seem really happy, Shaney." – Leah

"I KNOW! And I really am, Lee. He's so much different than anyone else I've ever met, and not to be too graphic but if I never have sex with anyone else besides Max, I would die happy." I admit, with my cheeks rosy as hell.

"I knew he had big dick energy. It was all the brooding. He's changed though, ever since you guys started hanging out more. He's a lot less... grumpy. Now I guess we know why." Taylor wags her eyebrows. "I still can't believe you talked him into coming tonight!"

Taylor had been trying to talk me into going to the black hearts club for V-Day, basically since I told her Pete and I had broken up.

Even though it is technically a singles event, Max, Tucker, and Tank are going to meet us there separately. Ruby is also meeting us there even though I had hoped she would come to the house to pregame with us but she has to wait on the sitter to get there for Hendrix.

I was elated when Max told me he wanted to spend tonight with me. Even after I told him what I had previously committed to. He grunted over the fact that we would be at a club, seeing as he is not a guy who loves dark, crowded places. But after realizing I would be there without him if he didn't go, that kind of sealed the deal. Because *"I'll be damned if you're out dancing and anyone tries anything while I'm not there."* This man.

We are decked the hell out in all-black attire. I am wearing my black leather mini skirt, black knee high boots, and a black cinched bodice top with black sheer long sleeves. Lauren is giving me a more dramatic black winged liner and I decided on a dark red lipstick.

Lauren opted for her black leather pants and a black bodysuit with a deep v-neck that would bring any man to his knees.

Leah is wearing the cutest black baby doll dress I've ever seen in my life, and paired it with black suede booties. So fucking classy, just like her.

Taylor, in all her red-headed fierceness, is wearing black ripped jeans, black stilettos, and a cropped one-shoulder top that has red sequins sporadically placed on the sleeve. When I ask why she went against the all-black theme with the red statement pieces she says, *"It's the pieces of all my ex-lovers' broken hearts. It's on theme."* This bitch is a badass.

We take some pre-game shots at the house since we are taking an über to the club, then snap about a million photos before we actually head out the door.

When we all crawl into the car Taylor is already on her mama bear shit.

"If you even think of trying something, you'll be taking a stiletto to the head, you got it?" She points accusingly at our driver. This poor guy. He looks like he can't be much older than nineteen and Taylor is threatening him with a stiletto to the head. He shakes his head nervously and Taylor smiles at him, settling into her seat.

I post a photo to Instagram on the way since I don't plan to be on my phone again until I get home tonight. I pick my favorite photo of the four of us that we took in the full-body mirror in Taylor's room and a single photo of me raising my shot that Leah had snapped. I keep my caption simple – and tag all my besties.

`currently unavailable.`🖤 `#blackhearts`

As soon as I hit post, we pull up to the club. "Thank you, Zayn. You beautiful young man, one day you'll be spending Valentine's Day with a beautiful woman, or beautiful man, whatever you're into." Taylor says as she puckers her lips blowing an air kiss at him. She is definitely feeling her pre-game shots now. We walk in and for some reason, so many people all decked out in black on Valentine's Day makes me smile. A bunch of jaded hearts all partying together and I'm here for it. Even if my heart is no longer jaded.

We all opted for our small wristlets tonight so we don't have to worry about losing our things since ¾ of us don't have pockets. We make our way over to Ruby who is waiting at the bar for us and greet each other with a round of hugs. Yeah, we're all feeling out shots now. We do another round, then quickly hit the dance floor.

Ruby is already a baddie, but the all black outfit she's wearing tonight screams stunner. She has on black leather pants that lace all the way up the sides, black strappy shoes, and a black tie front crop top. Pair that with her jet black hair that she's wearing straight down her back tonight and even I want to hit on her. We are only out on the dance floor for about two songs before a pair of warm hands wrap around my waist, a familiar woodsy vanilla and leather scent surrounding me.

"Need a partner, Sunshine?" his deep voice growls into my ear, making me tingle all over.

I turn around and take in the sexy man in front of me. I told Max this was a blackout event and that he was required to follow the dress code, but to make it hot, and he fucking delivered. He's wearing a fitted black t-shirt, his black leather jacket with a gray hoodie attached, black jeans, and his biker boots, which tells me he drove his motorcycle and that makes him even hotter. His dark brown hair is a perfect mess and his deep blue eyes are staring directly into mine.

"You look sexy as hell, Max Mullins." I say looking him up and down.

"Back at you, baby." He pulls me into his chest, leaning down to kiss me. When he pulls away, I notice my red lipstick smeared a little on his lips.

"Oh no!" I cry, wiping it from his lips.

"That's gonna look so good around my co–" Max starts.

"Down boy, this is a public place." Tucker playfully interrupts, clapping him on the shoulders. Max snarls at him then looks back at me and winks. Oh yes, I know where you were going with that, and I can't wait to make that happen.

"Hi, Tucker. Hi Tank." I greet them as they move onto the dance floor with us. They say their hellos, then start talking to the girls, Tucker to Taylor, and Tank heads over to Ruby. We all grab a round of drinks from the bar, the guys only committing to one since they all drove here. When Dirty Thoughts by BONNIE X CLYDE starts playing, my eyes go wide and I look at Max, dragging him onto the dance floor with me.

He tilts his head as a warning that he doesn't want to go, but once I bite my lip in protest, he's mine. He follows me willingly after that. We get out on the dance floor and the rest of the group follows close behind. I walk up to Max, pressing the front of my body to his, moving my hips back and forth, and he matches my movements. We're bouncing to the music, and he leans in, kissing me senseless. He moves his kisses to my neck, making me moan from the sensation it sends down my spine. The flashing strobe lights in the club make everything feel like it's moving in slow motion. When Max stands back up to his full height and swipes his tongue along his bottom lip, looking completely primal, I am ready to ditch the club and beg him to take me home. Before I know it, someone's hand is wrapping around my elbow, spinning me around. I see a familiar face that sends an ice-cold chill through my whole body.

"What is this, Shane?" his pompous, entitled voice hits me at the same time as his condescending glance.

"Pete?" I am flooded with feelings of confusion and anger. Why is he here?

In Nashville. At this club. In my fucking face.

"Pete," I hear Max's voice growl behind me. About that time Taylor notices him and leaves her position dancing with Tucker and storms over.

"You scrawny, cheating bastard. I'm gonna kick your fucking ass." She says, before Tucker pulls her back.

"Though I'm sure you're *fully* capable, I'll handle this," Max says, stepping up from behind me.

"Who the hell is this, Shane?" Pete asks, ignoring Max standing right in front of him. I grab Max's hand before saying anything. Pete looks down and then back up at me.

"Her date. So why don't you take your hand off of her if you plan to keep it." Max warns.

"Well you may be who she came here with, but I'm who she'll be leaving with. Shane, can I talk to you? In private maybe?" Pete mindlessly asks. I feel Max's grip tighten on my hand.

"Whatever you have to say, Pete, you can say it right here," I tell him, unmoving.

"I came to apologize in person since you never took any of my calls. I messed up, I know that now. I was being stupid and I want you to come back home. I miss you, baby. It was just a stupid mistake. I'll treat you better now I promise. Come back home with me where you belong." Pete stands there with a dumbass smile on his face. Does he really think that worked?

I feel bile in my throat at everything he just said. But when he called me baby my eyes shot up to Max's face. His jaw ticks and I feel every muscle in his body stiffen.

"Over my dead body she'll be leaving with you. Shane doesn't concern you anymore, so why don't you head on back to California? Alone." Max states, wrapping his arm around me and pulling me closer to him. Pete looks between the two of us as I give him a go-to-hell look. When he realizes I sure as shit won't be going *anywhere* with him, he scoffs putting a smug look on his face.

"Whatever man. Just remember I had her first. You can go ahead and have my scraps."

Fucking. Asshole.

My jaw drops open as my friends all add in commentary at the same time:

"Oh hell no." –Taylor.

"Is this guy serious?" –Leah.

"Mm. That was a fuckin mistake" – Tucker.

Before I know it Max rears back and punches Pete square in the jaw.

"Shit!" Pete yells out. Max stalks over to him, pulling him up by the collar of his shirt.

"If you ever try to speak to or about her, if you ever even *think* about her again, it will be the last fucking thing you do. I will hunt you down and rip the lungs from your chest myself. Understand, motherfucker?" He tosses Pete backwards as Tucker and Tank walk up beside him. Taylor, Leah, Lauren and Ruby surround me as the guys stand there waiting for Pete's next move.

He rubs his jaw and then nods once before leaving like the coward that he is. That's probably the smartest decision he's made in a year. When he's out the door I see Max take in a deep breath and then he turns to face me, hurrying back to my side.

"You alright?" he asks, looking directly into my eyes as if no one else is around. I glance around, seeing my girls, my new friends Ruby, Tank, and Tucker – and Max, I have never felt more loved in my life. I nod my head and smile.

"Of course I am. I have you." I reach up on my toes and kiss Max, my hands running wildly through his hair. When he pulls away I recognize the fire in his eyes, because it's the same fire burning in mine.

"Let's get out of here." He commands. I nod my head eagerly in return.

"We're out, take care of these ladies." Max says to Tank and Tucker.

"You know we will." Tucker assures him.

Max grabs my hand and leads me through the crowded dance floor, all the way out the door. When the cool air hits us as we walk outside, Max pulls me around the corner, pressing me up against the side of the building. His hands wrap around my neck, kissing me with such passion and desire. I grab his leather jacket, pulling him in to kiss him harder. Letting him know I want him as badly as he wants me.

People start to whistle and yell at us to get a room, making me laugh beneath his kiss. He pulls away and grunts at the attention.

"Let's go." He says, pulling me to his bike. I have no idea where we're going, but if I'm with Max, I really don't care.

WE RIDE ALL the way to my house on my motorcycle, in the pouring rain. It started almost as soon as we pulled away from the club, and hasn't let up since. I could have ripped that Pete guy limb from limb, showing up, thinking Shane would ever take a sorry cheater like him back. Thinking he was going to take her away from me. He's got me fucked up. She's *mine* and I am never letting her go. He's lucky to still be breathing after calling her scraps, like she's not the best thing to ever happen to planet earth.

When we pull up I roll into the garage, parking the bike next to my truck, which I probably *should* have driven tonight. I bought this house a few years back after getting my investments sorted and had enough money to my name to do so. It's small, which is perfect for me and Riles, and it's in a nice neighborhood. The exterior is painted black with brown river rock around the bottom of the house, and the same rockwork wraps around both columns on the front porch. There's a single rocking chair on the porch with a pillow on the ground beside it for Riley, it's where I like to sit before sunrise to enjoy the peace and quiet. I'm holding Shane's hand, leading her into my place for the first time and I honestly can't believe she's never been here before. There's a simple green doormat outside, and the front door is a dark wood that matches the brickwork of the columns. It was the only house in the neighborhood that felt like *me*.

When we first step inside the small entryway, I toss my keys into a bowl that's set on a small table to the right, by the front door. The only other thing on the table is a photo of me and Riley on deployment. I look over at Shane who is taking in her surroundings, her beautiful blue eyes taking it all in.

"Let's get you out of those wet clothes." I say, looking at her soaking wet, all black outfit. I take her hand and lead her through the house, not stopping until we reach my bedroom. Riley lifts her head to look at us as we pass by the brown leather couch, but otherwise doesn't move.

When we walk into my bedroom, I immediately slide my leather jacket off, dropping it onto the floor in the corner. Then I pull the wet t-shirt off over my head, throwing it to the side with the leather jacket.

Shane's mouth is hanging open as she watches me undress until I walk over and close it with my own. Wrapping my hand around her neck, I kiss her while walking her backwards until the back of her knees hit the edge of my bed. I run my hands over her sweet little body, my thumbs trailing over her perky breasts, then along her ribs, making her whole body shiver.

Our kiss breaks just long enough for me to pull her shirt over her head, then I'm back for more, sliding my tongue right past her lips. I brush her wet hair off of her neck and behind her shoulder, running my lips along her neck. Nipping at her ear as I unhook her bra. It's black lace, coordinating perfectly with the rest of her outfit, which doesn't surprise me one bit.

It falls to the ground as I work my lips down her neck, planting kisses on her collarbone before moving down the slopes of her breasts. Taking one of them in my mouth, holding the other firmly in my hand, her full breast fits perfectly in my large hand. Running my tongue along her peaked nipple, I tease the other with my fingers. She lets out a soft moan and it's music to my ears. I'll never tire of hearing how good she feels when she's with me.

"Every single part of you tastes fucking perfect." I growl, as I move my lips to her other breast. Giving it the same attention I gave the first. I kiss my way down her stomach until I reach the waist of her black leather mini-skirt. "You better have fucking panties on under this, Sunshine." I warn. She rolls her lips together, trying to hide a smile. I am going to lose my damn mind if she doesn't.

I quickly rip the skirt from her hips, and I am met with a pair of black lace underwear, a perfect match to the discarded bra she was wearing. I raise a brow at her and smirk.

"Good girl," I praise before tossing her onto my bed. I take the thigh high boots from her feet, before stripping out of my sopping wet black jeans. Then I'm on the bed with her, hovering over her perfect body. "Here's what's going to happen, I am going to taste that sweet pussy of yours until you shake from the pleasure and come all over my face," I lean in, kissing and biting her neck. "Then, you're gonna take as much of me as you can in the pretty little mouth of yours, making me feel so good, just like you did the first time," I look up and her cheeks are rose colored.

"Once you do that," I start trailing my fingers into her underwear, discovering just how ready she is for me. "I am going to worship every inch of your body. Until you forget there was ever a time you didn't feel good enough for some prick who never deserved you, because you're the only thing I have wanted, no – craved, for months." I tell her, seeing emotion well in her eyes. "Do you understand?" I ask.

She nods before choking out. "I understand."

"Good girl." I praise.

I move my fingers into the waistband of her panties and slide them off her legs. Running my hands back up her thighs, squeezing and sliding them to either side, making room for myself to rest between them.

I drag my tongue along her seam, making her eyes roll back in her head. I slowly work around her clit, feeling her relax beneath my touch. Listening to her beautiful moans as I feast on her perfect pussy, picking up the pace when she begins to rock her hips, matching my rhythm. She's absolutely intoxicating, and I can't get enough of her. When I slide a finger inside of her, followed quickly by a second, her own fingers find their way into my hair. I continue like this, just the way she likes it, until she's right on the edge.

"Max," she whispers, letting me know she's close.

"That's it baby, show me how good it feels to be mine." My tongue is back to work instantly. Her back arches off the bed, her grip tightening in my hair when she comes.

"Max!" she moans, curling her toes where they're propped up perfectly on my shoulders.

When she looks down at me, my primal stare is locked on her. I stand up and my erection is at full attention in my black boxer briefs. She bites her lip, still the perfect shade of red, looking ready to take me just like I told her to. I drop my underwear, grabbing onto my length and stroking it once before beckoning her with a wave of my finger.

"Bring that pretty mouth over here," I command. She slides to the end of the mattress, looking willing and ready to take my cock in her sweet pouty mouth. Before she does, I take the hair tie that lives on her wrist and throw all of her hair into some version of a bun on top of her head. It's not perfect, but it's not stuck in her face anymore.

I stroke myself once more, bringing my tip to her sweet lips, and she opens her mouth wide. *Fuck.* She slides her hand down my length, and her mouth follows after. Bobbing her head back and forth, taking me as deep as her throat allows. I watch her take as much of my cock as she can, and when she looks up to watch me I lose it.

"Damn it baby, that feels so good." I praise. As my hand helps rock her head back and forth, pressing myself further into her throat. I'm getting close to my release, and I think she knows it. She begins picking up her pace, but I stop her before she can go on, pulling myself from her mouth. She pokes her lip out in a pout, making me laugh.

"Don't pout. baby. Lay back and take my cock like a good girl." I command.

I push her legs open with my knee, settling between them. I tease her entrance as I kiss her neck, making her eyes flutter shut. Lifting my lips from her neck, I press into her, stopping at just the tip.

"Eyes on me, Sunshine. I want to see you take all of me again." As soon as her eyes open, I slide into her all the way, not bothering to go slowly this time.

She sucks in a breath as I press my full length inside of her. She wraps her hand around my neck, pulling my lips to her own. My tongue slides across her lips and she lets me in eagerly. As my tongue explores her mouth, the movement of my hips picks up speed. I can feel her everywhere. My whole body feels electric with pleasure from being inside of her. She takes my breath away with every thrust.

"Fuck, you feel too good," I say lifting my lips from hers.

"Max, I'm so close." She lets out breathlessly. I move a hand down, rubbing her clit just how she likes, as I bring my lips to her ear.

"I want you to scream my name when you come. Let me know you're mine. Just mine." Like the good girl she is, she does exactly that.

"Max, I'm coming," she screams. I can feel her orgasm through my whole body, as she shakes against me.

"Good fucking girl," I growl, as I empty inside of her.

Once we've both ridden out our high, I roll over pulling her with me. She curls up resting right under my arm. "Max..." she says shyly.

"Yes, Sunshine?"

"Your come is dripping out of me..." she giggles, glancing down at the comforter now covered in the evidence of both of our releases.

"Good." I wink at her before taking her lips in mine.

I want to be dripping out of her. I want her to feel me even when

I'm not around. I want to ruin her for anybody else, making damn sure she'll always be mine.

"Alright, come on." I say, scooping her off of the bed. She shrieks as I carry her to the bathroom.

"What are you doing, you crazy Viking?" she laughs kicking her little feet.

"Did you just call me a Viking?" I quirk my brow at her.

"Um.. Yes, that's what I called you after you slammed into me that first day." She rolls her lips together like she's holding in another laugh.

"I've been called worse." I shrug.

"You didn't answer my question." She says, crossing her arms over her chest.

"We're taking a shower." I kiss her forehead as I turn the shower on.

When we finish in the shower, I get one of my Navy t-shirts from the drawer and let her wear it. We grab some food from the kitchen then crawl into bed and talk for hours before she finally falls asleep in my arms; it's the best Valentine's day I've had – ever. Shane Thompson has completely tilted my world on its axis in the matter of two months. I went from some grumpy asshole, with the weight of the world on his shoulders, refusing to let anything or anyone who dared to bring me joy into my life, for fear of losing it, to some simp who can't imagine living without the girl laying next to me, and I fucking love it.

Chapter 28

Shane

After Max punched Pete in the face and whisked me back to his house for another round of earth shattering sex, we took a shower, grabbed some food and stayed up talking for hours. I finally gave up and fell asleep with my head on his chest as he ran his fingers along my back. I'm guessing I was out for the night after that, because the light shining through his bedroom window is now waking me up. I finally open my eyes, but Max is nowhere in sight. I get up and look around, seeing my clothes from last night are no longer discarded on the floor, but hung neatly in the bathroom to dry. "Max?" I call out, as I walk into the living room where I see Riley laying on the couch. "Hey girl, where's Max at, huh?" I ask as I rub her ears.

When I run my hand along the island countertop in his kitchen, I bump into a note.

> Sunshine,
> If you wake up
> before
> I get back,
> I ran out for coffee.
> Be back soon.
> —max

I take a minute to look around, since we basically walked straight to his bedroom last night, not that I'm complaining. His house is absolutely gorgeous. It's small but in a really nice neighborhood, and the outside is such a vibe. He has the only all black house on the block and the brown stones surrounding it, makes it even more beautiful.

But the way the inside is decorated is immaculate. I wonder if he did it all himself or if someone helped him. The entire house is painted a beautiful taupe color and has white trim.

His kitchen is probably my favorite kitchen I've ever been in. He has forest green cabinets with bronze hardware, light, natural wood countertops, and matte black appliances.

In the living room he has a brown leather sofa, with no throw pillows or blankets in sight. *Tragic.* There's a unique epoxy coffee table in front of it, with only a stack of bar coasters and a TV remote on it. The wood burning fireplace is located on the wall to the right of the couch and has built in bookshelves on either side. One side is full of books and decorative art pieces, the other serves as a mini bar. The fireplace mantle has a folded american flag in a shadow box and a photo of Max, Tucker, Riley, and another guy, at what seems to be a military base. Judging by his bright red hair, I am going to assume that's Red, the friend he lost in battle.

I pick it up and study the picture, all three guys are smiling, and I swear to god it looks like Riley is too. She's wearing Max's helmet and they all seem to be laughing about it together. It brings a smile to my face seeing Max so happy, doing something he was so passionate about. You'd have to be passionate about it to spend 12 years of your life doing it, right? I hear the front door close as I place the photo back on the mantle.

I turn around to see Max walking through the door with two coffees in hand and a pastry bag in his teeth. He shuts the door with his foot before walking over to me and I take the bag from his teeth. He smiles before leaning in to kiss me.

"Good morning." He says, his deep voice driving me wild.

"Good morning." I smile up at him. He leads the way into the kitchen as I follow closely behind.

"I didn't have any coffee in the house, but I figured you might want some when you woke up so I slipped out. Sorry if it worried you when I wasn't here." He says, poking the straw through my cup and sliding it over to me.

"Nah, I figured I was in good hands with Riley here." I wink at her and she walks over to me, brushing up against my bare leg. "Plus, I saw your note." I smile at Max, waving the paper in the air.

"Good, then it served its purpose." He says, pulling me into him. He looks just as sexy as he always does with his backwards baseball hat, a hoodie with a seal on it, and a denim jacket over it. Paired with black joggers and white running shoes. Damn, I think I'm drooling.

"So, what can I make you for breakfast?" he turns to open the refrigerator.

"Hmmm. Toaster Strudel." I answer. He stops moving and turns slowly to face me.

"Toaster Strudel?" he looks at me like I just said I would like the sacrificial firstborn lamb from his nonexistent flock of sheep.

"Yes. Apple if you have it." I tilt my head in confusion. I thought it was normal for a freezer to be full of Toaster Strudel, but maybe it's just me... and Taylor.

"That's your idea of breakfast?" he asks, leaning against his fridge.

"That's my *favorite* breakfast, actually." I correct, pointing my index finger at him.

He shakes his head in disbelief. "I can make you eggs, waffles, pancakes, french toast..." he offers. I blink at him a few times trying to decide how to answer, because all of that sounds amazing.

"Surprise me?" I shrug. He turns around and begins digging through the fridge for ingredients, muttering, "Toaster Strudel," then snickering.

"Hey, apple Toaster Strudel is the superior strudel and you will not change my mind, no matter how sexy you are." I lean back on the barstool, bending over to pet Riley.

"Whatever you say," he winks at me as he moves around the kitchen, making our breakfast.

I watch him for a while, admiring how hot it is that he knows how to cook so well. Everything smells amazing. At one point I walk over and toss a little powdered sugar at him, prompting him to chase me around the bar. When he grabs my waist and picks me up to set me on the island top, he notices I'm still not wearing anything under the t-shirt he let me sleep in. So let's just say he had a little, pre-breakfast snack.

When we finally finish our food my gaze makes it way back over to the photo on the mantle. Once he sees what I'm looking at, he gets up and walks over, grabbing it from its spot and bringing it over to the island.

"This is Red, the man behind Chattahoochies name." He says, as if to introduce me.

"He looks so happy, you all do." I say softly.

"He was the happiest person I knew. Always helping people and wanting to make them smile. There wasn't a single thing that Red couldn't twist some positivity into." He says, smiling at the photo as he remembers his friend.

"I'm so sorry you lost him, Max. Truly. He sounds like an amazing person and I wish I had gotten the chance to meet him." I say, running my hand along his arm. He takes a deep breath and looks up at me, a calmness to his eyes I've never noticed before.

"You remind me a lot of him, Sunshine. Always thinking of others." He says, pinching my chin and winking at me.

"Hey Max…"

"Yeah?" he takes a sip of coffee before setting it back down on the counter.

"I started to ask you this the first time you ever said it. You told me maybe one day you'd tell me, but I haven't brought it back up; secretly because I loved that you had your own nickname for me and I really didn't care why. But I'd be lying if I said I wasn't curious… Why do you call me Sunshine?" he takes my hand in his, placing it in his lap.

"The first day I met you, I felt something I hadn't felt in a long time. It was weird for me because it was instant. The second I looked into those beautiful ocean eyes of yours." He looks over at me and I'm hooked.

"What did you feel?" I ask, hanging on to every word. He sighs, staring right into my eyes as he brushes a piece of hair behind my ear.

"I felt like I was seeing the sun shine after being in the middle of a storm I thought would never end. I didn't know it until I saw you that day, how desperately I was waiting for sunshine. How desperately I was waiting for *you*." He admits, pulling one corner of his mouth up into a half smile.

Just like that, any part of my heart I thought wasn't already his, was. Max is completely different than any other man I've ever met. He is everything I'd hoped to find in someone one day, I just didn't realize that day would happen so soon after leaving California. He is strong and brave, loyal, kind, and trustworthy. And he looks at me like I am the only woman in the world for him. I hope I am, because after being with Max, I'm not sure how I could ever be with anyone else.

TAYLOR

You okay?

TAYLOR

If you don't respond soon I'm sending a search party

TAYLOR

Bitch you're lucky I have your location.

TAYLOR

The sex can't be that good, freaking text me back!!!

My best friend is absolutely insane, and I fucking love her for it. I finally made my way back to Max's room to grab my phone, which he had put on the charger at some point. He literally thought of everything, but I had forgotten we were supposed to be planning Lauren's surprise party today.

ME

I'm okay. I'm at Max's house. The sex IS that good, thank you very much 😌 and he fucking made me breakfast bitch 💀

TAYLOR

Well damn girl. Bout time you had a man worth a shit. But also, get your ass home we have a party to plan!

ME

Be there soon.

Don't get me wrong, I'm excited to go home and plan Lauren's party but I could easily stay here with Max all day. As soon as I toss my phone down on the bed and turn around, Max is standing over me ready to sweep me off the ground. He wraps my legs around his middle, hands planted firmly on my ass.

"Any plans today, Sunshine?" he asks, his deep voice something I'll never tire of hearing.

"Actually, yes." I say, scrunching my nose.

"It better be staying in bed with me all day." He teases, nipping at my neck.

"Mmm. I wish I could, *believe me*. But Taylor, Leah and I are planning Lauren's surprise party today while she's in back to back showings at work." He lets out a heavy sigh, leaning his head back to look at me.

"Then I guess I'll make this quick." He says, tossing me back on his bed before pulling his shirt off over his head.

Everything he does has me squeezing my thighs together. He slides his pants off next before climbing back on the bed with me.

"Don't rush on my account," I say, biting my lip.

He lowers his head, settling between my thighs, then spends the next hour making me wish I never had to leave his bedroom. When we finally manage to get dressed and out of the house I insist Max takes me home in his truck instead of the bike. Because if I learned anything last night, it's that motorcycles and mini skirts are not the best idea in the world.

"How's party planning?" I ask, as Shane and I walk out of the coffee shop and toward the gym the next morning.

"Oh my god," she grumbles.

"That good?" I tease. She takes a sip of her iced coffee and laughs.

"It's really not so bad. We want to make her feel special so we're pulling out all the stops, but it's turning out to be a lot more work than I realized." I reach down and wrap my fingers around hers as we walk down the sidewalk.

"Well, I'm sure it's going to be great. Lauren is lucky to have a friend like you. And Taylor and Leah too I guess." I wink at her, making her blush as we walk hand in hand into the gym. We walk in to see Tucker already there waiting for us.

"You know, I'm starting to get offended that you guys never bring me a coffee." He says, crossing his arms over his chest.

"Tucker, you're 37 years old. Get your own damn coffee." I lean down and kiss Shane's forehead before heading to put my stuff in a locker.

"What do you like?" I hear her whisper as I walk off. This woman. Heart of pure gold. I don't listen for Tucker's answer because my mind is too focused on how I got so lucky to have Shane show up in my life.

"Sorry, I'm late!" Leah comes walking in with her own coffee and Tucker tosses his hands in the air making Shane and I both laugh.

"What? What did I do?" Leah asks, wide eyed.

"Nothing, just Tucker pouting." I tell her as I slap Tucker with my gym towel.

"Come on, let's start our warm up." Shane locks her arm with Leah's and they go over to the treadmills to warm up while Tucker and I start on the pull up bars. By the end of the workout we're all dripping sweat and starving. At least I assume so by the way Shane's stomach is growling.

"Showers then Spurs?" Tucker asks.

"God, yes." Shane eagerly agrees.

"Okay, meet you ladies back out here in ten." Tucker says and we head to the showers.

We go to the diner and stuff our faces, having the most random conversations you could imagine. Leah has started joining us at the gym regularly and we've just kind of made it a routine to come to Spurs after to eat. Today's topic of conversation revolved around Lauren's birthday party in a couple of weeks, which brought up a very forgettable name.

"Okay, but I just really don't understand why he would *tell* people he has a pet turtle, ya know? Like sir you are *twenty* seven years old, not seven years old. Stop bragging about your turtle." Leah says as she tosses a fry in her mouth.

"Named *DONATELLO* no less!" Shane exclaims, making the whole table laugh.

"Yeah, I didn't say anything about it then because we were still a little new to the group, but that dude was weird as hell." Tucker says, picking up his sweet tea.

"Maybe so, but I kind of owe a big thank you to Luther." Shane shrugs, piquing my interest. I raise my brow in question, so she continues.

"Luther is the one who told Lauren about Chattahoochies. I never would have walked in to drink away my shitty week if it wasn't for him." She looks up at me and smiles.

"Oh yeah, I completely forgot about that." Leah remarks.

"I'm kind of seeing a *forgettable* pattern with this guy." Tucker mutters under his breath.

"I never would have met you," Shane says, her eyes so full of peace. Tucker clears his throat dramatically.

Attention whore.

"Or you, Tucker." She says reassuringly, smiling at him.

"You ready to go home, Sunshine?" I ask. The rest of the table seems to stop breathing at my question, making me look up at them. "What?" I ask. Looking at Tucker and his shocked to shit expression, I realize I just insinuated we shared a home. To be honest, I don't quite mind the thought.

"Yeah, I'm ready. Let's go." Shane smiles. I drop money on the table and we all stand to leave. Shane stays with me more often than not recently, and little pieces of her are starting to flood my house. We'd gone to the store for groceries not too long ago, stocking up on her Toaster Strudel and iced coffee, and she convinced me to buy some blankets for my living room. Some of her clothes hang in my laundry room, her bathroom products are overtaking the counters and her blonde hair is absolutely every damn where, and I fucking love it.

"I'll see you back at Taylor's later to talk party stuff?" Leah asks Shane. Damn, they weren't kidding, they're doing the most for this damn party.

"Yes, of course." Shane says, hugging her friend bye.

We hop in my truck and head towards the house while Shane looks for a good song on her phone. She stops scrolling and looks over at me. "Oh, can we stop by the store again? We need more paper towels and I want to get some treats for Riley." She says, not knowing how the word *we* sounds like music to my ears because so many things feel shared between us now, and I wouldn't have it any other way.

"Of course. But we gotta hurry, I have something for you back at the house." I say, grabbing her hand and kissing the back of it before letting our intertwined fingers rest in my lap. She looks at me curiously but doesn't ask for further information.

When we finally pull back up at the house, with not only paper towels and treats, but another damn blanket and some tiny couch pillows, I am eager to get to the package that arrived while we were out. I pick it up from the front porch, before opening the door for Shane. When we go in, she walks over to Riley to tell her about the new treats she got. She's spoiled my girl senseless and Riley just eats it up.

"I'll be right back." I tell her, taking the package to the bedroom. I rip it open and smile when I see that it turned out absolutely perfect. I find some dusty old gift bag and place the item inside before making my way back out to her.

When I round the corner back to the living room, I hear Shane talking to Riley.

"See, isn't this so much cozier? You gotta back me up on this Riles, us girls have to stick together." She says, fluffing the pillows and readjusting the blanket over the side of the couch.

"I think it looks great too, no need to gang up on me." I wink at her and a big grin spreads across her face.

"I knew you'd love it." She beams.

"Alright, come here. I have something to give you." I nod her over to the kitchen island where I've set the bag down. She looks at it curiously.

"You know my birthday isn't for another two months, right?" she asks accusingly.

"Yes, I know. This isn't a birthday present. This is just a regular present. One that's long overdue." I answer. "Go ahead and open it." I cross my arms, my fist covering my mouth, anxious to see her reaction. When she lifts it out of the bag, and unfolds it she looks over at me with a smile.

"You bought me a Chattahoochies sweatshirt?" she exclaims.

"I did. You told me I owed you a new sweatshirt, but instead of one that's ridiculously white and just waiting for a disaster, I thought this would be a safer alternative. Especially for you." I look down at the white and brown tie dye Chattahoochies sweatshirt that rests in her lap.

"The perfect coffee spill camouflage." She states, smiling down at the gift.

"That was the thought process I had, yes." I glance back at her. "You really like it?" she sets it down, throwing herself in my arms.

"It's perfect, thank you." Lifting her chin she kisses me hard and every part of me relaxes. I never want to live a life where Shane's lips don't find mine everyday.

"I'm gonna wear it right now." She says excitedly.

Jumping over to the counter she begins stripping out of the clothes she'd worn to the gym. Standing in the kitchen in her bright green sports bra that displays her perky nipples perfectly. She slides the sweatshirt over her head, disrupting my view, and holds her arms out to the sides.

"What do you think?" She smiles wide.

"Just like you said, it's perfect. But..." I quickly close the space between us.

"But what?" She pouts.

"But I'm about to have to take that right back off of you." I throw her over my shoulder and haul her perfect ass back to my bedroom.

"Max!" she squeals. "Put me down." Her words are coming out as laughs.

I toss her on the bed and rip my shirt off over my head. I pull her workout shorts off of her legs, being met with absolutely nothing underneath. My eyes snap to hers and she bites her lip, drawing a growl from deep in my chest.

"What the hell am I going to do with you?"

"Whatever you want." She teases. I lean in close to her grabbing her by the jaw, lighting the fire in those ocean blues.

"Ruining that damn sweatshirt was the best thing I've ever done. Now, take this one off before it's ruined too." I demand, taking a step back. I watch as she lifts the fabric over her head, painstakingly slow, her peaked nipples waiting to greet me through the bright green fabric. When she reaches for the zipper I hadn't noticed on the front of her sports bra, I grab her wrist to stop her. I take her other wrist and hold them both in one hand as I lay her back on the bed. With my free hand I reach for the zipper tugging it down until her bra pops open, freeing her perfect, full breasts. I bring my lips to her ear.

"I am ruined for you, Sunshine." I tell her, before biting on her neck, making her whimper.

"Then ruin me, too." She pleads, making my dick throb inside my boxers.

So I do. I stand up long enough to toss my pants to the side with hers before I take her wrists in my hand once more. I bury my dick inside her, hard and deep with every thrust, making the most beautiful moans fall from her lips. I move my hands from around her wrists, gripping her tight at her full hips, she reaches up, digging her nails into my back as my name replaces her moans when she reaches her release. Her back arches as her pussy pulses around my dick, biting her lip as she does. I take her lips in mine, emptying myself into her as she still rides out her orgasm. She grabs my face in her hands, kissing me with such ferocity, I can only hope she's ruined for me too.

THE LAST TWO weeks have been some of my favorite that I've ever experienced. Shane's been keeping busy as usual between the bar, helping out at the local art center, and planning Lauren's fucking birthday party. So I'm stealing every spare second she has. Who knew how much shit went into planning a party. What ever happened to beer, food, music, and a few people you can tolerate longer than an hour?

I've made it a point to hangout upstairs with Riley and watch her paint, even when she's there for hours on end. We've gotten to ruin a few corners of her art studio in the process and I'm not mad about it. There's probably more places in this bar we've broken in than most people would care to know about.

We're both scheduled behind the bar today so we can attend Lauren's party together tonight. I remember now why I don't schedule myself with Shane anymore. It takes everything in me not to drag her back to my office every time those ocean blue eyes land on mine.

She's on her way back behind the bar when Lenny gets into it with some asshole by the pool tables. Apparently this guy tried to weasel his way into Drengr after banging Lenny's daughter last year – but they found out he cheated on her so they told him no. *Obviously.*

Lenny rears back with a pool cue just as Shane is walking past and it hits her in the eye. My blood starts boiling the minute I see it happen. I rush around the bar and am stepping in front of her in a matter of seconds.

I grab the pool cue from Lenny as he's turning to see what, or better yet *who,* he just hit. He knows he fucked up when he sees Shane, then realizes how bad when he sees the anger that is living rent free on my face now.

"Oh, Shane. Sweetheart, I'm so sorry." Lenny says to her with panic in his voice. He turns to look at me. "Max, I–" I cut him off before he can finish.

"Lenny, you know I have a no BS policy in this bar. You've been coming here since I opened, you of all people know, you got a problem you take it the fuck outside. You just about took out my girl and I really don't wanna have to kick your ass over it." I snap at him.

"You. Leave." I direct at the asshole he was getting into it with.

"Lenny, I'll deal with you later," I say, tossing the pool cue to the ground. It echoes in the otherwise silent bar as I turn to Shane who is holding her head right above her eyebrow.

"Sorry again sweetheart," Lenny says quietly as he nods to his crew and heads out the door.

"It's alright Lenny, really." Shane says back sweetly.

"Like fuck it is." I growl, tipping her chin up to look at me. There's a small cut and a bruise forming around it already. I have a mind to go after Lenny and kick his ass after all for hurting her. She must see it on my face because she runs her hands along my arms, giving me a comforting smile.

"Max, really. I'm okay. It was just an accident." I take a deep breath, trying to meet her in the calmness she's somehow remained in. How she manages to be perfectly level-headed through shit like this blows my mind.

"Come with me." I direct, heading towards the kitchen.

"Marco, you're in charge for a minute." Marco nods and continues moving around the floor. He's not a bartender by any means, but if someone needs something besides a beer, they can fucking wait a minute. I grab some ice from the kitchen and wrap it in a bar towel, holding it up to her eye. Her ocean blues look up at me and everything in me goes weak.

"Thanks, Max." She says softly.

"What for, baby?"

"Well, this is the second time we've been in this situation at this bar. You're always here to swoop in and take care of me. So, thank you." She says, reminding me of the first night I held ice to her face here. The night I saw red for the first time over a woman. The first time I wanted to rip someone to pieces for hurting her.

"You know, that night was the first time I wanted to take a person out for hurting someone. Out of all of my years serving, I've killed because it was my duty, but that night – I wanted to because someone hurt *you*. It made my blood feel like lava, seeing you hurt." I admit to her. She smiles, holding a hand to my face, I close my eyes and lean into her touch – my favorite feeling in the world.

"That was the night I realized that I might actually be able to trust someone again. The safest I'd felt in a long time was all because of you." The words resonate with me deeply. I smile down at her and move the towel. The spot is a little red but isn't deep enough to need stitches.

"I told you, you'll always be safe with me. The good news is, *this* incident won't end with us in the ER." I tease.

"I can't believe I have this lovely mark on my face the night of the party." She rolls her eyes.

"You're still going to be the sexiest one there," I say, grabbing around her waist and pulling her into a kiss. Just then Marco busts through the kitchen doors.

"What the hell is a Gimlet?" he asks, making Shane bust out laughing.

"Jesus Christ, it never ends." I mutter, kissing the tip of her nose before heading back out front. "You sure you're alright?" I ask once more. She smiles and shakes her head.

"Yes, I'm fine. Go." She giggles, making my chest feel warm. Like the radiant sunshine that she is.

SHANE

Just as I am about to make my way back out to the bar to help Max, my phone rings. I lift it from my back pocket, figuring it's probably Taylor or Leah with some last-minute party needs. To my surprise, it's Hugh.

"Hello?" I say with hesitation.

"Shane! Good to hear your voice, how are you doing?" Hugh asks, his tone as smooth as ever.

"I'm doing well, how about you?" I slide myself onto the counter in the corner, settling into the conversation.

"I'm good. Listen, I'm in Nashville tonight on some business. I would still really like to talk with you, will you have some time today? I fly out again first thing in the morning." It completely slipped my mind that Hugh mentioned needing to speak to me when I was in San Francisco over a month ago.

"I am working right now and I have a party I am helping host tonight. It's for my friend Lauren, who you met at the event. You're more than welcome to come, I'm sure she'd love to see you again. Unless it's something you'd like to discuss in a more... I don't know, calm environment." I laugh out, making Hugh laugh along with me.

"Not at all, that will be fine. Send me the address and time and I will meet up with you there."

"Okay, See you tonight." I hang up the phone, then slide off the counter, making my way back out to the bar. My mind is racing with thoughts about why Hugh may want to speak to me. I remember him seeming kind of serious when he mentioned it. But it's been over a month since then, surely it can't be too important, right? At least I'll find out tonight. I shake my head, trying to clear my mind when Max walks up beside me.

"Everything alright? You look a little more serious than usual." Max furrows his brow.

"Yeah, just a lot on my mind. Nothing to worry about though, I'm okay." I smile at him but his expression doesn't change. He nods, accepting my answer as is, before getting back to work. I don't want to mention talking to Hugh yet. I don't even know what he wants right now, so I will fill him in when I have all the information. I am kind of excited for the two of them to finally meet. I spend the rest of my shift trying to hide the fact that my mind won't stop spinning. However, the way Max has watched me all day tells me I'm not doing a very convincing job.

We told Lauren that we are going out to celebrate Leah finishing her Masters' to make her less suspicious. The hall we rented is packed full of people and when we make our way through the threshold, the crowd of people yelling *"Happy Birthday Lauren!"* proves this was the best kept secret we've ever managed. She looks so surprised, her face turning red instantly. She turns to face us, with tears welling in her eyes, and brings us in for a group hug. Taylor, Leah and I all laugh at our success.

"I don't know what I ever did to deserve you girls." She says squeezing us tighter.

"It's truly a mystery," Taylor teases. "Now go mingle with your guests." She winks, waving her off.

I look up and find Max in the crowd, Tucker and Tank hanging out behind him. He's looking at me like he can't wait to get me alone and it has me tingling all over. I decided on wearing my sky blue suede shorts with a black sweater and black booties, my tan legs on full display. Max looks like a damn snack himself in his white undershirt, hooded denim jacket, black ripped jeans and his biker boots. I love when he has those on, it always means he drove the bike, which makes him sexy on a whole other level.

I prance over to him, letting him envelope me in a hug.

"You look radiant as always." He says, leaning in to kiss me.

"Are you ever *not* going to make me blush Max Mullins?" I ask, my cheeks already rosy.

"God, I hope not." He smiles, his perfect, straight white teeth on display.

We walk around saying hi to acquaintances and old friends of mine, Max never letting my hand go. I know he isn't a fan of crowds, so it means a lot to me that he shows up to things like this that are important to me, never once complaining. When he makes his way over to the bar to get us both a drink, I turn around and am met with an all too familiar face. Swagger fully intact as he makes his way over to me.

"There's my favorite rookie!" Hugh announces. I smile, closing the space between us to greet him. He opens his arms for a hug and I lean into him.

"Are you still pulling the rookie card on me? I feel like since you've displayed my art now maybe I should shake that title?" I tease. He laughs at my response, before taking a deep breath in.

"The place looks fabulous, and Lauren sure looked surprised. You did a great job." He says looking around the venue.

"Oh, thanks. It wasn't all me though, Taylor and Leah helped of course." I answer, glancing over at my friends.

"Of course, you ladies always have been a package deal." He

replies. I'd spent so much time with Hugh during my time in San Francisco, so he knew all about my best friends and the bond we had. He too became like family to me and I've really missed him.

"So, what was it you wanted to talk to me about? I would be lying if I said I wasn't racking my brain all day trying to figure it out." I admit. He laughs so casually, putting me a little more at ease.

"Okay, no beating around the bush then." He answers, placing both hands inside the front pockets of his slacks.

"I want you to come back to San Francisco to be my full time art curator. The position is open and I can't think of anyone better fit for the job. It's yours if you want it. Unless, of course, there's something keeping you here." He says, holding his hands up in hesitation.

My mind is absolutely frozen. I can't believe he's offering me this position. That he came all the way *here* to offer me the position. Well. I mean, I'm not sure that's the actual reason he's here, but still. Is this really happening?

"Well," I open my mouth to speak, but I hear someone else do it for me.

"Of course there's not." My head snaps to Max, standing behind me with our drinks in his hands.

"What?" I ask, completely shocked by his response.

"Don't worry about putting in a notice at the bar. This is clearly what you're meant to do. You shouldn't be wasting your time or your talent bartending. You're better than that Shane. You're better than anything this town has to offer you. You should take the job. Consider this your official termination from Chattahoochies." Max forces a half smile.

"Chattahoochies?" Hugh laughs. Max narrows his gaze at him before turning around and walking off.

"Max, wait." I chase after him, leaving Hugh standing in the middle of the venue alone.

"You don't mean that. Tell me you don't mean that." I say pleadingly. I stand there waiting for him to tell me he's joking.

"Did you know he was here? *Why* he is here?" he asks surprisingly calm. Stunned, I try to come up with a response. I take a deep breath and try to explain it to him.

"I didn't know he was in town until earlier today. He said he needed to speak with me back when I was in San Francisco, but I forgot to contact him when I got back. He called me today saying he was in town so I told him about the party tonight." I answer honestly.

"Did you know *why?*" his jaw ticks at the end of his question.

"No! He just said he wanted to talk to me. I didn't know he was going to ask me to go back to San Francisco." I feel the panic starting to rise in my chest.

"Do you want to?" he asks, studying my face for a reaction.

I freeze at his question, at how angry and hurt he looks. Sure, this is a great job opportunity, and it's something I wanted for a long time. But things have changed since I left San Francisco. Things are different now, I *want* different things now. Before I can answer, Max takes my silence as answer enough.

"Go to San Francisco, Shane. It's where you belong."

Just like that he's gone. He rushes out the door and gets on his motorcycle before my feet can catch up. I run out the door behind him, but when I make it to the edge of the sidewalk, I'm too late. I'm left standing there, tears falling from my eyes. Wondering how he could just let me go like that. Leave me like that.

He basically pushed me on a flight back to San Francisco, broke up with me and fired me in one fell swoop. Now I have to go back to my best friend's party and pretend everything is okay. Because even though my heart is broken, I will not take away from her special day.

When I return, Hugh is talking with Lauren, a smile spread across his face as wide as the ocean. When he sees me approaching he turns his full attention to me.

"So, what do you say?" he asks. Lauren cocks her head to the side, looking at me like she missed something. *Girl, you have no fucking clue how much.*

"Um, Can I let you know?" I ask vaguely, forcing a smile on my face.

"Sure, just try to make it sooner than later, if you don't take the position I have a stack of applications to thumb through to fill it." I nod in response, cutting my eyes to Lauren who is looking at me much more intently now.

"Be in touch soon then. Happy Birthday, Love. I hope it was a fantastic one." He kisses Lauren on the cheek and walks away, but I'm too numb to react.

My mind is still solely focused on Max, and the way he just left me and my shattered heart on the sidewalk.

"Babe, what on earth is going on? Where'd Max go and what the hell is Hugh talking about?" she asks. Damn Lauren, read the room.

"Excuse me," I breathe out as I walk away from her. I rush to the bathroom to try and compose myself. I see Tucker and Tank on my way out, both of their gazes following me in with concern. When I get to the bathroom, I'm almost immediately joined by Taylor, Leah, and the birthday girl herself.

"Do you guys have like a radar on me or something?" I half heart-edly laugh.

"Shane, what the hell happened?" Taylor asks. I try to think of a way to make it sound like nothing, to not take away from Lauren's special night that we spent literally weeks planning. But I can't ignore the lump in my throat when I go to answer. I let out a sob, and explain the events to them step by step.

"I don't know why he reacted like that. I didn't even tell him I was considering it or anything, he just told me to go, fired me, and left me. Literally left me standing on the sidewalk." My voice cracks as I try to understand it all myself.

"I'm sure he was just upset at the thought. Once you guys talk it will all work out." Leah reassures me. I hope she's right. I need her to be right. I go back to the party for about 30 minutes, before I realize I won't be fun for anyone anymore. I decide to head home and go straight to bed. But not the same bed I've grown used to sleeping in. Tonight I won't be surrounded by the woodsy, vanilla and leather scent I've come so familiar with and the warm body that puts mine at ease. Tonight, it's just me and a bottle of wine against the world.

ME

> Please call me tomorrow. I don't like how tonight ended.

ME

> Max, you can't just tell me to leave and then ignore me. I really want to talk to you about this.

ME

> Are you working today? We really need to talk.

ME

> I don't want to go, Max. Please just call me.

After trying for four days to reach him – going to his house, looking at the bar, checking the gym, and asking Tucker, who was apparently under some loyalty oath, I had nothing. Until my sweatshirt from Max showed up at our door with a note.

> Shane,
> San Francisco may not be cold, but there are clumsy people with coffee everywhere.
> Be safe.
> — Max

The wave of tears that came next hurt more than any other ones

I've ever cried. He is actually done with me. He returned this with a note pushing me even further away. In other circumstances, I wouldn't leave without a fight. I would wait outside his door until he came home from wherever the hell he's been. I would make him talk to me, or at least listen to me. I would tell him I didn't want to go until I was blue in the face if that's what it took.

But he's trained to be hard and emotionless, not only as a SEAL but it's who he's been as a person for so long, that I think he's done for good. I would normally stay and fight, but it hurts too much to be here without him. Without his flirty texts, his warm embrace, his passionate kisses, the way he looks at me. Nashville simply won't be the same for me if I don't have Max. And he's clearly not coming back to me. Plus, I'm jobless again since he fired me, so what other choice do I have?

ME

Looks like you have a spare room again, Tay. I'm going back to San Francisco.

TAYLOR

I'm gonna kick his ass too. I don't want my room, I want my best friend. Please don't go.

LEAH

Are you sure about this Shaney?

LAUREN

Don't make any hasty decisions over some guy.
Think about it, babe.

ME

I can't stay here. It already hurts too much.

I text Hugh to accept the position, then toss my phone on the bedside table. I curl up in bed, crying myself to sleep before I pack for my move to San Francisco, *again.*

SEEING her texts come through feels like a dagger to the heart every time I read them. Reading the last one makes me do something drastic though. She is only saying she doesn't want to go because of me, she has to be. She told me before how much she loved her job and how that would be the one thing to keep her in San Francisco to begin with. I know she'd stay because of me, which is why I'm telling her to go. I know I have to be the one to sever ties, I can't be the one to stand in the way of her dreams.

Even if I wanted to punch that guy in the face for offering her a job 2,000 miles away from me. I saw the hesitation in her eyes, and that was enough for me. I've been avoiding any place she'd look for me, and told Tucker I'd have him by the balls if he tells her where I went. I am doing this for her own good. She may not be able to see that right now, but she will one day. I hope.

I decided to take Riley and camp for a while. I just couldn't be there when she left. I couldn't see her, because I would have ended up telling her to stay, which would only be holding her back. I've seen what she's created. I know this Hugh guy is the person she needs to work with to get her art on display someday. It's the only logical thing to do. Even if it hurts like hell. I made the trip back to deliver her sweatshirt to her, knowing everything else at my house of hers was just spares. Maybe she'd still think of me while she was away, maybe she'd toss it out the window, but I still wanted her to have it. Regardless of her decision, it was hers to do with what she wanted.

She's been gone for two weeks now and I've been in a shit mood ever since Lauren's fucking birthday party. Tucker texted me the day she left letting me know I could go home without worrying about running into her, so I packed up our campsite and went home. When I got there, I put all of Shane's things in a box in the closet. I can't bring myself to actually throw any of it out. I'd hopped in the shower to wash off the days of camping, and when I got out, I fell straight into bed. When my head hit the pillow, the smell of lavender flooded my senses.

Not being able to pull her warm body into me and breathe her scent in deeper, not being able to stroke her golden locks, bury myself in her and kiss her perfect lips before falling asleep, was agonizing. It felt like someone was pulling all of the air from my lungs, with no plan to return it.

TUCKER

Range day?

ME

Not up for it.

TUCKER

You gotta leave the house sometime man.

TUCKER

Be ready in 20 minutes. I'm picking your ass up.

Persistent motherfucker. I get off the couch to get ready, grabbing my range bag from the closet. I get a strudel from the freezer since apparently I'm on a time clock today, and as soon as I finish it, Tucker is honking outside. I call Riley and we head out the door. Tucker yammers on about the project he's currently working on, but all I can focus on is how this damn Toaster Strudel isn't followed by the taste of Shane today.

She convinced me to try it the day we got back from the store, buying enough to last through the damn apocalypse. I told her that strudel had never been a favorite of mine but she insisted I try it anyway.

"Your taste buds may have developed into something worthwhile since the last time you tried them. Plus have you ever had the apple flavor? They're superior to all the other flavors." *She'd argued, waving the frozen pastry in my face. I grabbed her wrist to move it from between us to make a deal.*

"I will try your damn strudel, on one condition," I told her.

"Name it." She narrowed her gaze like she was ready for battle.

"I get to cleanse my palette with the taste of you after." I yanked her towards me by her wrist, causing her to gasp.

"Even if you like it?"

"Even if I like it,"

"Okay, deal." She smiled, her cheeks turning pink before she rushed to the toaster. She started humming and swaying her hips to whatever song was playing

in that beautiful mind of hers, and I was completely captivated by everything she did. She took the pastry out of the toaster as I closed the space between us. When she turned around, her hand bumped into my chest. Her eyes shot up to mine and she smiled so brightly.

"Open." She said, holding the icing-glazed strudel to my mouth. I raised a brown and huffed, doing as I was told. I took a large bite, making her laugh when half the pastry was gone after. When I'd finished, I licked the icing off of my lips, catching her gaze following the path of my tongue.

"Well? What do you think?" she asked impatiently.

"Disgusting. Absolutely terrible." I said evenly. She studied me for a minute to see if I was telling the truth. I wasn't, surprisingly it was pretty damn good.

"You're lying! You liked it." She playfully yelled, bringing a smile to my face.

"Hmm.. guess you'll never know. Now get your ass on the counter, and spread those beautiful legs for me." I demanded, nodding to the island behind us. She did as she was told, and my pallet was thoroughly cleansed.

Every morning after that when she would stay with me, I would have fucking Toaster Strudel and Sunshine for breakfast. So today, this strudel fucking sucked.

After I've blown through about two boxes of ammo, Tucker finally breaks the silence between us. "Max, man. What the fuck are you doing?" he asks, in his disappointed older brother voice.

"Planting roses. I'm slingin' lead, Tuck what's it look like?" I mouth off, loading my next magazine.

"First of all smart ass, you could never. Second of all, put the mag down and talk to me like a man. You know damn good and well I meant what the fuck are you doing with Shane." I think this is the first time in our entire friendship Tucker has sounded pissed off at me.

"I'm not doing anything with Shane. In case you haven't noticed it's hard to do anything with someone that's 2,000 miles away." I slam the mag down on the table getting pissed off right back at him.

"Yeah? Who's fucking fault is it that she's even there dumbass? Huh?" he yells at me, shaking his head.

"Watch it Tuck." I warn, my jaw clenching so tight I think I might break a tooth.

"You know, I watched you for years try to grieve the loss of your mom when she passed. You had a new woman every other night, always gone before sunrise. Sleeping all day and drinking all night. Then you finally cleaned up to go on a few more deployments with the SEALs – and then we lost Red, and you completely shut down." He lays into me, not holding anything back.

"I know, Tucker. I was there." I remind him in a clipped tone.

"Yeah? Well so was I Max. In case you forgot, I lost him too, we all did. But you're the one who shut the whole world out after that. I watched every single light inside of you burn out completely. No trace of hope or joy was left behind. Now, correct me if I'm wrong, but a certain blonde with a personality straight from God himself lit that fire back in you. She brought that lost joy back to life?" He waits for a response that isn't coming.

"Then you all but throw her on the next flight to San Francisco at the first mention of an opportunity out there for her. Without so much as asking her what she wanted first. I told you once before that she's happier with you Max. I saw you change over the years, and we've been best friends for decades, but I saw her the first night she was in town too. It didn't take a genius to see how much shit she was dealing with. Then I saw her after you finally let her in, when she was happier than anyone else I've ever seen. Then I saw her the day she left. You broke her man." My eyes snap to him, my heart aching at his words.

"And you're making the worst mistake of your life if you don't open your eyes and fucking do something about it." My jaw ticks as I work through everything I just heard.

You broke her man.

"You done?" I ask harshly, making Tucker scoff.

"Yeah, I'm done." He says, his tone sounding defeated.

"Let's go. I gotta get to work." I grab my bag from the ground, throwing it in the back of his Bronco. Probably looking like a child throwing a tantrum, but I don't really give a shit right now. My brain feels foggy and I don't want to talk anymore. Not to Tucker, or anybody else. We load up our stuff and head back to the house, riding the whole way in complete silence. When I get back home, I toss my range bag back into the closet, and when I do the box of Shane's stuff falls over. I stare at it a moment, letting Tucker's words replay in my mind. I start to pick it up but decide against it. I can't go there right now, I can't let myself miss her, or think about how I could have possibly made a mistake. So I shut the door, and get ready for work.

Chapter 32

Shane

Hugh is the boss that everyone wants, and no one deserves. He is truly like family to me at this point, and I am so grateful for everything he's done for me since I met him. When I called him to tell him I would accept the head curator position at *The Gallery*, he told me he would have one of his small apartments set up for me. A simple one-bedroom, one-bathroom apartment that is in close proximity to work and conveniently enough, some of my favorite hangouts. I decided to walk down the boardwalk today since I have the day off.

I stop to look out at the ocean, letting the salty breeze wash over me. I pull my phone from my pocket and scroll through my photos. My eyes start to sting as I stop on pictures of me and Max. There are pictures of us from the club on Valentine's Day – before he rocked Pete's jaw and rushed me back to his place. There are photos of us at his house, and one of him and Riley asleep at the studio that I snapped during one of my prolonged painting sessions.

The one that I love the most is one I took super sneakily while he was making breakfast one morning. He hadn't gotten dressed yet and wore only his black boxer briefs and a backward baseball cap. His tattoos on full display on his perfect, tanned skin. Riley had jumped up, placing her paws on the cabinet beside him while he was making french toast and he looked down at her and smiled so big his whole face lit up. It was a moment I wanted to remember forever.

I don't even realize I'm crying until I see a teardrop hit my phone screen. I look back out at the ocean, groaning and wiping the tears from my cheeks. I am so sick of crying all the time, but I can't help it. I miss him so much. When I look back down at my screen I see a text come through from Lauren.

LAUREN

Meet me at Mario's in 10.

I blink a few times in surprise because – what the hell is she doing in San Francisco?

ME

You're here?

LAUREN

Sure am. And I'm starving, so I hope you're hungry.

Seeing as how I barely eat most days, I'm in a perpetual state of starvation.

I pull up to Mario's and make my way inside, the smell of pasta and garlic bread flooding my senses. *I'm getting the chicken alfredo.* I spot Lauren at a booth in the corner, smiling at me when she looks my way. She stands up and opens her arms just as I finish closing the distance between us.

"Shaney!" she says excitedly.

"Hey, Lu. What on earth are you doing here?" I ask, trying to hide the sadness in my tone.

"I'm here on business." She says professionally, tossing her brown hair behind her.

"You don't have a realtor license in California. Do you?" my brows pull in questioningly.

"This is friend business, babe." She cocks her head. Drawing a deep breath from my chest.

"I'm *fine*, Lauren." I roll my eyes playfully. Not at all hiding how much of a lie that is.

"Shane, come on, you are so not fine." She says giving me a sympathetic look, causing tears to well in my eyes again.

"I don't know what you want me to say... I'm *trying* to be fine. Doesn't that count for something?" I pick at the hem of my shirt, trying to look anywhere but at her.

"It counts for everything. You are legitimately the strongest woman I've ever met. The past year alone would be enough to make me never get out of bed again. It took you what? A week, and you're back out here painting and working and doing the damn thing." She sounds so proud of me when in reality I'm barely dragging my ass out of bed at all.

"Fake it til you make it, right?" I say, with no hint of playfulness in my tone.

"I came out here to check on you, give you a hug if you need it, and tell you that Max is an idiot. He'll see that eventually." She grabs my hand in hers, squeezing it reassuringly.

"I'm not so sure he will," I argue. "He wouldn't even speak to me, Lauren. He heard about a job opportunity for me across the country and didn't let me get so much as a word out before basically packing my bag for me and sending me on my way. I'd say he's pretty done with me." I can feel myself falling deeper into my own sadness again. Playing the events over and over again in my mind was all I seemed capable of doing these days. She grabs her menu and studies it for a moment.

"I'm no expert. But I think you're wrong." She says leaving no room for discussion. We order our food and continue to catch up, laughing like we always do when we are together. I miss Nashville so much. I miss seeing my girls almost every day. I miss the weekly girls' nights we had. Trips to Topgolf, Chattahoochies, my studio, Riley, Max. I miss it all. But I guess I just have to let it go.

I reach into my bag and pull out an envelope with Max's name on it that I have been carrying around since I unpacked it.

"I need you to return these to Max for me please." I hand Lauren the envelope and she studies it for a moment. Noticing it's way too bulky to be a note.

"I shouldn't have his dog tags. I didn't even realize I packed them with my things. Can you return them for me?" I ask, ignoring the burning sensation in my throat.

She takes the envelope and hugs me goodbye, reassuring me one more time before leaving that Max will come around. I still don't think he will ever speak to me again though, so I decide to go to the gallery and continue working on the painting I started the day I got back in the studio. Because through the years, I could always count on my art to get me through things.

Chapter 33

EVERYONE at the bar has been more annoying than usual today. I almost got into it with Jackie of all people, which really goes to show how bad my mood is. I thought after spending the morning at the range with Tucker I may have gotten some of my frustrations out, but the conversation he decided we apparently needed to have left me feeling even more aggravated than before. Just when I think things can't get any worse, the asshole Lenny got into it with before almost taking Shane's eye out with a pool cue, comes into the bar.

He sits down on one of the stools and orders a whiskey. He nods over to Lenny, who's at the pool tables, with a smug look on his face as he tips his drink back. He finishes it in one gulp and orders another. Jesus fucking christ, it's only noon. He's trying to have a conversation with me about the bar – how I got started, where did the name come from, why I work the bar when I own the place. All things I don't engage with him about until he asks one question that has an answer I can't let slide.

"Whatever happened to that sexy blonde you had working back here?" he asks, finishing off his third whiskey. "She had an ass on her, didn't she?" he asks absentmindedly. My head snaps up, my narrowed eyes locking with his. I'm not sure if steam is coming from my ears, but with the way my blood is boiling, I wouldn't be surprised by the fact.

"Oh. Touchy subject. You hit that?" he asks, seeing how his question has clearly pissed me the hell off. I sure as shit hope he's drunk, otherwise this is going to hurt. I walk around the bar, dragging him outside by the shirt collar. After all, I have a no BS policy. Once we're out on the mostly empty sidewalk, he turns around trying to fix his shirt.

"What the hell man?" he asks, sounding shocked by what just happened. He better fucking buckle up. I rear back and rock his jaw so hard, he takes a few steps back.

"Son of a bitch!" he yells.

"You're going to keep your ass out of my bar, and her name out of your fucking mouth." I huff out.

"I don't even know her name, asshole." He says while holding his face. "But if you give it to me, I won't say it to *you*. I'll just call her myself."

That's it, this guy is dead. I turn my hat around backward, my hands fisting at my sides as I get ready to punch him again. The bastard is lucky Tank is working today and sees what's happening through the window or I'm not sure he would have made it off the sidewalk. He comes running outside from the bar, grabbing my attention.

"Max, hey, what's going on?" he asks, stepping in between us.

"Nothing that concerns you, Tank." I bite out. He must see the red flashing in my eyes because he turns to face the guy behind him.

"Get the hell out of here man." He nods to the guy, who scurries off in the other direction. "Care to tell me what that was about?" Tank asks, pointing in the direction the guy ran off.

"Nope." I say as I walk back into the bar. People all around are staring at me as I make my way back behind the counter.

"Jesus man, you've gotta get it together." Tank shakes his head following behind me. Some girl sitting at the far end of the bar pipes up in her low breathy voice.

"Wow, that was intense." She says, smiling over at me. I cut my eyes her way, not giving her my full attention. "If you need someone to help you calm down later, give me a call." She slides a napkin in my direction with her phone number written on it. I look at her fully now, her brown hair straight down and her bright green eyes staring insanely hard at me.

"No," I say, taking the napkin and crushing it in my fist. She looks shocked and a little offended as she stands from the bar and walks out. I toss the napkin in the trash below me, then continue wiping glasses clean. It's not her fault that there's only one woman I would want to calm me down in a heated moment. The very same woman I would kill a man over.

"Wow Mullins, seems you have a bit of a chip on your shoulder." A familiar voice calls from the opposite end of the bar. "She happen to be blonde, radiant, and approximately 2,000 miles away?" Lauren asks. What the fuck is it with everyone today? My jaw ticks but I ignore her question.

"What can I get you?" I ask, walking over to her.

"Margarita, rocks." She answers. I begin making her drink as she sits quietly at the bar. The look on her face tells me the wheels in her mind are spinning, which is frightening. Taylor is loud and scary, but the quiet ones are the ones to truly fear. She finally sits up ready to let me in on whatever she came here to say.

"Look, I don't typically poke my nose in places it doesn't belong, but I am making an exception today." What is this, unsolicited opinions day?

"Lucky me," I say dryly.

She narrows her gaze at me before sitting back on her barstool.

"You are the biggest idiot I've ever met if you think you did the right thing with Shane. That girl has been through shit this past year. You of all people should know that. She deserves to finally have something good in her life, something that makes her happy." She says.

"That's why I did what I did. She deserves that job more than anyone." I reply, pouring her drink and placing it in front of her.

"No… Well, yes of course she deserves it, but that's not what I'm talking about." She lets out an aggravated sigh. "Look, Mullins. If you can't see how absolutely sick in love she is with you, then maybe you aren't the one for her. But I think you can, I think you can see it but won't let yourself believe it. You were scared of losing her, so instead, you pushed her away. You broke her heart and sent her 2,000 miles away because that's what you *thought* she'd want. When what she really *needed* was for you to tell her there was something worth staying for. Shane always talks about how brave and loyal you are, but it sounds to me like you had a big ass coward baby moment and probably lost the best thing that's ever happened to you in the process." She sits there, staring at me while I let everything she said sink in.

"You done?" I ask, my exterior not giving away an ounce of how I feel inside.

"Yep. Just needed to make sure you knew you were an idiot." She says as she tips her drink to me.

"Enjoy the drink," I say, turning to walk back to my office.

"Oh, wait. I forgot one thing." She says, pulling something from her bag. All I want to do is be alone, can she hurry the hell up with it?

"I was asked to return these to you." She slides an envelope across the bar with my name written on it. I look inside and see the dog tags I had given to Shane before she left for San Francisco the first time for the art event. My jaw clenches and a cold chill falls down my spine. I look up at Lauren who is studying me like a textbook. She finally shrugs while giving me a knowing look. "Now I'm done." She answers, taking another sip of her drink.

When I shut the door to my office, I pace the floor a few times before slamming my fist on the desk. I am pissed the fuck off at everything she just said. Not because she's wrong, but because she's dead fucking right. Except, I wasn't being a coward. I really *did* think that accepting that job was what Shane wanted. I didn't want to hold her back and have her only stay for me. I didn't want to see what would happen if she stayed for me and it turned out to not be enough for her in the future.

I realize now that I never knew true love until I met Shane. I have been afraid to open myself up to it because I'm afraid of losing someone else I love. When in the end, I'm the one that pushed her away. I thought I was doing what was best for her, that I was giving her what she really wants. Because that's what you do when you're in love with someone right? I sent her away because I wanted her to be happy, not because I didn't want her. I guess I never took a second to think it's a possibility, that being with *me* is what makes her happy.

I would walk through fire for her, I feel like I can't breathe when she's not here. Every good thought I have includes her. I would kill anyone who dared to hurt her. But it turns out, I broke her heart and mine right along with it when I told her to go back to California. What kind of fucking idiot pushes away the only woman he's ever been in love with?

If Lauren is right, if she is just as in love with me - or was before I fucked it all up, maybe I have a chance to get her back. To show her that I did what I did because I thought it was what she wanted. When I should have dropped to my knees and begged her to stay.

I should have told her everything I felt when I heard the offer for her to move back to San Francisco came out of Hugh's mouth. I'll be damned if I don't even try. Before I can second guess my decisions, I pick up the phone and call Tucker.

"Hey man, I need your help," I say as soon as he answers the phone.

"Everything alright?" he asks cautiously.

"Yeah, I just need you to watch Riley for a bit."

"Oh. Alright man, bring her over whenever. If I'm not home she can hang out in the backyard."

"Thanks, Tuck." I say before quickly hanging up the phone.

After ending the call with Tucker, I rush back out to the bar. Lauren is just finishing her margarita when I make it over to her.

"I need your help with something," I say, her gaze narrowing on me.

"Alright, Mullins. Whatcha got?" she says, leaning into the bar.

Chapter 34

Shane

I'm in the same room I used to paint in all the time before I left San Francisco four months ago. It took everything in me to get up and come to work that first week. I couldn't stop crying long enough to do my makeup, so most days I came in with puffy eyes and waterproof mascara, trying to pretend I didn't look like a grieving widow. When I finally got back into a groove of painting here, things started to get a little easier.

My mind spins nonstop most days, replaying what happened with Max. I will remember everything from the first day I met him, to the day he left me. He told me once how the first day he met me felt like seeing sunshine after a storm, ironic how a storm rages inside me every time I think of him now.

I could feel my heart breaking a little more every day that I spent in that town without him. Every place I went reminded me of him. The coffee shop, the gym, the bar. My whole life in Nashville has something to do with him. I decided to take the job after Max clearly ended things by returning my sweatshirt from his house. I couldn't stay there if he didn't want to see me anymore. Plus, I'd been fired so I was in need of a job.

I have never loved anyone the way I loved Max. I still love him. I'm so in love with him that the only way I could cope with the pain of losing him was to leave, just like he told me to. I wanted to scream and beg him to see that I really didn't want to move back to California. I wanted to stay with him.

Even if it meant I worked at Chattahoochies for the rest of my life and never had art displayed in a gallery. My life completely changed when I met him. Every broken and grieving piece felt complete when I was with Max. I felt safe and protected, as if he would never let another part of me break. Until he broke them all.

When I walk out of the creative space, my headphones playing at a volume I thought could drown out my thoughts, I run straight into someone in the hallway, and I'm suddenly covered in ice-cold coffee. Is this ever going to stop happening to me? I look up and am face to face with the last person I ever expected to see. Maxwell Mullins just spilled my favorite coffee all over my white painting shirt.

"Dammit, Sunshine. We have to stop meeting like this." He smiles a sad smile at me and I freeze in place.

I blink a couple of times trying to make the hallucination of him disappear, but alas, the coffee is still leaking into my bra, and the deep blue eyes I have fallen in love with are still staring back into my own.

"Max, what are you doing here?" I ask quietly, looking around.

"Can we, uh, go somewhere to talk?" he asks nervously. I shake my head and hold a hand out directing him into the room I just came from. The same place I have the rawest and most vulnerable in-depth painting I've ever done; sitting front and center.

The canvas on the easel that I hope will show him all the things I never got a chance to tell him. He walks in and freezes in place, staring directly at the painting. I hear a shaky breath come from him as he studies the canvas.

It depicts the story of my life, before and after meeting Max. There are a few happier moments from my childhood, like fashion shows I put on as a kid or the family game nights we used to have once a week, leading up to the day I lost my parents. The tragedy begins with the flipped car and the emergency room where I found out I had lost them both forever. I show the pain of being left to live my life without them, but how painting saved me.

It shows how my first relationship left me feeling like I wasn't good enough, and that I believed I would never trust again. Then the part of my life where I am reunited with my three best friends. Where I meet Max, Ruby, Tucker, and Riley. Followed by the night of the robbery when Max not only saved me from the asshole in a ski mask but how he saved me from my own anxiety that same night.

I painted our night at Topgolf where I felt the freedom of riding on the back of Max's motorcycle with him, and the day after when Max gave me the studio to paint in. My favorite part of the painting is the pool table where he finally let go of his grief, and showed us both how capable he is of love. There are moments of us in his kitchen together making breakfast with Riley waiting for the food fights that always guarantee her scraps on the floor. The Toaster Strudel he kept stocked in his freezer for me since I became a more than regular house guest.

The end of the painting is the day he broke my heart. Only in this depiction, I tell him how I would throw away every other dream I have ever had, just to have him in my life. I would leave the gallery and San Francisco and teach at the art center, painting only for pleasure if it meant I got to keep the man who finally showed me how I should be loved.

If I got to keep the person who protected me at all costs and made me feel things I never knew possible. Someone who quite literally did the one thing they vowed to never do - love someone and lose them again - just to let me chase my dreams. I would give it all up for *him.* Because I am madly and deeply in love with him. Only that didn't happen, he pushed me away and I had to start over *again,* so I have no idea what he's doing here now.

"What are you doing here Max?" I let out a deep breath trying to keep my voice steady. He turns to face me with tears streaming down his face, catching me completely by surprise.

"I came for you, Sunshine." He chokes out. "Baby, I fucked up so much by letting you leave."

"You *told* me to go, Max. You didn't let me leave, you basically bought me a ticket yourself then avoided me until I was gone." I remind him, not hiding the pain in my voice.

He swallows hard taking a step closer to me, I glance up at him and he looks so hurt. The same sadness behind his eyes that I saw the first day I met him was back.

"I know I did, I guess I was being a coward when I thought I was doing the right thing. I thought I was doing what would make you happy, Shane. I didn't want to be selfish with you and ask you to stay. I didn't want you to stay because of me and give up this amazing opportunity, only to wonder what you missed out on later in life. So yeah, I pushed you away before you could leave me, or stay and resent me. If I could go back to that night though, I would be the most selfish I've ever been. I would drop to my knees and beg you to stay. I would tell you that I will do whatever it takes to keep you, that you're mine, and that I will never let you go.

"I'd tell you that I will build an art gallery myself and give it to you if that's what you want. Whatever it takes to have you stay with me. Because I am so in love with you, Sunshine. I feel like I can't even breathe without you. It almost killed me the night I drove away from you. Leaving you on that sidewalk all alone was the hardest thing I've ever done. I need you back, baby. Because if I'm being honest, I never really let you go."

He looks desperate for me to say yes. Like if I tell him I've moved on, that I'm staying in San Francisco to run this gallery with Hugh, it might actually kill him. The whole time I've been out here all I have wanted was to know that it was killing him as much as it was killing me. That he didn't really just give up on us like that. He's finally fighting for the love he never thought he would allow himself to have, and I'm planning on fighting right alongside him.

"So, what, you think you can just show up in San Francisco with iced coffee and get me to come back home?" I look down at the now-empty iced coffee cup in his hand.

"Um, no. Actually…" he answers, tossing the cup in the garbage bin by the door.

"Max, If you hadn't left me on that sidewalk that night, and avoided me for days, you would have heard exactly what I wanted. You wouldn't have had to wonder at all if you were doing the right thing, or if it was what would make me happy because I had planned to tell you all along." I say, the look on his face is still nervous.

"I never wanted to leave you. I only came here because being in that town without being with *you* was too hard." I say, beginning to see the brave shell he wears like armor crack. "I want to work at the bar and deal with Lenny's crazy ass and listen to Tucker complain when we don't bring him coffee. I want to fall asleep listening to your irregular heart-beat and make breakfast with you and Riley. I want to ruin every possible surface of your house and bar with you. I want you and Riley to watch me paint in the studio you gave me until my stomach starts growling.

"Then when you make me the best burger I've ever had and I'm stuffing my face with french fries, I want to talk about all the random bullshit in life whether it matters or not. Because whatever I'm doing, I'll be happy as long as I'm yours. I love you, Max. I've loved you for longer than you know." I tell him, tears welling in my eyes.

"Say it again, baby." He pleads as he grabs each side of my face, tears beginning to fall from his eyes.

"I love you, Max," I say again, staring into his gorgeous blue eyes.

"I love you, Sunshine." He says, before bringing his lips into mine. He sweeps me up, wrapping my legs around his waist. When I remember something he said, I pull away and look down at him curiously.

"Wait, you said you *didn't* come here with iced coffee to win me back?" I look at him with a raised brow. He sets my feet back on the ground before clearing his throat and answering me.

"Right. I uh... I didn't come with just iced coffee..."

"Do you have Toaster Strudel hiding somewhere?" I laugh, crossing my arms over my chest.

"Not exactly." He cocks his head to the side. "I'm sure you remember the first day we met. Today being a jolting reminder and all." He says, holding a hand out to my shirt.

"Yes, of course, I remember," I smile, reminiscing on the day.

"Well, I remember you standing in the middle of the sidewalk that day for some reason. So I took a walk on that side of town one day when I was missing you, and it hit me. I know why you were standing there." He answers, grinning over at me.

"Oh? And why was that?" I tease. He couldn't possibly know.

"You were picturing your art studio there." He answers, making my heart drop to my feet.

"How did you–" I start.

"Because I can see it too, Sunshine." He grabs my hand in his. "The paintings you could display, the classes you could teach. Whatever you wanted to do. You could accomplish it there." His answer brings a smile to my face. This man knows me so damn well, big dreams and all.

"So, I bought it." My eyes grow wide. Did I hear that right?

"You– you... *Bought* the building?" I stutter out.

"I'm desperate for you Sunshine. I need you in my life. I need to walk down the street with your hand in mine. I need your lavender scent to cover every inch of my bed. I need to spend every morning wondering how on earth you run on Toaster Strudel and iced coffee. I need to watch your beautiful mind work as you create absolute masterpieces. This way you can do that somewhere other than a dusty old attic. So yeah. I bought you the building. I would do anything to bring you back to me. To see you smile. To help you chase your dreams. I love you too much not to." He answers. I can feel the lump in my throat and the tears falling down my face. He bought me a building? My very own art studio. "Come home baby, please. Come home with me." He pleads, picking me up by my thighs, placing his head on my heart.

"Max Mullins, I never took you as the begging type." I laugh and look down at him. He lets out a sad laugh and sets me back down, towering over me again. "Haven't I made it clear, there's nothing I wouldn't do for you Sunshine?" He grabs my chin and smiles. "So will you?"

"Will I, what?" I tease, biting my bottom lip to drive him crazy.

"Come home with me." He pulls both of my hands up to his chin.

"Home for me *is* you, Max."

"You're home for me too, Sunshine." He pulls me into a kiss and I wrap my arms around his neck, savoring every moment of his lips back on mine. "Oh and if you think for a second you're going back to live at Taylor's, think again." He says, nipping at my bottom lip.

"What are you saying?" I furrow my brow.

"I want you to move in with me. You can buy all the tiny pillows, unnecessary blankets, and Toaster Strudel you want. What do you say?" he asks, smiling that panty-dropping smile of his.

"I say – the blankets are absolutely necessary." I tease, making him tickle my sides. A laugh bellows out of me before he stops and looks at me for a more serious answer.

"I would love to move in with you, Max." I smile back at him. He grabs me around my neck and kisses me more fiercely this time.

"Let's go home." He says, in his sultry, deep voice. He fought for me. When I thought he'd given up for good, he kept fighting. For *us*. "Oh, and before I forget." He adds, reaching into his pocket. "I believe you misplaced these." He wraps his dog tags around my wrist, the same way I wore them when I was here for the charity auction a few months back. I look up at him and smile. "And don't you dare ever try to give them back." He commands, kissing my forehead again.

"I pinky swear," I hold out my pinky to him, and he takes it in his. Then we add another room to our list of ruin.

Epilogue

Max

nine months later...

CHRISTMAS DAY

Shane and I are closing down the bar together and the smile on her face has everyone in here feeling some sort of Christmas magic. I finally got my shit together nine months ago and went to San Francisco to drag her back home with me. I went with a coffee in hand and an art studio up my sleeve, hoping that I could prove to her just how much I love her and need her in my life. That I am willing to do anything to make her happy. The coffee gesture went over about as well as the first day we met, but if she's not mad about it, I'm not either.

The painting I walked in and saw that day had me feeling like the wind had gotten knocked out of me. It was a depiction of her life through tragedy. It hurt like hell knowing that I had put her through so much pain, even if it was only for a short amount of time. I was going to spend the rest of my life trying to make that up to her. Because there was no way I was letting her go after I got her back.

With Shane helping run things around here this year the bar now has a Christmas tree set up in the corner by the pool tables. It is full of the most unique ornaments you could imagine. From military-related ones to biker ones, to Viking style ones that expand on that aspect of the bar. And of course every single alcohol-related one she could find. She sure has a way of making even the smallest things special. It's one of the things I love most about her. Just as she's locking the door her phone starts to ring. I look down to see Hugh's name come across her phone.

"Any idea why Hugh is calling you on Christmas Day?" I ask curiously.

"Oh my gosh." She says bringing her hand to her forehead before rushing behind the counter to answer. "Hello?" she answers anxiously, still not answering my question. "Merry Christmas to you too." She smiles, running her hand from her forehead to her cheek. Tears began to well in her eyes and I already wanted to punch him for it. "Are you serious?" she asks, biting her lip and running her hand through her hair. *What the fuck is happening?*

"Hugh, that's the best news. Thank you so much. Okay. Yes, we'll talk soon. Bye." She hangs up the phone and squeals before running into my arms. That's more like it.

"What on earth was that about? Are you okay?" I ask, still curious as to why that phone call seemed to be so important.

"Um... Okay, I have something to show you." She says, leading me toward my office. We head upstairs to her old art studio which has me a bit confused.

"You are aware you have an entire art studio about a block away from here, right?" I hike my thumb over my shoulder.

"Yes, I am aware. But I had to keep this hidden from you for a while so I decided to work here so you wouldn't happen across it at the new place by accident." She says, stopping just at the top of the stairs. "Close your eyes." She says excitedly, making me raise a brow in question.

"You know, pushing me down the stairs would be the worst Christmas gift ever," I tease. She rolls her eyes playfully and groans. "Close your eyes, Max. Please." So of course, I do.

"Alright, Sunshine. They're closed." She guides me a little further into the old attic studio. When we finally stop, her hands drop from mine.

"Keep them closed. One more second." She says as I hear her moving things around the space. "Okay. Open your eyes." I open my eyes, blinking a few times to let them adjust. She stands a few feet away from me now with a nervous smile on her face, surrounded by some of the most detailed and amazing paintings I have ever seen.

"What do you think?" she asks, fidgeting with the oversized sleeves of her sweatshirt.

I take a moment to let each and every painting register in my mind. They are all military-based paintings. There are paintings of heroes with their service dogs, some carrying their dogs over their shoulders, some playing around at the base. There are men carrying their brothers over their shoulders, and some carrying their caskets.

There are dual versions of events where in one moment the guys are laughing and playing cards, then the next moment they're in the middle of a battlefield. There's a photo of a soldier back home with a folded flag next to him as he finishes a bottle of whiskey and his duty weapon on the table next to him. There is one painting that resonates with me so deeply that I almost hit my knees. Two soldiers, closely resembling Tucker and myself, at the national cemetery, pouring one out for a fallen brother. It's the most incredible thing I've ever seen.

"Baby, what is this?" I ask, trying to swallow past the lump in my throat.

"It's a service based art collection. Hugh wants to do an exhibit on it at *The Gallery* to raise money and awareness for soldiers. People have no idea what you all go through, and I wanted to shine some light on it in any way I could. I wanted to show the soldiers that they are seen, that they aren't alone, and also help others see that sometimes help is needed even when it will never be asked for. It's a tribute to all the men and women who serve; to those who don't make it home physically, and to those that never make it home mentally either." She says, making me fall in love with her even more. Which I didn't think was even possible.

"Do you like it?" she asks timidly.

"I fucking love it. I think you are the most talented artist I've ever encountered. You portrayed the message perfectly. You never stop amazing me, you know that?" I tell her, walking over to scoop her into my arms. I kiss her lips then peck kisses all along her cheek and down her neck.

"The fact that we actually get to do the exhibit is the best Christmas present I could have imagined." She says, looking at the collection that will soon be displayed.

"Not so fast there, Sunshine. We still haven't exchanged presents." I wink at her.

"Oh my gosh, what time is it?" she gasps, her eyes going wide.

"Yeah, It's almost seven we better get going," I tell her, before setting her down. We head back to the bar, I lock up my office and shut off all the lights. "Come on Riles," I call, making her hop down from her regular booth. Shane convinced me that we should host Christmas with all of our friends this year. I didn't really fight the idea either, because thinking about having our favorite people with us on a day that was so hard for the both of us for so long, makes me happy. Shane grabs the food we prepared for tonight and we head out the back door.

The house is full of love and laughter as we all eat, drink and listen to Christmas music. I'm sitting on the couch, watching Shane talking with all of her girlfriends as they're all gathered around the kitchen island. Ruby has become the newest member of their friend group and they are all laughing at something Taylor is going on about. No surprise there.

"You ready to open presents?" Tucker asks as he plops down on the couch next to me.

"Let's do it." I agree. He announces that it's time for gifts and Shane makes her way over to me, sitting down in my lap. We all go around and open gifts from one another, and when it comes time for Shane to open mine, I don't think I've ever been this excited, or nervous. I ask her to hop up so I can grab it from our bedroom. When I get back, I take a seat in the chair next to her current place on the couch and hand her the big box.

"For meeee?" she sings out playfully. I nod and hand her the box. She tears through the paper and peels the tape from the sides, laughing when she reveals what's inside.

"My very own leather jacket." She smiles brightly at me, pulling it from the box.

Gasps draw from each of the girls when she holds it up, the back turned to the group as she examines the front. She drops it back in her lap, looking around at them.

"Oh my god, have you never seen a leather jacket before?" she sarcastically asks.

"Turn it around, bitch." Taylor almost screams at her.

When she holds the jacket back up and turns it around, I take my next position. She gasps now, dropping the jacket in her lap once again, the words *Mrs. Mullins* are stitched across the back of her jacket. When the jacket drops from between us, no longer blocking her view, I am down on one knee with a ring box in my hand.

"Max…" she whispers through her tears.

"Shane, I'm not sure I could ever put into words how much you've changed my life. The first day I met you, a fire lit inside of me that had been dormant for so long. With each day that passed, being in your presence warmed every part of my cold and bitter heart. You stormed through walls I had put up and so effortlessly waltzed right into my heart. You help me overcome decades worth of grief just by being you.

You helped me to see there *can* be love after loss, and you've allowed me to love you through it all. I spent so long waiting for sunshine, and now that I've got you, I'm never letting you go. I have been so lucky to call you mine for almost a year, but I would consider myself the luckiest man alive if I could call you my wife. Shane Thompson, will you marry me?" I ask, tears threatening to fall from my eyes, as they fall freely from hers.

"Yes!" she exclaims in a now raspy voice.

The screams that come from our friends are almost deafening. She holds her hand out as I place the ring on her finger. She jumps into my arms as I run my fingers through her hair, bringing her in for a kiss. When she pulls away, tears streaming and her smile bright, she rubs my cheek with her thumb and I lean into her touch. A touch I get to feel for the rest of my life.

"I want to spend the rest of my life listening to you tell me that strudel isn't a real breakfast, and painting while you and Riley sit and watch me. I want to spend every Christmas at the bar serving people and maybe someday let our kids run around and drive Lenny crazy. I want to ride on the back of your motorcycle and explore any new place you're willing to take me. I want to fall asleep listening to your heartbeat and wake up every morning knowing I get to love you for the rest of my life. I love you so much, Max Mullins. I would be honored to be your wife." She says, filling every bit of my heart with joy.

"Alright, get a room," Tucker yells unnecessarily loud.

"Don't have to tell me twice," I growl, raising my brows at Shane. I pick her up and throw her over my shoulder. "Merry Christmas everyone, now get the fuck out. I'm taking my fiancée to bed." I announce.

"And on that note. We're gone." Taylor claps her hands together before hopping up and grabbing her things. I haul Shane to the bedroom, as everyone shouts their goodbyes. It's not like we don't see these fuckers every week, so I don't care about the formality of goodbyes tonight. I want to fuck my fiancée and I want to do that sooner than later. I walk into the room and shut the door, tossing her on the bed. I immediately pull my shirt over my head and start to pull her pants from her waist.

"Max! They're still out there." She whisper warns, as if that's somehow going to stop me.

"Then they can either get out quickly or they can hear my fiancée scream my name. Either way, I'm not waiting another second to celebrate the fact that I get to marry the most radiant and captivating woman I've ever known. Now lay back, and let me fuck you." I demand. So she does. I don't know if everyone makes it out before Shane climaxes and screams my name, and I absolutely do not give a damn. I love her in every way I know how. We're laying in bed now as I run my hand through her golden waves, her studying the ring on her finger as her hand rests on my chest.

"Max?" she asks, her voice so soft and sweet.

"Yes, Sunshine?"

"I don't want to wait to get married." She props herself up on her elbow looking over at me.

"What's that pretty little mind of yours thinking?" I narrow my gaze at her.

"How does a New Year's Eve wedding sound?" she pulls her bottom lip in with her teeth, remembering the first night I ever took her lips in mine. The first night I gave in to every good feeling I got from being around her. The night that proved to be the point of no return for me. She was mine from that moment on. Even if it took me a while to see it.

"You tell me the time and place and I'm there," I tell her, leaning over to kiss her lips. There's nothing I wouldn't do for this woman, and if she wants a wedding in 7 days, then that's what the fuck she's going to get.

"Mrs. Mullins," she whispers, "I like it," she smiles as she nuzzles back into my embrace.

"I like it too, Sunshine. As a matter of fact, nothing has ever sounded better." I kiss the top of her head, holding her close as we fall asleep. In six short days, I get to marry the woman who has changed my life. The one who saved me from drowning in my own grief, who shines light on every negative thing, who makes me forget there was ever a time I didn't love her. I don't know how I got so lucky, but I'm sure as hell not questioning it now. She's mine and I'm never letting her go.

The End.

Acknowledgments

I can't believe this is at the end of my very first, published book. The first people I absolutely have to thank are the girl who helped me realize I had a dream to follow, and the man who didn't let me give up. To Courtnee, you're a God-sent friend and I am so incredibly lucky to have you in my life. Your love and excitement for Shane and Max's story, as well as all their friends, made me want to give them my absolute best and nothing less. I'm not sure I would have picked their story to finish it if not for your encouragement and I will forever be grateful to you for that. To Pirtle, my real-life book boyfriend, thank you for never letting me give up, and for encouraging me to keep going when self-doubt dared to make me quit. Thank you for the inspiration, the music and for listening to me change scenes an absurd amount of times to get them just right. I love you and couldn't do this without you.

To my babies, Oliver, Tyr, and Stevie, who keep me on my toes and bring so much joy into my life. Thank you for always being there when I need hugs on a hard day, and supplying everlasting laughter in our home. I love you one hundred.

To Kate and Erica, who both took a chance on me and worked with me on this debut novel. I can't even begin to describe how much I appreciate you both. Your insight, excitement, and guidance helped make this book the best it could be, and I am excited to see what comes of this series.

To the authors who helped guide me in the right direction and answered so many questions, I had when first starting out. I wouldn't have known where to start if it wasn't for your kindness and willingness to help, even in the midst of your own book releases. I am truly so thankful for you.

To the readers who showed this book love and support before even knowing a single thing about it, you all are amazing, and I simply couldn't do this without you. I hope I delivered a story you could love, laugh and resonate with in some way.

To the family and friends, I hid this from until it was finished so that I wouldn't get discouraged or break my focus. The love, support, and hype-up you gave me is something I truly never imagined. I am grateful for every single one of you and honored to have you cheering me on during this new chapter in my life.

About The Author

Sarah Pirtle is an author who found her love of writing after starting a blog in 2018, a year after having her first son. When writing she hopes to give her readers a story they can not only fall in love with but also relate to in some way or another. She lives in Northern Mississippi with her husband and three children. In her free time, you can find her hanging out with her mom and sister, at Target, or binge-reading a romance novel. When she's not running kids to soccer practice or working on school lessons, she's likely writing ideas for your next book boyfriend.

Connect with Sarah

INSTAGRAM: instagram.com/authorsarahpirtle
TIKTOK: tiktok.com/@authorsarahpirtle